ANNE-MARIE

Anne-Marie

Michael Hankinson

Contents

First Printing, 2024

1

Eleanor Rosefield

It'd been dark for hours when Eleanor made her way home through the dark streets of London. Dim lamps glowed above her head at uneven intervals. They were pathetic sources of light, but the only ones available to guide her way.

Stone buildings, wet with evening dew, flanked either side of the street. The proximity of their walls formed a narrow corridor like a funnel, pushing on Eleanor's back with a bone chilling wind, as if the city itself were trying to suck her in deeper.

That night was hauntingly quiet; the silence only broken by the occasional bark of a tethered dog in a far-off alley, or the hiss of a startled feral cat. Eleanor had already spooked several of the timid felines as she passed by them digging through piles of refuse. Each one arched its back, baring sharp broken fangs before scampering away to a more secluded spot.

Most of London's night owls had returned home for the evening, their bellies full and heads swimming from cheap gin. Disapproving wives welcomed them home, calling them foul names while yelling obscenities.

Eleanor would've been home too if it hadn't been for the unusual lack of customers. Other women had claimed all the well-to-do gentlemen already. It'd been an unfortunate string of bad luck for Eleanor the last couple of weeks. No matter how long she waited, or how many pubs she stood next to, the only clients she could find were penniless drunks looking for a free handout. They were the opposite of the wealthy patrons she needed to stay decently clothed and fed. She was ready to give up for the evening but decided to try one more place before heading home.

It was one of her less frequented establishments. *The Pig Pen,* was open later than any other pub, meaning every patron in it was already piss drunk and more than likely broke. It was also the only choice Eleanor had left. She rounded a street corner and paused, staring down to where the pub waited for her. A small wooden sign hung askew over the front door. She could barely make out the painted pig snout adorning the rotted wooden background of the sign. Her stomach lurched from a combination of disgust and hunger. Her mother had always told her that beggars can't be choosers, but that was when life was easy and she'd had the luxury of being the chooser, not the beggar. Life had dealt her a shitty hand, gave her an unlucky roll of the dice, every phrase usable to explain the reason for her current predicament. Regardless of how it happened, the series of events added up to Eleanor being forced into a life of prostitution.

Two lanterns hung on either side of The Pig Pen's sign, partially illuminating the painted pig snout with orange flickering light. An array of tables sat outside the pub for customers to sit at and drink when the weather was pleasant or when the interior was full. That night it was due to the latter reason. Unfortunately for Eleanor, other ladies of the night had claimed every available lap around the exterior seating. The harlots bounced jovially on their suitor's legs, pretending to have a wonderful time.

Eleanor scoped out the exterior before peeking inside. There wasn't an open seat or sober soul in sight, apart from the bartender. They locked their eyes for a second. He shrugged and walked away after seeing the disappointment on her face. She stepped back outside and turned to leave, her stomach tightening again at the thought of going home empty handed. Tears began forming in the corner of her eyes. She would've let them run down her cheeks, but before they could accumulate enough moisture to drop, she spotted a figure standing alone in an alley directly across from her. With the heel of a palm, she wiped the preemptive tears away. She walked around one of the tables, giving it a wide birth while trying to get a better look at the man who stood apart from the rabble of the crowd.

From a cursory glance she could see he was short, standing only a head taller than her. His frame looked frail, and she wasn't sure if it was just the dim lighting, but something was off about his face. His cheekbones were high, his head narrow, the bony temples of his skull stuck out from beneath the skin. The contours of his face lead down to a prominently pointed chin. The man wasn't entirely unattractive, but there was certainly an awkwardness about him, as though his skin were holding his bones together instead of his muscle. What caught her attention more than his physical features, was the clothing he was wearing. The fabric was exquisite, at least the portions visible beneath an outer black cloak, which concealed much of his outfit.

Eleanor's stomach growled, aggravated at her lack of commitment to nourish it. *Fine, I'm going. Just hang on, would you?* She pleaded while firmly rubbing it in a vain attempt to settle the grumbling.

As she approached the alley, a man sitting at one of the outside tables bellowed a hearty laugh, startling her. The laughing man was large and repulsive. The corners of Eleanor's mouth curled downward in a grimace as she eyed him. A combination of gin and gristle from the meat he was gnawing on ran down the side of his cheek in a fatty stream. His clothes stained in a few places from the drippings. Despite all that, two women were laying on him, heavy petting every part of his chest and thighs. The fat fool was having the time of his life, unaware of what his female company was taking from him. A soft hand here and a heavy one there from the ladies, and all his possessions had disappeared by morning. You'd think after the first time it happened, they'd be more careful, but they never learned. They came back repeatedly, purses and balls full, both leaving empty.

With any luck, Eleanor had her own man to filch. It was common for her to swoon a couple gentlemen a night and make enough to get by during this time of year. Winter was ending and the available jobs in the countryside would start to pick up, which meant less men in the city, and even less opportunities for someone in her line of work. Sometimes she'd get lucky, and the gentlemen would be carrying their entire evenings allowance on them. She wouldn't have to go out for a couple of weeks in those cases. Lately though, there'd been more penniless men begging for food, drink, and physical entertainment.

The man in the alley wasn't one of them. No, this man had money, and she was going to do everything in her power to change that. His head faced away from the street, looking into the alley as she approached.

Eleanor closed the gap between them, stopping a few paces short of arm's reach before calling out to him. "Good evening, sir. I see you do not yet have a companion for this evening. Might I offer you my services in this regard?" She pinched the fabric of her dress below the hips, performing a curtsy and flashing a seductive smile.

The man said nothing. He turned his head to look at Eleanor. His eyes worked their way up and down her body, as if judging a cut of meat hanging in the window of a butcher's shop. He stepped forward, using a cane for balance as he approached. His left leg had a limp, making his movement slow and laborious. "Y- yes. I c-could use the c-company." He stuttered.

Eleanor had to bite the inside of her cheek as she smiled, to keep from laughing. She stood up straight. Her grip on the dress relaxed, letting the fabric fall back into place.

"Very well, sir. Shall we go somewhere a bit more private? This place appears to have reached its maximum occupancy for the moment." Eleanor offered her arm, and the man gratefully took it. She led him out of the alley and onto a neighboring street.

As they walked by The Pig Pen, Eleanor looked inside again. What she'd said was true, the small building had met its limit. She could see men and women jumping up on tables and the bar, singing songs, making a mess of the place. The bartender was running back and forth, yelling at customers to get down, while simultaneously trying to clean up the damage. It was a losing battle, but the bartender tried regardless.

"So, what's your profession?" A question Eleanor asked all her first time clients. She used it as a probing question to figure out how much money they'd potentially have on them.

"D-doctor." He replied, an answer that would've caught anyone by surprise.

Eleanor couldn't wrap her head around the idea of him cutting someone open. If his hands were as shaky as his voice, then his patients must've had a rough time on the operating table. She suppressed a chuckle, thinking about his fingers slipping while someone was under the knife and him saying "o-oops."

As if reading her thoughts, he held up the hand wrapped around her arm. "G-good hands." Pulling off a glove he revealed five long, bony fingers, holding them out to show their steadiness.

Eleanor, taken aback when the hands held firm without shaking. *Proof you can't judge a book by its cover,* she thought.

It'd only been a few minutes. The doctor's slow gate and speech made Eleanor feel as though they'd left The Pig Pen hours ago. The sun would be coming up soon and she wanted to get it over with. She decided she'd push him into the next alley they came across and get to work.

The farther they moved away from the pub, the more uncomfortable Eleanor became. She could barely hear the distant echoes of singing and cheering. The only clear and distinct noise was the doctor's cane as it struck stones on the road. This made Eleanor take notice of the cane's features. The doctor's hand covered the handle, but silver still shone through the gaps between his fingers. The back of the handle came to a sharp point, leading up to some kind of carving resembling a bird. *An eagle, falcon, hawk perhaps?* The shaft of the cane, a black rod that stretched from the handle to the ground was smooth as marble, and the tip capped with silver, like the handle.

The doctor struck a rock with the bottom of the cane, emitting a sharp ringing tone that broke her concentration. He raised up his hand, pointing a single bony finger at a barren alley. "H-here?" he asked.

Eleanor looked past him. The alley was close enough to what she'd been looking for. Something about it made her uncomfortable though. She took a moment to figure out what was wrong. A mouse scampered out from inside and that's when she realized, there were no streetlamps close enough to illuminate the area. It wasn't until the mouse had fully exited the alley that she could see it. Only a couple meters inside and the two of them would be invisible to anyone looking in from the street. *Come on, just do it. Push him up against the wall, right here in the street, and get it over with.* Her stomach grumbled in agreement. Before she could force him against the nearest building, the doctor pulled the two of them into the alley. His grip on her arm was monstrously firm. He was much stronger than she'd have believed possible given his build. Eleanor wasn't convinced she could pull away from him even if she'd wanted to.

Her heart hammered against her rib cage; its steady, rhythmic thumping, turned into a rapid beating. The instinct to run begged Eleanor to heed its command. *There's no way. This feeling can't be coming from him. If I wanted to, I could kick the cane out from under his leg. He'd fall over and be as feeble as a tortoise on its' back.* Despite these thoughts, she couldn't shake the feeling there was more to him than his awkwardness led her to believe.

They reached the edge of the alley. The doctor grip on Eleanor's wrist loosened. The blood flowed back into her fingers. He rested his back against the wall a few meters inside the alleyway. His frame was invisible against the stone surface of the wall. Everything Eleanor had learned *not* to do when working in her profession was ringing warning bells.

"W-well?" The doctor impatiently asked from the darkness. The combination of discomfort he gave her, and the pitch blackness of the alley made him sound as if the devil himself were beckoning her forward.

Eleanor took a deep breath, a small boost of assurance that it would be like every other job she'd done. With a little luck, she wouldn't have to do it again for a couple of weeks.

The cold sting of late winter air filled her lungs, a good reminder that she was still alive as she stepped into the alley and swallowed by the darkness.

Eleanor stretched out her hands as she stepped forward, feeling for anything familiar to the touch. The cold stone wall of the building next to her was a good start. The rough surface brushed against her fingertips, evening dew collected on her fingers, running down to the wrist before dropping to the ground. After a few more steps, she began to wonder if the doctor had abandoned her. Eleanor swept away the thought when she felt a tap against her shin from the doctor's cane.

With a little, if not aggressive aid, her hand brushed up against the smooth fabric of his cloak. She could now appreciate the true worth of the fabric; soft, smooth, and warm. The doctor was producing an astonishing amount of body heat from underneath, like he'd a lantern or small stove tucked inside his coat. Thoughts of hell and the devil resurfaced, but she suppressed them.

Don't be stupid Eleanor. She thought. *What would hell, and the devil for that matter, want with a doctor who can hardly speak, walk, or otherwise interact with a living person without stuttering. Either they've gone downhill in terms of standards or there's more to him than meets the eye. The idea of hell running low on worthy subjects was also laughable. The way the world was heading, they should have their pick of the litter. Look at where you found yourself after all...stupid woman.* Her chain of thoughts broke when her hands found their way to his face. The skin was smooth to the touch. She hadn't noticed earlier, her focus fixated on his clothing, walk, and manner of speaking more than his detailed features. The more her palm ran across the surface of his face, the stranger it felt. It wasn't just smooth; it was slick enough to be a newborn's skin. *Certainly, the doctor was old enough to grow facial hair. He didn't look young enough to not have had his first stubble. Being a doctor though, he must also be good with razors and blades.* The only thing more striking than the slick texture, was the frigid temperature of his skull below the surface. For a body that put out enough heat to drive back winter frost, his face was ice cold.

Despite the chill, she placed the palm of her other hand on his opposite cheek and went in for a kiss. Men often liked it when the woman buttered them up before servicing and it gave her an opportunity to dig around too, both literally and figuratively, to find his coin purse. Her lips touched his, but it wasn't the familiar rough, cracked skin of unpampered lips. They were smooth as river rocks and scalding hot as if pulled from a fireplace. She tried to push away, but the doctor slipped his free hand onto the back of her head, forcing their mouths to remain in contact. The intense heat blistered her lips; tears streamed down the side of her face, sizzling into steam as they ran by their mouths. The doctor kept their faces together until Eleanor smelled cooked flesh.

Tearing away from the man was futile. The doctor's hand was in complete control of Eleanor's head. When he was satisfied that she'd suffered enough, he moved the hand from the back of her head to the top, forcing her down into a squatting position. His hand was like an iceberg, a frigid anvil applying immeasurable pressure. His hand continued to apply force to the crown of her skull until her knees touched the unforgiving, dirt coated alley. Small, jagged rocks stuck out of the ground pressing sharply through the thin fabric of her dress, stabbing both knees.

Whether it was luck or divine intervention, the downward pressure finally stopped as her buttocks joined her legs on the ground. Eleanor had a terrifying thought. *I've never met anyone this strong before. I've run into my fair share of abusive and brutish men to be sure, but this...if he really wanted to, I think he could've kept pushing until my spine shot out my back and the rest of me crushed into a puddle of gore on the ground.* A shiver shot through her body causing thousands of small bumps to riddle her skin.

The doctor released her head. The spot on her scalp where his palm had been, began to warm back up. Eleanor was certain there'd be a red mark at a minimum and in the worst case, frost bite. She only now realized that her hands were still out in front of her, shaking uncontrollably. She rubbed them together to get the blood flowing, before trying to find the front of the doctor's trousers. He set his cane down against the wall. There was a small *clink* when the silver handle hit the stone.

Eleanor's hand brushed up against a small satchel. There was a light jingle of coins inside. In the alley, it sounded like a cascade of metal clanging together. She now knew where he kept the purse, which was the first step. The second was deciding when to grab it and run. *Do I dare even try? I think it'd be best if I just gave this one away for free.* Her belly twisted in disagreement, easily swaying her thoughts the other way. Her fingers began their work on the buttons of his pants, pushing them out of the small slits in the trousers that held them together. It was tough work in the dark. Normally she'd have at least a miniscule amount of light to work with, but Eleanor was conducting the task through feeling alone. She started from the top and worked her way down. After undoing the third button, she knew there'd only be one or two more to go. The tips of her fingers felt the bump of the last one and pushed it free.

The doctor grabbed one of her wrists. She felt the same freezing, burning sensation as before. Eleanor winced and instinctively tried to rip her hand away, but his hold was adamant. The pain was excruciating, and her hand naturally opened. The doctor put something in it. She couldn't tell what it was above the throbbing pain in her wrist. He dropped her arm.

It took a minute for the pain to subside before she could feel the weight and shape of the coin he'd given her. It was quite large, larger than the currency she normally received from clients. It was heavy too, much too heavy to be a pence or even a pound. For a second, she let her imagination run wild, dreaming that he'd given her a gold piece. She buried the payment between the cleavage in her dress. The shock and excitement sent her hands into a frenzy trying to get the last button undone.

He was ready. She could feel the doctor was at full mast. With one hand she got to work on the shaft, while the other began to grope around his backside. Her searching hand started low, working its' way higher while looking for a string or thread that held the rest of his coins.

Where is it you bastard?

It was tricky work, trying to make it appear as though the heavy petting was all part of the deal, without revealing her true intentions. Normally, the gentleman she serviced were drunk and wouldn't notice her picking their pockets. The doctor was painfully sober, making it that much more difficult.

Eleanor grew paranoid, afraid that what she'd felt earlier hadn't been the satchel with the rest of his coin. Her servicing hand worked on him with added gusto, to give the other one more of a distraction to work with. She felt around his backside, around the waist, and even the area leading up to his chest, with no luck. The doctor's body quivered. Her working hand was too effective.

Damn it. Don't you do this to me. You better hold it in until I find the string to your pouch...Eleanor had a sudden, terrifying thought. *Did he even put the coin purse back after he handed the money to me? He could still be clutching it in his other hand. If that's the case, I'll just have to be happy with what I got. There's no safe way to check is there? I just hope I'm wrong.* That's when she felt it. Her fingers snagged on a loop hanging down from the back of his coat. *I was wrong, I found it.*

Eleanor's fingers pulled on the loop. When it failed to loosen, she tugged harder. This time a bit too vigorously, almost dragging the whole coat down. She was certain the jig was up, but he hardly noticed. She moved her hand back to his body, now knowing the height and location of the string. The only thing left was to provide herself with the proper level of distraction to untie it and catch the purse. She focused on finishing off the doctor, and he started convulsing. The instant his body trembled and seized up, she shot her free hand around his back, pulling the drawstring of the knot. The coin purse dropped free. She caught it with the other hand before sprinting out of the alley.

Eleanor left the doctor in the alleyway with his pants down. She ran out into the street, not caring which direction she was going, so long as it was away from that monster. Her feet carried her past The Pig Pen, the bartender working hard to drag a drunken patron out of the building. She passed three intersections until she felt safe enough to duck into a small hollow between two shops. Her heart was racing. She tried to catch her breath, but the purse and the coins in her cleavage were digging into the soft tissue of her breasts every time she inhaled. Taking the satchel out, she noticed the bag was leather, with small metal tassels hanging down along the edge of a sewn seam. Forcing two fingers into the small opening at the top made her heart stop.

Inside the pouch were gold coins. She pulled one out, holding it up to the nearest streetlamp. It looked genuine, from the weight to the sheen. With this money she could make it almost two years without having to work out in the countryside or the city. Eleanor realized how stupid she was to be holding the coin out for anyone nearby to see. Her fingers shoved the single coin back into the pouch with the others.

Cautiously, Eleanor left the small hollow, looking up and down the street to see if anyone was watching. The road looked deserted. Walking down the edge of the street, she looked for a sign that would point her back home, where she could enjoy a well-deserved rest. Tomorrow she'd decide what to do with the money with a clear head. Her heart and mind had conflicting desires. The last thing she wanted to do was make a rash decision that could waste the excellent opportunity.

It took a few city blocks before familiar scenery presented itself. She smelled the comforting scents of salt and fish from the ocean. They indicated she was heading in the right direction. Eleanor had lived next to the port of London most of her life, finding odd jobs where she could get them as a young girl. From scaling and weighing fish to managing the stands for stall owners putting them out for sale. There'd always been a love-hate relationship between Eleanor and the sea.

On the one hand, it brought her and Johnathan together. She thought he was her ticket to a better life and for a time she was right. Johnathan was a trader, selling spices and other commodities between the port of London and the orient. The two of them married young and for a while, life was bliss. He made enough for them to have their own place while Eleanor continued to work odd jobs while pregnant with their first child.

After a miscarriage, Johnathan grew distant. He was still the loving and supporting man Eleanor had married, but inside him something broke. He took on more voyages, leaving home for months at a time after only having returned from the earlier one for a week or two.

When they lost the second child, Eleanor's life fell apart. Johnathan left on another spice run, but never returned. To this day she still didn't know whether he was alive or not, but before he left, Johnathan made it clear he no longer had faith in her or their marriage. She refused to give up though, working her fingers to the bone to keep their home afloat in the hopes that one day he'd return, so they could try to make a family again. She even had a speech prepared that would hopefully convince Johnathan to change professions, so he could be around more while they tried for their third child. Despite her best efforts, Eleanor couldn't afford to keep their home any longer. She'd already sold off every asset worth any value, to no avail. Cast out into the streets, she worked the only profession that made enough to survive. Her dreams and aspirations of motherhood with a loving and supportive husband, lost forever.

The gold brought all those painful emotions and memories flooding back. With proper planning, she could live more of those days again. Eleanor was so ecstatic she hummed to herself without realizing it. Unfamiliar streets turned into well-known shops and scenery. The street ended in a T-intersection along the bank of the ocean where a stone wall helped prevent flooding in the neighboring area. Within the harbor a few ships sat docked, bobbing in the water.

Eleanor took a right at the intersection and was about to open her stride, when her ears picked up on a soft *clink* noise from behind. It was distant, so she didn't give it much thought at first. *A stray cat in the nearby alley knocking over empty bottles most likely.* She took a couple steps and heard it again.

Clink.

She walked a few more meters and again her ears picked up on the sound.

Clink, clink.

Two this time and I swear they're getting louder.

Eleanor quickened her pace, walking swiftly down the street. Her heart raced and small puffs of white air escaped as her breathing grew heavy. She hugged herself, rubbing the upper parts of her arms with her hands. She knew being right next to the water made the air cooler, but it must've dropped ten degrees within seconds.

Clink, clink, clink.

The echoes chimed. They weren't only getting louder; their frequency quickened.

Just ignore it. Have to get home. Must get home.

Clink, clink, clink, clink.

Anger replaced the fear. There were few things Eleanor hated more than stalkers. With her cheeks flushed from frustration and the cold, she whipped around to face the noise.

"Leave me the hell-" She looked back towards the T-intersection where she'd turned. Eleanor saw the doctor standing there. His black coat hanging down from his neck to the ground. The cane stuck out from underneath the cloak like a third leg, the silver bird shimmering via a nearby lantern.

That's impossible. The doctor could barely walk, let alone run. I covered damn near half the city it felt like. How could he have caught up with me? It can't be the same man. No don't be stupid Eleanor. That cane is one of a kind. I can't see his face so there may be a chance...

"What do you want?!" Eleanor shouted out to him.

The figure didn't reply.

"I gave you what you wanted, now go away!"

They didn't move.

Rage swelled up from Eleanors stomach to her chest. Mostly anger, but also fear. Her nerves were taking a beating. She managed to stand firm, but she wasn't prepared to confront a stranger alone this late at night.

"Go away damn you!" The yelling gave her the confidence to turn around and walk away.

Clink, clink.

This bastard... she thought as she picked up speed. No matter how fast she moved, the sound of the cane accelerated at the same rate, as if she were trying to outrun her own shadow. She fought the urge to peer over her shoulder, but curiosity won in the end. Eleanor couldn't believe her eyes; the doctor was walking with a swift gait. The clang of the cane was audible but not his footsteps. If she didn't know any better, she would've thought he was floating, using the cane as some kind of device to pull him along. What mattered was that he was following her and gaining ground. Eleanor cursed under her breath. *Damn-damn-damn!* She ran, all decorum and feigned innocence now gone. The run turned into a sprint as the doctor continued to close the gap.

The cane was tapping on the stone at a rapid-fire pace.

Mind overcome with disbelief; Eleanor dared to look back again. *He's a god damn monster.*

The doctor was still walking, each step covering as much ground as four or five of her own strides. It was like he had the legs of a giraffe.

In a desperate attempt to slow his progress she reached into the bag nestled between her breasts, gripping a few of the gold coins and tossing them frantically behind her. They struck the ground, some rolled off the edge of the dock into the water while others bounced where they'd landed before falling and kicking up little tufts of dirt when they hit the street.

For a moment it appeared to work. The doctor halted at the first coin he came across. His forward momentum stopped with such swiftness that the wind finally had time to catch up, it blew past him with enough force to sweep the cloak around his body like a shroud. His legs bent as he squatted down. He picked the coin up off the ground, flipping it through his fingers. The coin cartwheeled down the front of his hand and then back up, the way street performers did while entertaining a crowd.

Eleanor saw all this take place over the comfort of her shoulder. *Finally, some luck...he'll have to spend some time if he wants to pick them all up. By then, I'll be long gone.* Her hope evaporated at once.

The doctor turned his head away from the coin and back towards the woman. Without looking, he placed the coin on the tip of his thumb, pointing it at the water to his left. With a flick of his thumb, the gold piece launched into the air. It glimmered in the pale moonlight with every arial flip. There was an audible *plunk* when it struck the harbor's surface. The coin sank to the bottom of the water. Eleanor's heart drowned along with it.

Without realizing, she'd stopped running and was staring at him. She wasn't convinced she'd seen it the first time, but now there was no mistake. The doctor's mouth stretched into an impossibly wide grin, the whites of his teeth the only thing visible under the brim of his tricorne hat.

The doctor leaned forward; the devilish smile disappearing beneath the hat's brim. He was once again in pursuit, legs stretching to unreal lengths and reaching speeds that seemed impossible. Eleanor had no chance to outrun him directly. She needed a place to hide long enough for him to go by so she could slip away.

Eleanor looked desperately for a nearby alley. Being next to the harbor though, all the buildings smashed together like layers of a cake to maximize space. There were no gaps to even duck into for a second. At least not until the next main street, still a few hundred meters away. She'd never make it there before he caught up to her. Turning her attention to the harbor, Eleanor realized her only real chance to escape was to jump in the bay, hoping the doctor couldn't swim. Winter was still not over, and she knew the risk of death from the freezing waters was as likely as the man in pursuit murdering her. Given the two options she decided to take her chances with the bay.

The nearest dock was only a few strides away. Eleanor took a sharp left turn, sprinting towards the end of the dock and was about to launch herself into the pitch-black water. Her feet were ready to launch the rest of her body into the air. They never left the ground as a freezing pressure wrapped around her neck. The doctor hadn't only caught up, he was now keeping her from falling in with a single hand. She stared into the black water. Small ripples spread across the surface with each teardrop that fell from her chin.

The doctor pulled her back from the edge of the dock and picked her up by the neck. Eleanor felt the full weight of her body pulling down against the base of her head. The doctor had caught her like a rabbit in a snare.

With every fiber of her being, Eleanor wanted to fight back, but the fear paralyzed her. Suspended in the air, the doctor carried Eleanor away from the water, and back to the dock. She watched as he walked her down the wooden platform towards the street. Instead of continuing down the road or returning the way they came, he turned, walking up the gang plank of a ship. They ascended to the main deck of the vessel. Eleanor could make out the sails, folded and secured with rope at the top of the masts, waiting patiently for the crew to unfurl them. It wasn't until he started making his way to the hatch leading down into the belly of the ship, that Eleanor broke from her trance and fought back.

"No, no, no, no...don't take me down there!" She clawed at his hand with her fingernails. Scratching, pinching, and squeezing failed to loosen his grip. All she managed to do was to make the grip around her neck tighter, until breathing became laborious. Flailing her arms and legs only compounded the pain in her neck, as her body twisted below his hand, like a fish held up by its tail. Eleanor was barely conscious as the doctor dragged them into the darkness of the hold.

2

Mathias Crane

Captain Mathias Crane sat inside the captain's quarters of his newly acquired East Indiaman vessel. He named it Anne-Marie, after his wife, who'd died only a couple years prior. He was surprised when given the honor from the charter company to complete the trading contract. It was to be his first official campaign as the commander of his own ship. At 22 years of age, he'd be the youngest captain in history to successfully complete the voyage. The going rate of compensation far surpassed anything he made in the royal navy. Before any of that could happen though, he'd have to finish reviewing the manifest cluttering the entirety of his desk.

He sat on a plain wooden chair in his private quarters near the rear of the Anne-Marie. Most of his first investment went towards the ship's rigging and its crew, leaving hardly any money left over to spend on comforts or proper furniture. The cabin was situated directly beneath the helm and had a beautiful view out the stern windows. For Mathias, the view and privacy were enough of a luxury to compensate for the rest of the room. The only piece besides his basic desk and chair was a small, worn-out wardrobe sitting on the port side of the room. On the starboard side was the same hammock he'd slept in while serving in the royal navy. Beneath that was a large trunk where he kept most of his tools, writing utensils, and important documents.

The cabin was brighter than normal that night from the light of the full moon. Its glow was so brilliant, he almost didn't need the small lamp positioned in the corner of his desk. It produced a comforting glow that warmed his writing hand.

After spending an hour on the stock list his focus waned, so he switched attention to the crew manifest. The document listed who he'd be spending the next few months with at sea. Mathias stacked the shipment papers into an organized pile and placed them in the opposite corner of the lamp. He grabbed the crew manifest, working his way down the list to verify the names, positions, and levels of compensation. The manifest had the names listed from the highest paid sailor to the lowest. It was a mixed sensation of pride and fear seeing his name at the top. Mathias had no qualms with working under pressure and shouldering responsibility, but to be solely in charge of an entire ship; it was enough to give any man a reason to pause and reflect.

At the top of the page was a crew count total of 125. The number was a standard sailor provisioning for a ship and expedition that large. The only issue more painstaking than keeping count of them all, was keeping order.

Of course, it wasn't his job to watch them every waking moment. That's what he had his first mate and second in command for. Regardless of what responsibilities the first mate had, it was the captain's responsibility to care for and safeguard the wellbeing of the crew. For this first voyage, Mathias was planning to take extra precautions, requiring a daily count of all crew members.

Below Mathias' name on the manifest was Frederick Howser, someone he knew well from his royal navy days. They'd sailed together many times, and it was Mathias getting the captain position that convinced Frederick to leave the service and work with him. The pay wasn't much different from his job in the navy, but it paid slightly better at 2/3 shares. The exceedingly loose restrictions of a trade vessel versus military ships were a nice incentive too. On their last trip together, Mathias asked whether Frederick would join his crew if he were to ever get a position as a captain.

"Ey boyo, if you manage to convince a load o' crusty old geezers ta make ya cap'n. I'll quit this here navy bus'ness and join ya as yer First Mate." Frederick laughed heartily from his belly.

That conversation took place a couple months before Mathias convinced the trading company to hand him a ship and a crew. Frederick was the first to sign his name atop the manifest. He locked eyes with Mathias while signing the document, a crease forming at the end of his mouth in a smirk. "Deal's a deal, lad." Mathias couldn't help but smile back.

The next few names Mathias didn't recognize, which was concerning, since they were some of the highest paid crew members on board. He wanted to have a strong central control over the men and that was difficult when he wasn't sure how much he could trust or work with the others in charge. A couple of them, like Bob Hardy the cook and Vincent Carroway the doctor, Frederick had personally referred to Mathias.

"They may be green around the gills, but they's fine gents to be had on board." Frederick assured him.

"Does the physician not have his own practice?"

"Aye, he did at one time, before the uhh..." Frederick put a thumb to his mouth and tipped his head back. "...drinking problem made him lose most his business." He could see the concern in Mathias' eyes. "He's right as rain now though, clean as a whistle. I promise ya that. He lookin' for a fresh start is all."

Continuing down the list Mathias recognized one of the cox-Cranes, Jonathan Crenshaw. The other was Norman Bailey. There was also the midshipman, John Winterbury. All three of them were reliable crew members and had served with Mathias in the royal navy. Mathias was certain they were expecting special treatment since they left the navy to join him, which he couldn't say wasn't a fair assessment on their part. However, it being his maiden voyage as a captain, Mathias was planning to be firm on the reigns until getting his authoritative feet wet.

Underneath each of the main positions, there was an indentation for the assistants to those positions. Their direct superiors had chosen them since they'd all worked together and were trustworthy to get their respective jobs done. Mathias didn't recognize many of the names, but that was normal with a new crew, especially one that large.

Towards the end of the list, were the more miscellaneous occupations needed around the ship. Deck swabbers, rope wranglers, scrubbers, and so on. Most of these were young sailors looking to get a foothold in the industry. Others were gentlemen much older than Mathias who needed work and seafaring was the only life they knew. Regardless of their reasons, each one was a vital member of the crew in Mathias' eyes.

All in all, he was satisfied with the manifest and had few reservations about the success of the expedition.

He set the manifest aside to reveal the last bit of documentation he wanted to review before calling it a night. It was a map of the route they planned to take around the horn of Africa and into the east where they'd deposit their load. As he set the manifest documents down, the door leading into his quarters creaked open. He peered over the edge of the desk, watching the door move inward as the dark crease around its frame grew. That alone wasn't concerning, given the breezy conditions outside, but when the flame inside his lamp shook violently the hairs on the back of his neck stood on end.

Certainly, I would've heard footsteps if anyone was to come aboard. The thought was shy of comforting. He was potentially too enveloped in reviewing the manifest, not noticing an intruder. "H-hello?" He called out. Mathias cleared his throat, calling out more authoritatively the second time. "Who goes there?"

There was no response. The lamp's flame continued flickering as shadows danced across the desk. Mathias reached for the cutlass leaning against the right side of the desk's leg. His hand clutched the leather hilt, gently pulling the blade out of the sheath. It was only halfway out when a black ball jumped onto the desk scattering papers everywhere. Mathias jumped out of the chair, holding his hands up to block whatever was attacking.

The sword fell back into its sheath and toppled to the floor. Mathias peeked over his hands. Sitting atop the desk was his cat, purring and rubbing itself around the map.

"You scared the life out of me Lucy! Took a couple years off at least." Mathias laughed, his heart rate dropping as he regained composure. He picked up the chair and cutlass off the floor, placing them both upright. He sat back down in the chair when finished.

Lucy wasted no time rubbing herself against Mathias' arm before rolling over, looking for further attention. He obliged her, running a hand across her soft belly. She appreciated the pets, pushing her stomach into the palm of his hand with every stroke.

"You're going to take good care of us aren't you girl?"

As if to respond, she looked into his eyes and let out a familiar "Mew!"

"Aye, we'll have good fortune with you aboard. I have no doubt."

Mathias had found Lucy on a royal naval vessel, the Quantico. Unfortunately for her, there'd already been a ship cat; a fat, lazy tabby, which wasn't suited for the job of catching mice. Lucy accidentally found her way on board while chasing a rodent. The other cat on the ship didn't approve and they often got into fights chasing after the same mouse. It was after a brutal brawl that Mathias happened upon the two of them. Lucy took a liking to him at once, deciding to spend the rest of her voyage at Mathias' side. They became inseparable. Now that Mathias was in charge of his own ship, Lucy had free reign of the Anne-Marie, killing all the game she liked without fear of replacement.

After Lucy reached her petting quota, she jumped onto his lap, wrapping her tail around her face to fall asleep. Mathias swept up the papers that slid about when she jumped up, placing them back into their neat piles before turning his attention to the map. With one hand he stroked Lucy's back, with the other he reviewed the chart and timetables for the voyage.

The two of them were blissfully unaware of the woman running for her life past the ship to the edge of the dock. Mathias could've sworn he heard footsteps leading up to the gangplank but with Lucy as calm as she was, he assumed it was his imagination.

Below the main deck of the Anne-Marie, the doctor held Eleanor by the neck as he surveyed the confines of the ship.

Eleanor couldn't understand how he was able to see anything. Her eyes couldn't see a meter in front of her face, let alone anything across the room.

The doctor's neck creaked while looking around. It was as if he could see clear as day, like an animal in the night, his eyes fully dilated, glowing if looked upon directly. Eleanor was certain she'd see the same glow if his eyes were her way. She'd stopped resisting as the pain was reaching a pinnacle that wasn't bearable any longer. A combination of the pain and the tight grip on her throat almost caused her to lose consciousness a few times. She desperately wished she could lose consciousness for a couple seconds and wake from the nightmare.

The doctor took a few calculated steps forward. After thorough examination of the hold, he decided that the room would serve its purpose. There wasn't anything to obstruct his path to the main mast. He stopped just short of the massive wooden pillar jetting up through the middle of the ship.

Eleanor faintly made out the mast's shape as her eyes started adjusting to the lack of light. Panic set back in as the doctor hoisted her into the air. He lifted her up as easily as a child lifting up a doll. Before she realized what was happening, he hurled her back against the mainmast. The bones in her spine cracked, but the air forcibly removed from her lungs overshadowed the sound of snapping vertebra. The whiplash of her head trying to catch up to the rest of her body made her skull strike a nail head protruding from the metal ring of the main mast.

In some ways Eleanor's wish came true. A small stream of blood dripped down the back of her neck while her head faded in and out of consciousness. The corners of her mouth cracked grin.

The doctor thought about letting her enjoy the moment but decided otherwise. With one arm wrapped around his body like a wound spring, he whipped a hand around with blinding speed. The back of his hand struck the side of her jaw. The force was powerful enough to knock her over, but the mast kept her upright.

Eleanor's smile was gone in an instant. The blank expression on her face was of contempt and acceptance.

"Don't you *dare* smirk when you look at me. If I see a glimmer of that expression again, I'll make you suffer for it." The doctor's voice was deep, with a growling undertone. It was how she imagined a bear would sound if they could speak.

Eleanor wasn't sure if it was the knock on the back of the head or the jaw rattling slap from the doctor's back hand, but Eleanor swore his voice had changed. He was no longer the skinny, weak, whining, stuttering doctor she thought she'd duped. It was clear he'd been acting.

"I know that look. It's one of my favorites." The doctor used the cane to support his body as he lowered himself down to her level. Her extremities were limp, arms laying effortlessly at her sides, palms up, head cocked in the opposite direction of where his hand had hit her face. "You see I…oh wait, let me help you with that." Using the end of his cane like a boy using a stick to poke a dead animal, the doctor pushed her forehead away from him, so it rested against the mast. They would've been looking at each other eye to eye now if Eleanor's eye wasn't filling with blood and swelling. Her eyes saw nothing but black, except for spots dancing like stars from the doctor's blow. "That's better. Now where was I?"

Eleanor wanted to retort with a snide remark. She only managed to cough violently as her chest heaved against the mast, regaining some of the air it'd taken from her.

"It won't do you any good to struggle, so you might as well sit there and listen. Think of these last few minutes as my gift to you, for such *excellent* service. Now then, there's the issue of my payment. Personally, I felt as though the amount I gave you was fair, all things considered, but you disagreed. You wanted to make off with everything I intended to spend this evening, and I must say that's very rude indeed. Since I had nothing better to do, I decided that we should spend the whole night together. I'd say that I more than paid for it." He reached into the top of her dress and pulled out his satchel. Eleanor didn't resist or react, even though his hand froze the inside of her breasts. The remaining coins jingled inside the bag as he shook it up and down.

"Feels a little lighter than I remember." With the palm of his hand, he smacked the center of his forehead. "Of course, silly me. I had almost forgotten that *yooouuuu...*" he prodded her chest with the butt of his cane, "threw a handful or so my way when I gave chase. But it's neither here nor there. I'll just mark it down as a cost of doing business." He pulled out a small notebook and a pencil, mumbling under his breath while scribbling down numbers. "We got the five...minus the...with the other...and..carry that with the..." The doctor started laughing. At first it was a chortle, growing steadily into a full-on cackle. "Unfortunately for you my dear, this money is fake." Eleanor's face contorted in disbelief. "Ooooh I like that reaction. They always make the same one when I tell them." The doctor clasped his hands together and pressed them to his cheek like you'd see a damsel in distress do at the downtown theater. "Inside they're all screaming 'NO! NO! It can't be true! It mustn't be true! I died for a handful of fake gold coins. Woe is me, how could this...'" tears rolled down her cheeks as she sat helplessly listening to the man's ravings. "Oh no, now I don't like that face at all, no not one bit. Let's clean you up." He reached into his cloak again, this time pulling out an ornate silk handkerchief. Delicately he wiped the tears from her cheeks, starting at the chin and working his way up the contours of her cheek, taking extra care and time around the eyes until they stopped flowing. After placing the handkerchief back into its pocket, he looked at her dried face. "That's' better."

The doctor took a deep breath and exhaled a sigh. "I'm sure you have a million questions, as they always seem to do, and since you're not in the mood to ask them yourself. I'll go ahead and answer a few of the common ones if you don't mind. *Ahem."* He cleared his throat with a cough. "Yes, the money is actually fake. Yes, I use the money to lure creatures, such as yourself, to their untimely demise. Yes, I am *actually* a doctor. No, I am not a weak stuttering buffoon, but it sure makes it easier to trick ladies of the night. Yes, I am married but she can be a real cold-hearted bitch at times. Ironic I know. Yes, I do this all the time, about once every couple of weeks to be exact, or just whenever I get..." His body shook, as if a chill had run up his spine "...the itch. No, there isn't anything you can do, or offer me, to change my mind or the outcome of this evening." He stood up, taking another deep breath, pulling his arms in towards his chest, as if he was about to announce the beginning of a show or performance in front of a grand audience. "AND YES! YOU WILL DIE TONIGHT! Not until after I've had my fun though."

A final, animalistic instinct kicked in. Eleanor found the strength to push herself away from the mast. Her torso lurched forward into a seated position. Her arms felt heavy and unresponsive, but they moved begrudgingly to help push off the wooden boards she was sitting on. Her body didn't get far when she felt something pressed against her right shoulder.

The doctor had lifted his leg, shoving the heel of his shoe against her clavicle. "Yes, this is going to hurt." Using his full strength, the doctor kicked off with the foot, slamming Eleanor's back against the post. The blow brought forgotten pain in her back to the forefront once again. Strange numbing and throbbing sensations in her limbs coursed through her limbs as the nerves in her spine fired frantically.

With his foot still pinning Eleanor to the main mast, the doctor held his cane with one hand, unscrewing the top of it with the other. She paid him no mind, pushing with all her remaining strength against his leg near the ankle, but to no avail. She heard the sound of metal rubbing on metal. Despite the darkness her eyes could make out the faintest glint of light traveling one edge of a blade from the top to the bottom as the point slipped free of its casing.

The doctor's arm was fast as lightning, only a blur in the already distorted darkness of the hold. The tip of the blade slid through Eleanor's chest like a hot knife through butter. Her ribcage, heart, spine and even the hardened ship mast were no obstacle on the sword's journey. His thrust was powerful enough to split the post down the middle. Only the silver bird bauble at the end of the cane was protruding from Eleanor's chest. It looked as if she was wearing an oversized necklace, with an invisible chain holding it in place around her neck.

At first there wasn't any blood. The blade had penetrated clean enough to only cut away what was necessary for it to travel through Eleanor's body. Her heart took a beat. The initial cut grew as the muscle contracted and expanded, sending blood through her veins while the rest returned to its source. Her heart contracted and expanded, the cut in her chest growing in size with each repetition.

Several beats later, the heart was pumping as much blood into her chest cavity as it was the rest of her.

Eleanor and the doctor didn't move. Their eyes locked together. He was seeing her clear as day. All she could see was the shadowy outline of his figure. It was quiet enough to hear the beats of her heart and he knew that she could feel each one. A smile stretched across the doctor's face as he reveled in the moment.

Eleanor's body was incapable of keeping its precious, life-giving fluid inside her chest cavity. A warm trickle of blood snaked its way down her chest towards the floorboards of her floating grave.

The doctor leaned in, close enough to her ear so she could hear, but it wasn't clear whether he was speaking to himself or to her. "Perfection..." The doctor whispered under his breath. He dropped the cane and with a single finger, wiped some of the blood away. He stuck it in his mouth. The blood sizzled on his tongue, a wisp of smoke escaping his lips. The doctor's mind went blank, his body launching into action. His member stood at full attention as his hands tore away the fabric of Eleanor's dress, like he was tearing open a present.

By the time he reached his goal, the trickle of blood trickling down Eleanor's chest had become a proper stream. The blood stained every part of the dress it touched on its way down, pooling on her stomach where the fabric bunched together. The cheap wool was quick to soak up the liquid, as if ravenous for saturation.

The doctor was getting his money's worth before the pain and loss of blood caused Eleanor to teeter back and forth on the brink of consciousness. Her eyes struggled to maintain clarity as the dizziness took over most of her senses. She couldn't feel anything below the neck while her head slipped into a world of hallucinations.

Fields Eleanor used to play in as a child came in and out of focus. She wanted to run through them, feeling the sun on her face and the sweetbriar roses nipping at her heels with each step. In the distance she saw a man, their shape a blurry mess. It could've been her father or her husband. Either way, she ran towards him with arms outstretched, waiting for a loving embrace.

Lucy was fast asleep on Mathias' lap. His hand rested on the curve of her back where it'd stopped mid stroke, after he too had fallen asleep sitting in the chair. The lantern was still burning in the desk corner, the flame struggling to stay alive as the basin ran out of oil. It held on for as long as it could, desperately grasping for more sustenance to continue flickering. As the last drop of fuel burned out the flame danced slowly, shrinking until it was no more than a flicker, before fading out.

The light disappeared and Lucy awoke with a start. She could see perfectly well in the darkness, but it was her ears, not her eyes that gave her alarm. They turned, searching around like sails trying to catch wind. Her ears stopped at the door. Behind it, Lucy heard a couple of soft thuds. She sat up on Mathias' lap, pawing at his chest. She meowed softly while digging her claws into the fabric of his shirt, but he refused to stir.

Lucy was about to give up, circling atop Mathias' legs before preparing herself to lay back down. Before she got comfortable, a massive cracking sound like a cannon ball tearing through the wood paneling of the ship, reverberated through the room.

Mathias shot up, his royal navy nerves kicking into overdrive as he stood from the chair. The light, wooden frame of the chair flew rearward and fell to the floor with a dull thud. Lucy launched off his lap. She landed on the desk, her legs outstretched, trying to catch herself before sliding off the edge. She hissed from the sudden jolt. She tried to jump off the desk, but the stack of papers prevented her paws from gaining traction with the desk. Her feet scattered the pages in all directions as her paws tried to find purchase with the wood.

Mathias grabbed the nearby cutlass by its sheath, placing the other hand on the hilt. He was ready to draw and face whatever opponent had caused him to awaken so violently. As his eyes scanned the empty cabin, the only enemy he faced was darkness.

"What was that?" Mathias asked Lucy. "It definitely came from the ship." His grip loosened on the hilt of the sword without releasing it. His ears were alert, listening for any other sounds that could show where the first one originated from. "Maybe it was loose cargo falling over from the rocking. What do you think girl?"

Lucy was cowering under Mathias' hammock, where he'd set up a small bed for her to sleep in next to his trunk of personal items. Mathias made her bed from a wooden crate, filling the frame with a gracious amount of hay and blankets for padding. She still preferred to lay inside of the hammock or on top of Mathias' stomach at night. Whenever she found a rat or got scared though, she ran to her bed for comfort.

Lucy cautiously stepped one paw out of the crate, her eyes fixed on the door. She heard another soft thump from outside, a thump Mathias' ears hadn't picked up on. She scurried to the cabin door, pawing at it with her claws while looking back at Mathias to let him know she heard noises.

"I'm coming girl, let's go check it out." Mathias grabbed the lantern that miraculously hadn't fallen during the uproar. He gave it a shake. There was no splashing inside the reservoir. "We'll have to check it out in the dark." He placed the lantern back on the desk. "You'll have to be my eyes, Lucy."

With one hand still clutching the hilt of his sword, the other was free to pull open the door leading out to the main deck. He cautiously pulled the handle. The door creaked loudly on its rusted hinges. Mathias felt like a thief aboard his own ship. He knew that he should've barged through the doorway, yelling, demanding whoever had dared to come aboard unannounced in the middle of the night to show themselves. That wasn't Mathias though. That's what he expected his first mate Mr. Howser to do.

Idiot you already decided that it was probably some loose cargo that fell over. This is your ship and you're in charge now, there's no reason to be so bashful. Mathias' false bravado did not convince him. Internally, he'd prefer to slink back into his quarters and ignore the potential problem until morning, when the rest of the crew was supposed to arrive at first light.

Mathias had cracked the door open far enough for Lucy to slip out. She scurried across the deck towards the main hold's trapdoor. Mathias was more reserved in his movements. The moon was bright enough to illuminate the general shapes on deck and none of them looked out of the ordinary. Mathias took a few more hesitant steps, his confidence growing with each one. He followed Lucy to the hold. A few paces short of the hole he heard sounds coming from below. It was a groan, one that came off more as a growl but difficult to decide. *Maybe a stray dog found its way on board looking for food. It'd make sense that they'd knock over loose barrels looking for scraps. Pitiful creature probably can't find its way out and is bumping around in the dark.*

Lucy had already descended into the hold. She was waiting for Mathias at the bottom of the stairs.

Mathias was prepared to throw caution to the wind, laughing at himself for working himself up over a couple of bumps in the night. Still cautious, he stepped gingerly down the first step, taking it one board at a time. It was easy to miss a step and fall to the bottom with how steep the stairs were. He'd known a couple sailors who'd missed a step or two during rough storms, their necks breaking after landing on their heads at the bottom. He hunched over, craning his neck as far as his shoulders would allow. He was trying to see inside the hold without moving his entire body inside. Even though the space was dark, he could make out familiar silhouettes as his eyes adjusted. The only light he had to work with came from the moon. It provided nothing to illuminate the space below.

There was a large object in the middle of the hold resting against the main mast. Squinting and focusing with all his might wasn't enough to figure out the shape's identity. He'd have to move in closer to know for certain.

The growling continued, masking Mathias' approach. The last few steps down the stairs were slow. His hand was prepared to draw the sword at a moment's notice. Although he couldn't see them, Mathias knew the tops of his knuckles turned white from his choking grip on the hilt. As he took the last step down, one of the deck boards at the bottom creaked. The growling ceased, but after a short pause, they started up again.

Mathias walked down the center of the ship, the shape and main mast grew clearer. As he approached, the growling and moaning intensified. The bulging shadow he saw first coming down the steps gyrated in the darkness. The form was too large for a dog, especially a starving stray. A few meters away, the scent of iron struck Mathias' nostrils, knocking him backwards a few steps. The tip of his nose wrinkled at the aroma. If he didn't have one hand on his sword, he would've covered his face with them for relief.

The shape reared back and let out a blood curdling scream. "AaaaaaaRoooAwww!"

Instinctively, Mathias unsheathed his sword at the sudden noise. The sword's wooden sheath clattered when it hit the floor and Lucy hissed loudly behind him.

The shape pivoted in place, looking for the source of disturbance.

Mathias raised the sword.

The shape screamed again, lunging at Mathias.

Mathias swung the sword with both hands in a sweeping, downward arc. He felt resistance as the blade contacted flesh.

The shape collapsed at Mathias' feet. An object rolled past him, heading in the direction of the stairs.

Mathias ran back to the steps, tripping on the object that'd passed by him only a second prior. He had an even tighter grip on the sword now. It was sheer luck he didn't manage to cut himself while scrambling on all fours to the main deck. Once he was safely in the light of the moon Mathias swung around, pointing the tip of the blade at the hole. His chest heaved as his heart raced. Each gasping breath a struggle. The edge of the cutlass blade glimmered in his shaky hands. Mathias watched the hole for movement. If the shape ascended the stairs, he'd be ready.

A few seconds passed, followed by several minutes, nothing appeared from the hold.

Mathias regained control of his breathing and emotions. As if to prove it, his hands stopped shaking, the sword held motionless in front of him.

What the fuck was that? Mathias lowered the sword and walked to the gangplank. *I better find some help.*

WAIT! A voice echoed through his head. It sounded like his own but came forth involuntarily. ***We don't even know what it is you struck. What if you killed someone? Are the authorities going to accept that it was self-defense?***

Of course it was self-defense, it attacked me.

Yes, you and I know that, but will they? Mathias paused, the voice in his head made it clear they had a consciousness of their own. ***Exactly, we should at least find out what you cut down first. If it was a stray animal, then no harm done. We can dump it in the harbor and the matter, finished.***

And if it was a person? Mathias was concerned to hear the voice's answer.

Then we still cast it over the side into the harbor. Mathias heart skipped a beat. ***Either way it doesn't make sense to get help in the middle of the night when you've potentially murdered someone.***

No, no, no, not true. If it was an animal and I only wounded it, then it could still fight back. We need help. Mathias continued down the gangplank, the voice refusing to abate. Without saying a word, the voice made his head throb. The dull pain formed in the back of his head, moving around to the front before returning to the back again making a full circle.

No! We still don't know what it is. If it wasn't an animal then you may have to forfeit the expedition, your career, and even your life. Look first.

The throbbing subsided enough for Mathias to think clearly. He realized the voice was right. He had to know what happened before he could decide on a proper course of action. Even if it meant facing a wounded beast.

Mathias returned to his cabin to fetch the lantern. He searched for the oil can inside of his trunk, knowing he should've refueled in the first place, instead of searching blindly in the dark. It took some digging to find the oil can. He'd packed the trunk full of extra clothes, maps, compasses, and other miscellaneous personal belongings. His fingers wrapped around the metal canister and pulled it out, knocking some of the contents of the trunk onto the floor. Grabbing the lantern, he unscrewed the cap to the reservoir and started pouring oil into the basin. The basin filled to the brim, spilling over, and pouring onto the floor before he stopped. He screwed the reservoir cap back on and grabbed the flint striking set from inside one of the desk drawers.

It took a several tries to generate enough sparks to light a piece of paper. Once it caught, he transferred the flame to the lantern. The wick burst to life, burning off some of the excess oil from the basin. Mathias lowered the glass housing to contain the fire. He let it burn for a couple minutes to get the flame and himself under control before returning below the main deck.

The light revealed a long streak of what looked like blood on his coat. The crimson stain streaked from the top of his shoulder across his body at a sharp angle to the belt. He knew he'd have to change before anyone saw him, but Mathias sensed it may not be all the blood he was going to get on him that night. With the prepared lantern Mathias left the cabin, walking hesitantly to the hold.

The miniscule flame of the lantern struggled to penetrate the dark staircase leading down, but the glow of light brought him a level of comfort he needed to proceed. After stepping down once, he felt something softly brush up against the back of his calf.

Mathias froze. A shiver ran from the back of his leg to the top of his head.

Soft purring made Mathias realize Lucy had joined him. He appreciated the extra company. With a single hand he reached down and scooped her up. The black ball of fluff let out an exaggerated meow as he hoisted her into the air. Mathias placed her on a shoulder, and she did her best to hold on with her claws.

They descended the stairs together. The small light from the lantern danced in both sets of eyes. There were no noises coming from inside the ship this time. The growling and moaning had ceased. They could only pick up on the creaking stairs and the soft rocking of the ship as it bobbed in the harbor. These sounds normally calmed Mathias' nerves when he was trying to sleep in his hammock. At the present moment, they were ominous.

Lucy appeared calm. She held onto Mathias with her claws, digging them into his shoulder while purring as if nothing were wrong. Mathias knew animals could sense danger and if Lucy was calm, then maybe there was no reason to fret. With a new level of confidence, he took the remaining few steps down the stairs in stride to reach the bottom.

Initially, there wasn't anything to see. Rope strapped barrels ready for a long voyage sat scattered around the otherwise empty room. Tools sat on top of them, their small forms like oblong shadows forgotten by negligent dock workers.

It took only a single step farther in for Mathias' mustered courage to evaporate. His ankle caught the side of a solid object, and he kicked it away. A shift of the ship rolled it back against his foot. He lowered the lantern down to find himself gazing into a pair of solid black eyes, like a doll's eyes void of color or emotion. Underneath the blank stare, a mouth hung half open. Two rows of razor-sharp teeth, filed to spear like points ran around the top and bottom.

Mathias wanted to turn and run. The thought hammered over and over in his mind, but the severed head on the floor fascinated him more than the desire to flee. He developed a morbid curiosity that prevented him from leaving. Analyzing the head further revealed stark white skin, sharp, high cheekbones tapering to a pointed chin. The neck stretched down to a clean cut where Mathias had separated the head from its body. Blood already dried around the cut, congealing into a crimson mass of flesh.

At least now I know he's dead. Whatever the hell he is. Can't imagine what would've happened if it'd gotten the jump on me instead of the other way around.

Lucy hopped down off Mathias' shoulders, sauntering over to the head. She lapped it around it twice. When she reached the mouth a second time, her head cocked curiously to the side while gazing into the blank eyes. She batted the forehead with a paw. The head lolled slightly, returning to its original resting position shortly after. Lucy found a level of amusement in this motion, hitting it harder using both paws. Mathias snatched her up and placed her back on his shoulder.

Mathias studied the bottom of the neck, noticing a trail of blood on the floor where it'd rolled over to him. He followed it to a limp, headless body. There was no doubt it was the owner of the head. Touching the fabric of the coat covering the body, Mathias rubbed the soft texture of exorbitant material. *If this is a lord or prominent figure, there could be dire consequences if anyone were to find out what happened.* He placed the lantern on the floor and pulled on the body's shoulder with both hands to roll it over. The clothing under the coat was of equal quality, adding evidence to the deceased man's height of station. Mathias rummaged through the pockets, finding little value or evidence of the man's identity.

Over the body's right shoulder, Mathias picked up on another trail of blood leading away from the carcass. He grabbed the lantern, holding it up to see where the blood led. The trail grew wider the closer he moved to the main mast, like the mouth of a river opening up to the sea. Sitting atop the bloody stream's origin were a pair of shoes, the soles worn through and the fabric holding them together riddled with holes.

Raising the lantern higher revealed a pair of bare and attractive legs. Near the top of the thighs was the hem of a dress. The original color of the dress was indiscernible due to the congealing puddle of crimson liquid that had absorbed into the fabric. The dress and legs belonged to a woman sitting motionless against the mast; her head lolled to the left, dead eyes locked on the stairs. Both eyelids were open, an expression of frozen longing haunting them.

Mathias gently closed her eyes with the tips of his fingers. Grabbing her shoulders, he tried to lay her down, but the body wouldn't budge. He analyzed the area around her body with the lantern to discover the cause of the resistance. What he initially thought to be a necklace, ended up being the hilt of a sword. A sliver of the blade was visible beneath a silver bird effigy. With both hands he grabbed the bird, tugging on it, trying to wiggle it loose as best he could. He only managed to shake the poor woman's corpse back and forth against the post. The blade, firmly planted in the woman's chest. He tried a few more times but failed to make progress. He sat down, heart pounding, looking at her. Directly above her head was a crack in the wood, a split that ran straight down her back like a spine. He peered over to the man's body and couldn't help but wonder. *What in God's name were you?*

A monster. A monster trying to take what's rightfully ours. A monster sent against you to keep us from achieving what we've set out to do. We're not going to let him, or anyone else for that matter.

The disassociated voice made his head throb, short tangs of pressure from the back of his skull circling around to the front, a maypole of pain. The pain wasn't going to stop him. He'd worked too hard to let anything get in the way.

I'll grab a couple of sacks, shove the two bodies in them, and toss both into the harbor for the fish to take care of. Even chop them into pieces first if I have to.

Mathias felt regret for the woman. It was an awful way to go, but he'd decided there wasn't anything he wasn't willing to do now to ensure the success of this voyage. If it meant chopping up a couple of bodies, stuffing them in sacks, and tossing them overboard, then so be it. He grabbed the lantern and climbed up to the deck, where sacks laid stacked neatly in preparation for the final loading that was to take place at the coming dawn. Each bag was large enough to put at least a couple of limbs into. Maybe even a torso could fit if he got them in at the right angle.

The sacks were sitting where he'd expected them to be, near the bow of the ship on the side where the dock workers had tied the ropes off to the dock. There must've been at least a hundred or so sacks in evenly stacked piles. He counted off eight, placing them one at a time in the crook of his arm. They were bulky and itchy, but they would get the job done. He spotted a woodworking saw resting next to one of the stacks. Arms already full, he grabbed it and threw it on top of the pile under his arm, balancing it on top. He knew that he'd have to hurry though, looking out past the harbor at the open ocean, the early signs of morning approached. Rays of light on the horizon broke through the darkness.

With arms overflowing and growing heavy, Mathias ran back to the stairs leading into the hold. One hand carried the pile of burlap sacks with the saw on top and the other swung with the lantern. He took the steps two at a time. Lucy stayed with him, keeping a meter or two away from his feet to avoid Mathias' frantic steps.

Upon reaching the last step, Mathias threw down the saw, all but one of the sacks, and set the lantern down on the floor. He opened it, searching around the base of the stairs for the decapitated man's head. It wasn't where he'd left it earlier. Searching around in the darkness around the stairs revealed no sign of it.

Must've rolled away.

That was fine. There was plenty of other work that he needed to do. Mathias looked for the saw and for a minute had trouble finding it, too. Panic was overtaking his senses, clouding his head. He dug through the bags frantically, throwing the ones on the bottom out of the way. When he reached the last one and found nothing, he looked around. Only a little part of the blade was visible in the light. It'd bounced a surprisingly far distance from where he'd thrown the sacks down.

With one hand he grabbed the saw and the sack he was originally going to put the head in. With the others, he snatched up the lantern and went to the main mast, where the horrible job of cadaver deconstruction was waiting for him.

Except, Mathias couldn't find either one.

All that remained of the man was pile of clothes in a rough outline of where he'd collapsed. It was the same with the woman, a dress bunched up into a pile at the foot of the main mast. What startled him most was the lack of blood. Not a single drop remained on the mast or the floorboards that had guided him to the bodies only minutes ago. All signs apart from clothing, gone.

Before looking around more, he decided to clean up what he could, and worry about the rest later. The sacks were large enough for body parts, which made the single bag more than enough to hold all the clothes they'd been wearing. After grabbing the overcoat, pants, hat, and all the accessories from the man, the sack was still half empty. The woman had only been wearing the dress and a tattered pair of shoes. He shoved those on top before discovering a small satchel, a money bag that had surely been the man's based on its quality. Inside it were a few flat rocks, a strange thing for him to have been carrying around. Even stranger still, finding them in the woman's clothing and not the man's. The last piece of evidence was the blade still sticking out of the center of the mast. After more futile attempts at pulling the blade out of the main mast, Mathias decided to leave it there.

No! No evidence! The inner voice bellowed.

"Ach, fine!" He yelled out loud to an empty room.

Mathias placed the bottom of one foot against the mast near the blade to get as much leverage as he could. The other foot rested behind him, trying to maintain balance if the blade were to suddenly pull free. To his astonishment, it snapped in two. The sword hadn't pulled free like he'd planned but the result was acceptable. The ornate hilt tumbled across the floorboards, making metallic pings as it tumbled. He snatched it up, shoving it in the sack along with the clothes. He was careful not to push so hard that the broken tip could potentially puncture the sack. If he hadn't been in a hurry, Mathias might've tried to find a way to salvage the hilt. The metal alone could fetch a high price, and the carving could be repurposed by the right smith. Unfortunately, there wasn't enough time and the risk of someone recognizing the design wasn't worth the risk. He inspected the part of the mast where the sword had broken off and was convinced no one would notice the sliver of metal wedged inside it. Even if they did, it would look like no more than a nail hammered in too far.

Mathias conducted a final sweep for any other articles of clothing or accessories that might've moved around during...whatever it was that happened down there. He looked around every barrel, pile of netting, and rope that was sitting on the floor. He even inspected the areas around the bundles of cargo in case other loose belongings had managed to roll behind them. His focus enveloped completely by the search; he didn't hear the footsteps approaching from behind.

The sack of clothes still clutched in Mathias' hand, he leaned over a barrel, feet sticking up in the air behind him. The top of his head was poking halfway out one of the port holes, swinging from side to side looking at the bow, then the stern of the Anne-Marie.

"Oy, who be that stickin' out the winder?!" A man called out, looking at the feet dangling above some of the ship's cargo, head half stuck out a window. This wasn't the first time he'd had to deal with a stowaway or someone trying to make off with a set of goods right before a voyage. He'd told the captain that they should've hired some portside security to watch the ship the night prior, but the captain insisted that he'd be on board and handle any issues that arose.

Mathias jumped. More like flopped in place atop the barrels, hitting his head on the port ring in the process of pulling his head back inside the ship. "It's me, Frederick." He replied, rubbing his scalp with the hand free of bloody garments. He had to rock back and forth to wiggle his way off the barrel so his feet could touch the floor.

"Thought we had us a problem already." Frederick said. "Not my favorite way to start a voyage, tusslin' with stows and the like. Have to say it's also not my *least* favorite. Puts some salt in the blood 'fore even settin' sail."

"Aye it does at that. But unfortunately for you, it's only me." Mathias walked over to Frederick, for a second, almost forgetting what he'd been doing.

"Ey, are ya alright lad?" Frederick asked, giving Mathias a concerned look.

He'd picked up the lantern Mathias left by the staircase and was shining it directly on his captain's chest. Mathias had completely forgotten about his clothes covered in crimson; his head wrapped up in grabbing the garments off the two dead individuals.

"Oh uhhh, rats. I was helping Lucy kill some of the rats, or at least picking up the dead ones." Lucy rubbed against Frederick's shins and calves, purring as she weaved in between his legs, validating Mathias' claim. *Good girl.* He thought.

It was apparent Frederick wasn't convinced, but he was also a man that respected his position enough to not dig where he didn't think he belonged. He gave a sidelong look at the sack, and then went back to Mathias. "Rats?" He questioned, indicating towards the bag Mathias was holding onto with a clenched fist.

"Yes. Quite a few, which is why I'm glad Lucy's here. Should make for a rodent free or at least, rodent reduced trip."

Frederick swapped the lantern to his other hand, walking back to the stairs leading onto the main deck. "Aight, then Cap, best change out of those clothes though, 'fore everyone else gets aboard. I'm all for puttin' some fear into the men, but that might be goin' a tad overboard fer first impressions."

"Aye, that it would." Mathias agreed.

Frederick was halfway up the steps before Mathias finished his reply. Lucy stayed behind, sitting where Frederick had been standing, looking up at Mathias. She let out a soft meow before licking her paw and rubbing it against her head. "Good girl." Lucy ignored the compliment while continuing to clean herself. Mathias left her sitting below deck and went back to his cabin to change out of the clothes he was wearing. They were some of his finest garments and he was wearing them to present a professional first impression to the men. In their current state though, Frederick was right. He'd be displaying the wrong kind of first impression.

By the time Mathias made it up top, a few other sailors had come aboard, working on the rigging in preparation to set sail. Mathias avoided them as best he could and was able to make it to his cabin without too many crew members noticing his clothes. Most of the men were busy focusing on their individual tasks, while others thought it better to avoid looking in his direction altogether. Sailors avoiding confrontations with the captain was a savvy strategy employed by most.

Closing the cabin door behind him, Mathias tossed the bloody sack of clothes into the nearest corner of the room. Then he got to work unbuttoning his coat, throwing it on top of his desk. He pulled the white undershirt from inside his trousers with a firm tug, dragging it over his head, and chucking it into a pile next to his hammock. The morning light was in full bloom now, pouring into the room with orange light. The blood covering his undershirt was vibrant in the morning sun, but his overcoat only had a couple of hardly noticeable droplets. Most men wouldn't spot them, and even if they did, it was easy enough to assume they'd come from non-nefarious origins. Above him, he could hear Frederick calling out commands to the crew. "Tie that down, release that rigging. Not over there ya tosser! 'ave you ever even been on a ship before?!" His voice boomed with every order.

Mathias grabbed a fresh white undershirt from the bureau standing next to the cabin door. The previous tenant had left him the bureau and while he' wouldn't have chosen that particular design, it was hard to turn away free furniture. He put the clean shirt on, grabbed his overcoat off the desk, and put that on top of everything else. He left most of the buttons undone, to let the sea breeze make its way through to help him cool off as beads of sweat formed on his brow.

The stomping from above was becoming more frequent and the shouting showed no signs of abating either. Mathias figured he should get on deck sooner rather than later before Frederick cursed them all off the ship. He appreciated having an enthusiastic first mate, and no one fit the job better. Like many leaders though, Frederick could be too overbearing at times and Mathias hoped as captain he could help balance the first mate out.

Mathias was about to leave when he spotted the bag of clothing in the corner of the room. He'd almost forgotten why he was changing clothes in the first place. There was also the bloody undershirt, still sitting adjacent to his hammock, that he knew he had to do something with. It was a shame to throw it away seeing as how it was brand new, and it would mean that he'd already be down one shirt for an already long voyage. However, there wasn't much he could do about that anymore. He decided the best course of action would be to get rid of it all. He went over to his hammock, picked up the shirt, pulled the mouth of the sack open, threw it inside, and twisted the top closed. He opened the window in the back of the cabin and popped his head out, looking as far up and down the dockyard as his neck would allow. When he was certain there was no one taking an early morning walk or fisherman poking their head around where it didn't belong, he brought his head back in, chucking the bag out the window in its place. He watched the sack drown from the weight of the sword handle inside. The oblong shape of the sack grew darker as it absorbed the saltwater. His eyes followed it down, until the object was no longer discernable from the rest of its surroundings.

Hopefully, that's the end of it. Somehow, Mathias knew better. It wasn't a good omen no matter how you sliced it. Two people murdered aboard his ship the morning he was going to set sail. He was surprised the sky wasn't a deep red, premonitions of a disastrous journey ahead. Unlike many of his fellow sailors, he wasn't a superstitious man by nature. Frederick on the other hand, knew every bad luck and foul omen that could befall a sailor. That wasn't necessarily a negative trait. Mathias' logic and Frederick's spirit were both needed to keep the men in check.

The fact there was no evidence, other than the clothing now resting at the bottom of the harbor, was reassuring. Mathias didn't have the time or patience to figure out the details of what'd happened. After all, bodies don't disappear off the face of the earth or from within the stomach of a ship without a reason.

Another loud stomp broke Mathias' concentration. His focus returned to the task of preparing to set sail. It was always one of the most enjoyable times for Mathias and other sailors like him. The two most exciting moments for a sailor were getting ready to make way or pulling into port. Both were for varied reasons, but neither was any better or worse than the other. He always preferred setting sail though, if not for the simple fact there was a lot less trouble to deal with. It took about a week or so into a voyage before the men started getting bored and causing problems. That first week though, everyone was fresh and rearing to go. They followed orders without batting an eye and every man focused on the tasks at hand.

Mathias stepped out of the cabin and onto the main deck. There were more sailors aboard now than there'd been when he'd slipped into the cabin. Most of them were rolling barrels onboard and into places where they would sit for the majority of the voyage. Others helped them strap the barrels down with considerable amounts of rope to ensure they wouldn't roll around if the ship went rocking in turbulent waves. He looked up and saw a few sailors climbing the rope ladders, checking the sail tie downs, and ensuring the lines were in serviceable condition. That'd been one of Mathias' favorite jobs when he was younger. He could see for dozens of kilometers from up there, the vast horizon stretching out in all directions around him. He was reminiscing so much, he failed to see the stack of small crates cruising towards him from the starboard side of the ship. It collided with Mathias, shaking violently on their cart. The top crate almost fell on him, crashing down to the side of him. There wasn't any danger like the potential of death to kick your senses into overdrive.

Frederick yelled down from the helm. "Oy boy! Watch where yer goin'! You just broadsided the Capn'. Are ya nuts? People are killed for less I hope ya know."

The rest of the crates, the ones that' hadn't fallen, were set down on the deck and Mathias could see the boy hiding behind them. The lad couldn't have been a day over twelve, about the same age as Mathias when he'd set sail for the first time. The boy's face was red as a turnip from embarrassment.

"B-b-beg your pardon captain. I-I d-didn't mean it, I'm sorry!"

"That's alright. Just know that it's quite easy to miss where you're going and fall right over that railing there." Mathias put one hand on the boy's back and with the other, he pointed towards the port side of the ship at the wooden beam running horizontal to the deck. "The worst part is no one would even notice you were gone. At least not until the next rollcall. Of course, but by that time we'd be farthings away. You'd be alone. Maybe floating on one of those crates you were carrying if you were lucky enough to have one fall overboard with you. That's where you would stay. Stuck in the ocean, alone, paddling your arms off till they were numb from exhaustion, gasping for air, and screaming for help. You'd only succeed in drying out your mouth though." Before he'd finished speaking, the boy's face was no longer bright red. Instead, it all color had flushed away, closely resembling the hue of the severed head still rolling around the hold. Mathias could see all manner of thoughts and fears flood the boy's imagination.

The boy tried to swallow, but his mouth was already too dry. When he gained enough moisture back on his lips to answer, he said. "Aye sir, I'll be more careful. One crate at a time it is."

"That's a good lad." Mathias picked up the crate sitting apart from the stack and placed it in the boy's hands. He watched the boy walk away towards the hold. He could tell the boy was taking extra precautions to avoid colliding with anyone else, even giving barrels and crates a wide berth.

Frederick was watching the conversation take place from the helm. "You comin' up Capn'?".

"Aye." Mathias replied. He climbed the stairs leading up to the helm. His hand gliding along the banister railing, almost caressing it as he ascended. By the time he reached the top, Frederick had returned to barking orders at anyone he didn't believe was moving with enough purpose. "What's the status, Mr. Howser?" Mathias asked.

"Doin' fine sir. We should be able to get goin' on time, granted we don't have a crew full of boys like that one." Frederick pointed at the one who'd run into Mathias.

The boy was already on deck again, grabbing the second crate off the stack he'd left behind. His head was darting to the left, right, and over the crate.

"He's not a bad kid. Maybe a little overzealous and nervous, but not bad. I imagine we all started that way in the beginning."

"Bah! Not I. Been on a boat since b'fore I could even walk. Was swimmin' by that time too. Me thinks you were too easy on 'em."

Mathias couldn't help but laugh. "I'm sure you were, Mr. Howser. If you could've seen the look on his face, you wouldn't be saying that though. He'll be as quiet and careful as a mouse when moving anything from now on. It's a good skill to learn, one that will serve him well if he lives long enough to take advantage of it. Being a sailor is one of those jobs that will either make you or break you. Sink or swim in a manner of speaking."

"Aye, well Lucy will put 'at little mouse in line sure enough. Assumin' you 'aven't done that-." Frederick broke off mid-sentence when he spotted a sailor performing an improper tie off. "Three turns *around* the post ya toss pot. You got a brain in that head or just clam shells!"

None of the men on deck moved their heads because they knew Frederick wasn't yelling at them, all except for the one that did. "Aye sir!" The man yelled out from across the ship. They knew who they were, and they'd known they'd made a mistake.

"Thinkin' they can slip one by me'll be a mistake not soon repeated." Frederick half mumbled; half spoke under his breath. "Now where was I? Oh ye' that black cat of yours'll hopefully balance out all the other traditions you decided to spit in the face of."

"You mean the day I picked to leave?"

"Aye to that Capn'. You know well as I what 'appens when leavin' on a Friday."

"That I do, but you know as well as *I* do why we are. The trade commission doesn't care much about superstition and stories. They only care about ensuring we leave on time and return on time with their cut of the coin."

"Won't do them, or us, much good if we don't make it back in one piece though."

"That's true but I'm also not among the most superstitious of men either. I might be a lifelong sailor, but I never put much stock into luck, good or bad." ***Why don't you tell that to the bag of bloody clothes drifting to the bottom of the harbor? It's sitting down there right now, right at this very moment. Let's also not forget the two bodies that vanished from the face of the earth after being brutally slain. One of which was by your own hand, I might add.***

"I know, shut up. I don't need reminding." Mathias had both hands pressing on either side of his head. It looked like he was trying to squeeze his skull to keep it from pushing outwards. To Mathis, that's exactly what it felt like. It was as if the voice was trying to bust out from his skull in every direction simultaneously. A heavy hand fell on Mathias' shoulder, breaking him free.

"You alright there Capn'?" Frederick asked looking at him, concerned.

"Yes, just been dealing with some headaches as of late." Most of the pressure had subsided. Now he was having to deal with some of the aftermath. There was a lasting soreness around the temples that abated with light rubbing using his fingertips.

"I understand, 'appens to me on occasion. Especially after yellin' at these sea dogs all mornin' to-" Frederick broke off again. "Do you think I'm blind, or just fookin' stupid! Secure that barrel properly or I'll tie you off to the bow, throw you in the water as our chip log, and test the ship's speed with your face." That time a group of men turned to see where the anger and frustration focused towards. They saw Frederick at the helm shaking his fist while yelling.

In unison the men yelled back, "Aye sir!". Collectively they undid the knots of rope tied on top of the barrels in question. The proper method was to wrap around the barrels before coming back over the top of them. This ensured they wouldn't be able to roll around if a heavy wave were to slam broadside into the ship. Like the first sailor, they'd known better, but often times laziness was a disease that needed to be stamped out, before it could spread and fester.

"All my years, I've never seen such a useless bunch of sea dogs."

Mathias chuckled. "You say that about every crew."

"Oh, but I mean it this time." Frederick replied with a wag of a finger. "Normally everyone is doin' their best in the beginnin'. It's durin' the middle and the end when they always get lazy and do everythin' half arsed. Where'd ye drudge this lot up from anyhow?"

"You know guild assigned them to us. Half the reason I got this contract in the first place was under the stipulation that the company provides a majority of the crew. The only thing I really got to choose were a few key positions, like yours."

"Aye and I'm startin' to regret your decision in that regard." Frederick playfully punched Mathias in the shoulder.

"Oh, come now." Mathias returned the sentiment, smacking Frederick square on the back. "It isn't so bad, just a couple trips like this one and you can go be a lord somewhere. Live the high life on a farm. Start a family. All those things' we sailors are *so* well known for."

"Bah! I was born at sea, and I'll die at sea. If I have anythin' to say about it. Don't mean I like havin' to sail with a bunch o' bottom feeders, from a company that knows nothin' about sailin' in the first place. Other than it makes them money, for doin' nothin' other than bein' rich."

"That's why you're in charge and they're not. You have my permission to do whatever you feel necessary to get us there and back safely. Anyone steps out of line; you have free reign to do what you need to get them *back* in line."

"Thought that went without sayin'. No offense capn'. You're no jellyfish, not by a long shot, but you aren't exactly the most intimidatin' of men either."

Mathias took his hand back. "None taken. We all have our strengths and weaknesses. Like that boy down there." *He'll get his sea legs in no time.* Mathias hoped.

"Oy, what did I just say about them moorin' lines! It's a bowlin' knot, not a clove hitch! 'ave you pathetic excuses for barnacles never sailed before?!" Frederick stormed off the helm, putting his full weight into each step. Mathias felt the boards beneath his feet and the deck shake as the first mate descended the stairs. He even heard a nail or two squeak loose from the ends of the planks.

Frederick yelled obscenities that hadn't even caught on to mainstream sailors yet, but Mathias was certain if anyone could get them to become common vernacular it would be Frederick Howser.

Mathias stood at the wheel of the helm, looking down on the main deck. Some of the men he recognized. A few he'd picked out personally, while others he only knew by reputation or sparse interaction. The vast majority, however, were completely unfamiliar faces. That wasn't the worst, but it did make him nervous. You could tell how an expedition would go based on the crew, and that one looked rough around the edges. Since it was his first trip as captain, the potential for mutiny (if anything were to go wrong) was higher than normal. If everything was smooth sailing, there'd be little cause for concern, but these voyages were hardly ever that easy. There were always situations that arose, from running out of decent food and water, to the extremes of having to make emergency stops at ports for repairs. Heaven help them if they needed to deal with privateers. He'd have to handle all of those issues as they arose. It was futile, trying to imagine everything that could go wrong and take measures to prevent them from happening.

Mathias ran his hands over the wheel's spokes, feeling the smooth wood under his fingertips. "If we all take care of you, then I'm sure you'll take care of us." The wood around the base of the wheel creaked and groaned. He subconsciously picked up on the sound. He didn't put any stock into it. After all, wooden ships were always creaking.

Frederick returned to the helm, his face red with frustration. *No doubt from yelling his head off until his throat had gone dry.* Mathias thought.

"They're about done loadin' the rest of the provisions. Once the food and water's strapped down properly, we'll be ready to make way."

Mathias looked around the deck, spotting a few extra dinghy's swinging over the port side railing before being set down on the floor. "What's the story with the extra dinghies?"

"Oh tha'? Can't be too careful is all. I have no intention of going down with any ship moving forward. This ain't the Royal Navy after all."

Mathias couldn't argue with that logic. "Very well, excellent job Mr. Howser. Once that's done, gather everyone onto the main deck and we'll conduct our first roll call, check for any stows, and set sail."

"Aye Capn'". Frederick left Mathias alone again to spread the word.

Mathias moved to the stairs on his right, stopping at the edge of the highest step. He watched the men congregate on the main deck, in preparation to have their name called. A lot of sailors despised roll call. It could take hours if sailors weren't paying attention. A name could be called multiple times before someone would own up to it or realize that it was *theirs* and not someone else's.

A lot of the standing areas on deck filled up, so men on the rope ladders working on the rigging, turned around to face the crowd. Others opted to stay on top of the yard arms that ran perpendicular to the main mast. There were even a couple of souls in the crow's nest, looking down at all of them from high above. So long as they could hear from up there, it didn't bother Mathias. He always had a soft spot for the crow's nest. It was one of his favorite places to be on the ship. On hot days it was often the only place to feel a cool breeze. You were directly in the sun, but an accompanying breeze made it worthwhile. It was also a nice spot to see for leagues away, endless expanse of green-blue water. If you were lucky enough, you could catch sight of some whales breaching above the surface of the water, and that in itself could make the monotony of nest duty worth it.

Men continued piling into every available space. Hordes of sailors spilled out from the decks below. Mathias hadn't realized how many had boarded since he disappeared into his cabin. Many of their faces showed annoyance that the first mate had pulled them away from their work. Their demeanors grew worse when elbow room became scarce. Mathias was certain a fight was going to break out if one of them shoved another too hard.

Before anyone could start throwing punches, Frederick called out. "Listen up you lot. Now I know this isn't your favorite part, but there's a hell of a lot of o' ya, an' we don't 'ave time for your nonsense. Once you've been accounted for, go back and finish your jobs so we can make way, but if I 'ave to call your name twice you'll be hangin' upside down from the mast till mornin', is that clear?!"

Only half the men replied with an enthusiastic "Aye sir!" The other half either grunted apprehensively or didn't say anything at all.

Mathias heard Frederick mutter more of his favorite insults under his breath, but they weren't clear enough to make out.

Frederick held out the manifest and started reading names out loud. His voice carried far enough for everyone on the ship and passing onlookers from docks two ships down the harbor to hear. He got through five names before having to call one of them out twice. This didn't end well for the inattentive sailor, who got an earful from the first mate before they'd even been shoved off. "It's not even the second day and yer' already on my shit list. Not an effective way to start." This was Frederick's final comment to the sailor before letting him escape towards the stern of the ship.

Mathias was certain the man was finding a place to lay low before risk getting worse than a tongue lashing.

Captain Crane wasn't the biggest fan of giving out lashings from the whip, and neither was Frederick. There were times when it was a fitting punishment, however they found it wasn't as effective as one might think when it came to changing a sailor's attitude towards their duties. If anything, it only made them resent the leadership and crew even more, often times causing a downward spiral. Their morale could fall so low that they'd be locked in the brig until the ship made port again.

There wasn't another incident of a sailor missing their name until Frederick reached the bottom of the manifest. The majority of names had been called an all of those men were back to doing their share of work before they'd been corralled on deck. Any time a name was called that Mathias recognized; he'd give them a head nod in appreciation of them signing up to sail under him. He wanted as many friendly faces as he could muster, without angering the trading company.

"Paul Steiner!" Frederick yelled out. There was a quiet pause of longer than three seconds. The second time Frederick began to read the name, Mathias was afraid a blood vessel would burst in the first mate's head. Mathias could see it pulsing, just above the peak of Frederick's right brow. It grew larger as blood pumped from his heart to his brain. The anger was building, and tension filled the air. "PAU-"

"A-aye sir, here sir." A voice called out from the few men remaining on deck. The sailor took a step forward, away from the dwindling group.

Frederick sized Paul up, not a bit impressed. In fact, he was disgusted by Paul's physique. The sailor's inability to recognize his own name didn't help make him more appealing either.

Paul Steiner was short and disturbingly fat for a sailor. Typically, the lack of proper nutrition on long voyages kept a man thin. Perhaps it was because he liked to drink too much and work too little. It might also have to do with the fact that he ate more than his fair share of rations or snuck extra meals in when no one was looking. After all, it was easy to grab some leftover food without anyone noticing when patrolling the deck on night watch. It wasn't as easy to hide the evidence though. In Paul Steiner's case, the evidence was apparent in the form of a rotund stomach, sitting atop a barrel sized waste, and thick sausage thighs poking out below. There were also the extra chins running down the length of his neck like the folds of a discarded blanket.

"Are you Paul Steiner?" Frederick asked condescendingly.

"I am sir." Paul's entire face shook as he answered. Ripples of fat moved from his mouth to his chin. All the loose skin flapped with each wag of his tongue.

"Goo' lord, you even *sound* fat, if that were even possible. Very well, *Paul Steiner*. Since you don' seem to know yer name and ya didn' get enough exercise on yer last trip, you'll be walkin' the deck tonight as our first night watch. It'll give ya time to learn yer name again. You'll report to the helm at dusk. That understood?" Frederick asked.

"Y-y-yes sir, aye sir, dusk, helm...sir." Paul threw up his hand in an awkward salute. Frederick ignored it. Paul dropped his hand, shambling off as fast as his chubby legs would carry him.

After the incident with Paul, the remaining sailors had no issues responding in a timely manner when it was their turn to report in. Night watch was one of the least desirable chores a seaman had to endure. They were often long, boring, and resulted in the worst possible punishments if the sailors on duty were found sleeping, drinking, or eating.

Once the final name on the manifest had been called out, Frederick walked over to Mathias and handed him the list. "Everyone's all accounted for Capn'. All 125 souls."

"Very good Mr. Howser. Finish preparations and let's get the Anne-Marie underway for her maiden voyage."

"Aye sir."

Mathias returned to his cabin to discard the manifest onto his desk. The window at the keel of the ship was open, squeaking on rusted hinges. His initial thought was that someone had been in his lodgings during roll call, but even if someone had taken the effort to crawl around the outside of the ship (which would have been no easy feat to achieve on its own) they wouldn't have been foolish enough to leave the window open after exiting. No, he'd forgotten to close it in the first place after dumping the bag into the harbor, that's all.

The thought of the sack's contents brought gruesome images flooding back into his mind. Memories he'd have preferred to leave at the docks, permanently if he could. Realistically though, it would take a long time to erase them entirely. If he ever managed to. They say with enough liquor you can eventually forget your own name, but he hadn't reached a point yet where he wished to test that theory.

Mathias walked to the window and looked down into the murky, green water of the harbor. Bubbles rose up through the dark colors, popping as they hit the surface. It was most likely crabs or fish that'd sensed the contents of the bag and were trying to work their way into it for an easy meal. Mathias would be long gone before the animals would be able to succeed in getting inside. All that mattered was there'd be no sure proof way to connect the Anne-Marie to what took place. Aside from proximity, there'd be other ships that would come and take the ship's spot after she left.

Just like there'd been ships in that spot before she'd arrived a week prior.

Mathias closed the window, imagining that he was metaphorically sealing away the horrific events that took place. This was his maiden voyage as captain. Everything needed to be perfect. He'd not let anything get in the way of that if it was within his power to prevent it. Even though he was convinced he'd been the one to leave the window open, his subconscious mind couldn't help but wonder. Without thinking, he scanned the interior of the room before leaving. His eyes were looking for anything that might be out of place or missing. Nothing caught his attention, so he left without another thought, the case closed. He left the cabin and climbed the stairs to the helm where he waited for Frederick to give him the all clear so they could make way.

One of the two coxswains, Norman Baley, was standing at the wheel when Mathias arrived. He was patiently waiting to be given the order to release the rudder and guide Anne-Marie out to sea.

Frederick was on deck near the main mast, conducting his final inspections of the rigging.

"We're all set down here sir!" He called out to Mathias.

"As well Mr. Howser, well done! Load the gangplank and drop the rudder sail!" Mathias replied.

"Aye Capn'!" Some men on deck shouted. A couple of them hurried to the loading gap, an open section on the port side of the ship's railing. In unison they called out. "One, two, heave!" Pulling the long, wooden board, halfway onto the main deck. A second "One, two, heave!" was all they needed to get it completely on board. They laid it perpendicular to the deck boards and tied off the ends. That was where it would sit until the next time Anne-Marie made port.

Meanwhile, other men dropped the stern sail into place. The sailors held the sail's ropes in position while others tied off the tops near the peak of the mast. Before the end of the sail had even been secured, a small breeze was filling it, trying to move the ship away from the dock.

"Release the mooring lines!" Mathias commanded.

Frederick hung over the port side railing and relayed the command to the dock workers.

"Release the mooring line for the Anne-Marie!"

"God speed to ya!" A dock worker yelled back, before untying the rope and throwing it into the water.

Anne-Marie pulled the rest of the slack from the rope as it backed away from the dock. The free rope splashed into the water. Men on deck pulled it up through the bow hole. They consolidated it into a pile, looping the end around itself before tying it off to prevent the whole bundle from unraveling itself.

"Bring her out easy, Mr. Baley." Mathias instructed the coxswain.

"Aye Captain." Norman followed the instructions masterfully. The stern of the Anne- Marie moved deeper into the harbor before turning, so the bow could glide past the dock with sufficient clearance. Once the nose was pointed away from the heart of the city, Norman spun the rudder and adjusted the sail above the rudder. The maneuver changed how the wind moved the sail. Instead of pulling, the wind was now pushing the ship towards open water.

Anne-Marie was sailing away from the harbor within an hour after the completion of the manifest. All men had been accounted for and they all hoped that number would remain the same upon their arrival. Once the ship made it past the last dock in the harbor, the sailors sitting atop the yard arms let loose the main sails. With a jerk, the Anne-Marie picked up speed, carrying all 125 of the crewmembers away from home.

3

Paul Steiner

From the port side of the ship, the coast's edge was still in view. It was a sliver of green on the horizon, the trees near the water barely tall enough to be seen. The harbor, however, had been put far behind the Anne-Marie. It was as though it'd never been there at all when viewed beyond the stern railing. The ship was considered completely out to sea, the vast field of choppy water surrounding it, on all sides but one.

The men had agreed on their shifts of responsibilities earlier that day. Normally the matters settled agreeably, but the longer the trip went on, the less inclined the men were to continue behaving that way. Leaders such as Frederick would have to get involved and start assigning chores and timetables, who was doing them, and when they needed completed.

Paul Steiner had the unfortunate role of being the first night watch, along with James Corty. James was the other sailor who'd forgotten his name during roll call, thinking he'd gotten away with it. Paul assumed that James must've been hunted down by the first mate and given the honor of fellow night watchman.

Paul had reported to the helm as he'd been ordered, right as the sun was beginning to sag on the edge of the horizon, casting its orange glow over the domain of the sea. The first mate was elsewhere, finding someone to yell at Paul assumed. The captain was also nowhere to be found. The only men at the helm were himself, the coxswain Norman, and the other unlucky night watchman, James.

"Paul Steiner reporting for night watch duty as ordered." Paul stood at attention, back rigid, and his belly sticking out well past the lines of his legs.

"I'm here too." Was all James said. It'd been less than a day and he was already fed up with the voyage. Called out in front of the rest of the crew had been bad enough, but being forced to conduct first watch was something he considered to be 'excessive punishment', one that didn't fit the crime.

"Very well gents." The coxswain addressed both of them without taking his eyes off of Anne-Marie's bow. "The first mate left orders in case you reported before he got back. I'm not going to hold yer hand either so pay attention. This ain't yer first time at sea so I'm not going to waste time getting into it." Norman made small adjustments to the wheel as he talked. "Watch for any lights on the horizon, watch for fires, watch for sailors getting into things they shouldn't, ring the bell for emergencies, and don't fall asleep. Any questions?"

"No, sir." Replied Paul.

"No." Replied James.

"Very well. You'll be relieved at dawn. You can use the lanterns behind me. They've been filled with oil so they should last you the night. It'll be a full moon tonight, if the clouds stay away, so only use them below deck. No point wastin' any oil when we don't have to."

Paul and James each grabbed a lantern off the crate behind Norman and left the helm. Paul went to the starboard side and James walked port-side to begin their patrols.

Paul set his lantern down at his feet and leaned against Anne-Marie's railing. The wood creaked and groaned as he rested the majority of his weight against it. He watched the choppy water making sea foam in the water until it disappeared a few minutes later in the ship's wake as it bobbed casually on the waves. The sun was almost fully hidden beneath the horizon line. Soon, only the light of the moon among the glittering stars would provide company. He didn't move until the moon was the dominant beacon in the sky. The coxswain had been right. There was a full moon producing more than enough light so that he didn't need the lantern to navigate around the topside of the ship. The exception would be going below deck to check on the other sailors and the ship's cargo. There was plenty of time for that later. Paul still heard ruckus coming up from below deck as the sailors celebrated a successful launch. From experience, Paul knew they'd be at it for a while. This made him realize that's also probably where the captain and the first mate had been hanging out when he reported for his watch. Thinking about all of them down there getting fat, drunk, and being merry without him stirred ripples of anger. He wanted to be down there too, getting fatter, if that was even possible. He knew he should try to lose weight, but it was hard to prevent himself from gorging when the opportunity arose.

"It's alright." Paul told himself. "I'll have my own little celebration when everyone else is asleep." He knew the consequences if caught, but that didn't matter. It wasn't fair for everyone else to have all the fun while he was stuck on watch the first night. And for what? Answering a second too slowly for the likes of the first mate, *Frederick Howser?* A stupid reason in Paul's eyes.

That's all he could think about for the next three hours of his watch. The food and drink he'd enjoy in the belly of the ship. Filling *his* belly with as much salted meat and rum as he could handle, and then a little bit more beyond even that. He wasn't going to pay the hard tack any mind, no sir. It was only going to be the best provisions for Paul Steiner.

Paul continued his patrols around the edge of the deck, stopping every time he got close to the hole leading down into the ship. He leaned over the opening and listened for any commotion to come up through. The first few laps around the ship were as expected, lots of noise and merrymaking, with the occasional sound of breaking glass. The first mate would expect him to clean it up, no doubt. Songs sung and jokes told, a few of those jokes would be at Paul Steiner's expense, but he paid them no mind. He was going to have the last laugh after they went to sleep.

It was around midnight when Paul made his tenth lap around the circumference of the Anne-Marie. He saw James every now and again, moving around the outside, same as himself. Paul almost imagined James as a sort of shadow following him in the night, keeping that perfect distance like shadows always seem to do. Knowing there was someone else suffering the same as he was, brought him a level of satisfaction bordering on the sensational. What brought Paul even more pleasure was knowing that he was going to enjoy a feast that James wasn't invited to.

A couple more trips around the deck and the sounds below were settling down. The merrymaking was soon going to be at an end and Paul's merrymaking would begin. The accordions had slowed their pace, the singers were slurring their words, the storytellers had run out of tales to tell for the evening. Paul was certain most of the men had already found their hammock lodgings for the night, waiting to suffer the consequences of their overindulgences in the morrow. There were always those holdouts though. The sailors refused for the festivities to end until every last drop from their wooden steins emptied, and the last bit of meat stripped off the bone.

"Just one more. One more lap ought to do it." The verbal affirmation solidified Paul's resolve. Everyone else might have thoroughly enjoyed themselves but none had the same enjoyment that he was going to. Not by a long shot.

Paul scanned the deck of the ship, not looking for anything in particular, but interested in what he could see if anything. James looked like he'd taken up a post next to the stairs leading to the helm. His shape made it appear as if he was leaning against the handrail, no doubt already catching a few winks of sleep, the bastard. Towards the helm he could make out the contours of the coxswain, but much of his figure hidden behind constantly flapping sails, making it hard to discern much of anything.

It was when he looked towards the bow of the ship that he first saw a shadow he couldn't quite make out or recognize. Chances were rather good that it was a sailor coming atop to take a piss off the bow. "Giving a little bit back to the sea," they'd sometimes say. That description wasn't quite right though. Even the most seasoned sailor would be wobbling back and forth after having a few drinks, especially if their hands were occupied with controlling their sea serpent and not focused on balancing. No, this shadow was still, standing perfectly erect, not faltering even when the ship broke through a wave that knocked Paul off balance.

Paul took several steps forward. He'd made a trip around the ship a few minutes prior and hadn't seen anything out of the ordinary. He'd also been standing next to the door leading downstairs and he'd have heard if someone came up past him, despite being lost in thought about food. For a second, he thought about lighting the lamp but quickly parted with the idea. It was so bright from the moon that lighting a lamp would blind him more than it would help him.

As he approached, the shape remained still, not moving, not adjusting to the waves, stalwart. Paul could make out a few more of the features. The shape had a small head, slim shoulders that tapered down to a wide, curved waist, and long legs that stretched for several meters down to the wooden deck.

Paul had never been a charismatic or lucky man when it came to women. Mostly, he had to purchase their company from port to port, but the devil be damned if he didn't know what the contours of a lovely woman looked like. Not only was the woman beautifully shaped, but from what Paul could tell, she was also naked. The thought made his heart start to race. All the moisture was escaping his mouth, and he frantically licked his lips in an effort to get it back. His attempts were useless; his mouth was as dry as the hard tack he refused to eat. With a single hand, he swiped the top of his head trying to flatten what little hair he had left. He only managed to push a few hairs down across the length of his dome, which flopped right back over after he stopped pressing on them.

Paul's desire was so intense, he never stopped for a second to determine where the woman might've come from, or why she'd be standing frozen in place near the front of the Anne-Marie. None of that mattered to Paul. All he cared about was that it might be the luckiest night of his life.

That was, until he was standing only a couple of feet away from the beautifully curved figure. The slim contours vanished in the dark. It wasn't as though the figure moved to disappear, like smoke or haze. One second, he was moving closer to the shadow and the next, there was no longer a shadow at all. It didn't move, it didn't shift, it was simply gone. Paul refused to accept it, and he frantically searched around the bow of the ship. He dove around the forward mast rigging, searched behind crates, barrels, and even dug through spools of rope. Before Paul finished, he'd looked over every edge of the bow and even over the side of the Anne-Marie into the ocean, hoping for any sign of splashing water or human shapes.

Paul found nothing, unlucky yet again.

"I know I saw something. It was there…she was standing *right* there." Paul was still looking over the railing when a hand grabbed him by the shoulder. His voice cracked when trying to yell, so the only sound that managed to eke out of his throat was a squeak.

"What're ya doin' ya barrel lookin' idiot?" James had to practically drag Paul back onto the deck. Paul had nearly gone overboard looking for the shadow woman after being startled. Only one foot was on solid wood. The other was in the air from leaning over the railing. If it hadn't been for James, Paul might've gone overboard in search of his lost love.

"I…I…was just checking the…the lines." James looked at Paul, concerned. "You uhh, didn't happen to see anything did you? Shadow or figure wise…?" The more Paul talked the more concerned the look on James's face became. "Uhh nevermind, forget it."

"Uhuh, well you're going below deck first. I'm gonna stay up here, don't feel like going down."

Right, you're probably going to get some more sleep up here while I'm gone, leaning on that post of yours by the helm. What a stupid place to try and sleep on duty anyway with the coxswain and captain's quarters only a few meters away. How dumb can you be? Paul thought to himself.

"And don't go sleepin' down ther' neither." James added.

Yea you're one to talk, you hypocritical bottom feeder. "Aye, I won't." *One of these days I'm going to call you out. All of you. Bunch o' lying, food hoarding, miscreants. You can't keep Paul down forever, no sir. I'm going to have my time and you'll all be sorry when I'm in charge and running things. Just you wait. I'll start with the personal feast but who knows where it might go from there.* His mind was running through its typical ramblings about the injustices he'd faced and how his future was going to be different from his past. Even though after fifteen years he was no more than a glorified cabin boy.

Paul's conquest would have to wait though. That night he was only a night watchman and there wasn't much he could do about that at the time. His only option was to accept the duty and scrape a little comfort off the side for himself in the meantime.

James left Paul alone on the bow, heading back to his own perch below the helm.

Paul couldn't help but look around some more. *I know she was here, that woman was standing right here. I'm almost certain I wasn't imagining it. However, she was standing oddly straight, and the motion of the waves didn't seem to affect her at all. Almost like she's attached to the ship, like her feet nailed to the boards of the deck, to help her stay upright. Whatever, I know what I saw, doesn't matter right now. The sailors should be done downstairs and even if there's no women, I know there's rum and salted meat waiting for me.*

The thought of those two delights was enough to make Paul forget about his mystery mistress for a minute. He proceeded with his final lap around the edge of the deck. James was in his spot next to the stairs leading up to the wheel of the ship. He was leaning against the post again, picking his teeth with a broken piece of wood he'd chipped off the railing in front of him.

"Don't fall asleep." Paul mumbled while passing behind him, heading to the opposite side of the ship.

"What was that?" James asked, taking the chipped piece of wood from his mouth, holding it between his thumb and forefinger like a small knife.

"Nothing James, nothing." Paul replied, raising his hands in the universal gesture of innocence.

"Aye...nothin'." Was all James replied before going back to the task of removing an unwanted piece of food stuck between his teeth and gums.

Paul reached the top of the stairs leading down to the center of the ship, listening intently for any sounds coming up from within. He even put a hand up to his ear as he leaned down the top of the steps to get a better angle. He was unable to hear anything but the creaking of the ship's boards, the swinging of hammocks on rusted nails, and the unsynchronized snoring of dozens of drunken sailors. It was finally time, time for Paul to get what he believed owed to him by thunder. He brought his unlit lantern over to another one that was already burning on a post and grabbed the wick attached to it on a length of string. He opened the glass housing and lit the end of the wick, transferring the fire from the other lantern to his own. The flame took quickly. With a single puff, he blew out the wick and closed the glass housings to both lanterns. His hands were shaking from uncontrollable excitement, making him almost drop the lantern.

Paul took a second to calm his heart as it tried to pound through his chest. He took a few deep breaths, then turned around, heading to the stairs.

Paul didn't notice James, who'd turned around at his spot to watch the strange spectacle that was Paul Steiner. James shook his head, still picking his teeth and spitting over the edge of the ship whenever he managed to dislodge another piece of unfinished food.

Paul walked deliberately to the top of the steps, but before descending he glanced at the bow of the ship. It was only for a second, but he swore that the voluptuous female figure was standing there looking out over the front railing. She was unwavering, unmoving, like he'd seen her before. This time he had a lit lantern and could test to see if it made his vision better or worse. He raised it as far out in front of him as he could, stretching his arm to its maximum reach. The shape disappeared once more, even though the small flame wasn't powerful enough to reach from the stairwell to the bow. A concept lost on Paul, who accepted that it may have been a trick of the imagination all along. With a shrug, he proceeded down the steps to where his true loves were waiting for him.

Below deck, it would've been hard to imagine that the party was over. Even though all the sailors were either in their hammocks or on the floor asleep, plenty of noises still filled the air. Most of the men were snoring loud enough to wake the dead, others were tossing and turning. Mugs knocked over, bottles rolled across the floor with every ebb and flow of the ship, and the occasional instrument fell and played a couple garbled notes without an audience to hear them. Despite the noises they were making, each and every one of the sailors had passed out in a deep slumber.

There was one other time in his life where Paul had seen something that resembled the scene. It was during a voyage through the triangle where he found himself part of a mutiny. It wasn't a major mutiny. Hell, the ship only had thirty others on board, but the five mutineers ensured they would be the only five on board one night. Paul was on deck as a lookout while the other four took to slaughtering the rest in their sleep down below. When he didn't hear anything for a while, he went down to see how everything was progressing. The sight was similar to what he saw now. Bodies sprawled out in every direction. Arms, legs, heads, torsos of different bodies all mangled together in strange configurations. It didn't bother Paul, instead it brought back memories of a better time when he felt proud of himself for fitting into a group, even if it was as a mutineer.

The life of a mutineer was lucrative, assuming you could get away with it. You had to find an unsavory place to unload the newly stolen goods and a buyer willing to do business with criminals. They'd sold more than 100 barrels of food, spices, and different drinks, much like the ones stored on the ship he was standing on. *This* was a company trade ship though. Paul knew it contained much better spoils in the lower decks. Ones that would put the swill of that previous sloop to shame.

The trash provisions may be enough to satisfy these men tonight but not I. It's the premier cargo for Paul Steiner tonight. Paul thought to himself.

Paul worked his way through the room, to the set of stairs on the opposite side of the ship. He tiptoed between sailors laying sprawled out on the floor. Their legs spread wide, and he used this to his advantage, taking each step carefully. He had every right to be down there doing his routine checks, but it was common to get in a fight or two with drunk, ornery sailors who'd woken from a nice dream.

As he stepped between a pair of hairy legs with the pants rolled up nearly to their waist, something brushed up against Paul's back. He wheeled around to see who, or what, might've put a hand on him. As he pivoted, he realized it was another man lying in a hammock. The swinging sailor had rolled over in his sleep and their stiff arm tapped Paul on the back.

A couple of times, Paul had to suck in his gut to get through particularly tricky areas. In some places men packed together so tight, you weren't sure if they'd been only jolly close friends during the celebration, or a little bit more. Their arms and legs all mingled together to form a strange, hairy, ten-legged creature with arms protruding from what appeared to be random places around it. As Paul maneuvered around the harry amalgamation, a strong stench rose to greet him. There was the typical sailor stench, the one from long sprints at sea without bathing, but it hadn't even been a day, and this conglomerate of bodies produced a scent fouler than anything Paul was accustomed to. It curled the hairs in his nostrils and made his entire face scrunch together like a snarling canine.

And they call me *gross. Clearly, they've all gone mad. I've never in all my years been as disgusting as this lot's been tonight.* Paul thought as he spotted a strip of meat dangling half eaten in one man's hand. The arm holding the meat was part of the man-monster splayed out before him. If he didn't know any better, it appeared as though the creature fell asleep halfway through getting the meat to one of its many mouths. *Although...tonight may end up being the exception to that. I might not look much better when all's said and done.*

The mere thought of it, and seeing the half-eaten strip got Paul's mouthwatering. He lapped the moisture up with a flick of the tongue and proceeded onward, downward.

The lower deck was a pleasant change from the crypt of drunken, sailor bodies above. The space was far from empty. Cannons lined both sides of the ship. The windows where they poked out their barrels were all closed and their wheels securely fastened to the floor. A few of the cannons had company, as sailors found comfort in their iron flesh. One man had taken to mounting his cannon the same way he'd mount a wench. He lay sprawled on top of it, arms and legs hanging over the sides, with his britches pulled down well past the bottom of the knees but not quite reaching the ankles.

There wasn't much else of note on this floor of the ship. The space that wasn't taken up by cannons and sleeping sailors, was occupied by gunpowder, cannonballs, and rope. All of it was carefully organized along the edges of the hull, so that each cannon had its own supply of all three when needed.

Paul's trip to the opposite side of the Anne-Marie and the final set of stairs was uneventful. There were no portholes this deep in the bowels of the ship, which meant the lantern was his only source of light. Even after having been down below long enough for his eyes to adjust, there was only so much they could do against the darkness. He wanted to take his time to carefully descend, but his anticipation was mounting. His heart raced in his chest, and he could feel sweat forming on the palms of his hands.

The glow of the lantern lit his way, but there wasn't far left to go.

Upon reaching the base of the stairs, Paul's journey abruptly ended. A chest high wall of wood stopped him from going any deeper into the room. He could peer over the top of the first row and knew the barrels traveled all the way to the other side of the ship in long, straight lines. He recognized the crates and barrels immediately for what they were, treasure. He looked at the markings on the round barrel closest to where he was standing. It had '*PORK*', printed in big, beautiful, black lettering on the side. He wheeled around to look at a barrel on the opposite side, which had '*RUM*' written on it in the same fashion as the pork.

There was no containing the excitement now. Paul placed the lantern on one of the steps behind him without removing his eyes from the barrels. He ran a single hand over the top of the wood sealing the pork barrel. His fingers gently caressed the lid, until his stomach rumbled. Using both hands, Paul tore the top off with the strength of an elephant.

At first there didn't appear to be any meat inside. All he saw was a container full of tiny white crystals. He gazed at them the same way he looked at a night sky full of stars, except all the stars had been shoved together and forced into a barrel.

Paul plunged a hand into the shimmering pool up to the wrist. At first, the fingertips found nothing except the gritty texture of sand. His excitement was being replaced with dread, as he continued to have little luck in digging up any treasure. That's when he decided to dig even deeper. He drove his arm into the center of the barrel, almost up to his elbow, and his fingers finally struck something. The fingers brushed against a soft, squishy object. His joy was renewed. He clawed at the fleshy bits until he had a fistful. With a firm tug, Paul removed his arm from the barrel and stared slack jawed at the contents of his hand.

Four massive chunks of pink meat sat squished together in Paul's clutches. Each one looked perfect in his eyes. He stood there for a few moments, idolizing their texture, color, and consistency.

When the moisture in his mouth began to overflow the dam of his lips, Paul shoved the entire handful into his mouth. His teeth tried to work on the meat as best they could, but the tongue was already shoving pieces down his gullet before they'd had a chance to properly break it apart. One hand held pieces of meat for his gaping maw to pull from, while the other was busy digging out more pork from the barrel.

A couple of times, the salt became too strong. Paul paused to chew the larger pieces into smaller ones before swallowing. This only delayed his feast for a few seconds, until he got the pieces to a manageable size to swallow once more. He was well into his tenth handful before the saltiness forced him to quench his thirst. He remembered the barrel of rum, right on the other side of where he was standing. While still gripping handfuls of pork, he tore open the top of the rum barrel with his free hand. The lid didn't want to budge at first, but Paul was persistent. He dug his fingers into the small gaps at the top and yanked with all his might. The barrel creaked and groaned in protest, but it was no match against the ravenous sailor. There was a *snap* as the lid broke free and tumbled to the floor.

Paul saw a small reflection of light in the liquid. The area was too dark to tell precisely what the barrel contained. Based on appearance alone, it could've been water, but the scent was dense, and it couldn't have been mistaken for anything else but rum. He leaned his face towards the surface, not hesitating to look for a ladle or stein to scoop some up with. He moved his mouth so close that all he had to do was pucker out his lips to slurp it up. The sweet burning taste went smoothly down his throat. The rum dislodged fragments of salt crystals stuck on the lining of his throat. The flavor of salt and rum complimented each other, making Paul increasingly ravenous.

Rum was normally too strong and harsh tasting on its own for Paul to fully enjoy, but it was quality stock, sold for top coin in Asia.

With food and drink requirements satisfied, the real feast began. The one-man banquet became a relay race. Paul grabbed a handful of meat, shoving it in his mouth, and swallowing most of it whole. Then running over to the rum barrel, shoving half his face in it to get a mouthful instead of carefully sipping off the top like the first time. He was four laps in before the thought of slowing down crossed his mind. He swallowed a larger than normal piece of pork and it got stuck halfway down his pipe. He gulped a big swig of rum to break it loose. The piece went down without any further resistance, and he went to the stairs to sit down for a break after nearly choking. The scent of unwashed sailors wafted into his nostrils again. This time, he had only himself to blame as his armpits dripped with sweat. "Nothing like a good party to get the juices flowin', aye?" He said out loud to no one but himself. Paul prided himself on proper speech since it made him feel superior to his other sailor counterparts. When he drank though, that propriety quickly slipped away, and he began sounding like any other sea dog. "Thas' pert' good stuff I's say..." He wagged his finger at the rum barrel in approval. "You and I's gona' be good f-friends 'is veryage I can tell ya." The barrel didn't respond but he nodded in agreement as though it'd.

Paul's head was spinning faster and faster as the motion of the waves rocked the ship. He closed his eyes and enjoyed the sensation of floating. His body rocked in unison with the ship, almost dozing off a couple of times in the process. "Uhuh, can' be 'avin' none o' that. Still got mor' eatin' to do." He pushed himself off the steps, feeling something soft and squishy beneath his hands. He looked down, not realizing that he'd still had a large strip of pork in his fist when he'd sat down. Without hesitation he peeled the pieces of meat off the wood, like removing a bloody bandage off an open wound, and put it in his mouth. His teeth only bit the strip in two, before gulping both pieces down. "An' up we go." It took considerable effort, but with plenty of help from the rope banister and the stair steps, Paul managed to get himself back on his feet.

Once up, Paul couldn't decide if he wanted to get more rum or pork first. He played a quick game of eenie meenie minie moe. The pork was the victor. He leaned over the edge of the barrel, using the top rim for balance, and shoved his arm deep inside. The salt was reaching his armpit at this point before he was deep enough to find any meat. He rested his cheek on top of the salt pile while blindly digging for the pork. While his fingers dug through the white, sandy crystals, he peered towards the back of the ship, over all of the barrels lined up in perfectly straight rows.

The initial moments after coming down into the lowest deck of the Anne-Marie he could only see about three or four barrels back. With his eyes now well-adjusted to the dark, he could see almost ten barrels back, and there was something lying on top of them.

At first only a distorted silhouette was visible. A round object in the middle, with two long cylinders in the shape of an upside down 'V' on either side of it, holding the sphere shape up at the point where the two lines met. The orientation seemed strange at first, but then it grew clearer. The round object was a head and the two cylinders in the 'V' shape were arms coming out of it. Paul had seen this kind of pose before. The figure was a person, and they were laying on their stomach looking straight at him.

There wasn't much room between the top of the barrels and the ceiling of the storage deck. Paul figured the person would've had to crawl on their stomach, pulling on barrels to get in the position they were. He believed that even on hands and knees they would've been too tall to maneuver to where they were laying.

Paul pulled his arm out of the salt and turned his head so he could sit upright and get a better orientation. Once his body was straightened up, the shape was still there, unlike what'd happened on the main deck. He was staring at the silhouette while it stared back at him, only it didn't have eyes. The round shape of what Paul assumed to be a head resting on a set of arms was blank of any distinct features. His body was frozen in disbelief, but if there was one thing he'd learned to trust over the years, it was his sight. There wasn't much else in the world he trusted more than his eyes.

Neither of them moved while they stared each other down.

Paul's heart was racing. There was eerily disturbing about the figure lying there. The silhouette looked like that of a woman, and he wanted to deny it, but she *was* lying there. The idea of her being a stowaway crossed his mind, but that didn't seem quite right either. The bottom part of the sphere split open, revealing two rows of white teeth stretching out into a smile. His heart was still hammering in his chest. Droplets of sweat ran down the length of his face and neck, joining his already saturated armpits. He tried calling out to her.

"I-I saw yer on deck..." Paul's words fumbled weakly from his mouth.

The shape remained motionless, smiling.

"That was you was'n it?" Paul was trying, with every ounce of his being, to keep what he was saying coherent. The rum was doing a fine job of making that difficult. "How ye 'et over ther'?" He continued to make what he thought was eye contact, but the shape of the silhouette became blurrier with each passing second. "Are yu' a mermed er siren 'ome to terment' me?"

Curiosity turned to anger, which was common for Paul when he'd had more to drink than he could manage.

"Well fin' 'en. Stay ove' there ya sea' bitch!" Paul took the piece of meat he'd found before standing up, and threw it in the direction of the figure on the barrels. It flew a couple of meters, splattering against the ceiling before landing atop one of the barrels two rows back from where Paul was standing. It made a *plop* sound when it hit, like a soaking wet mop being dropped on the deck by a sailor who was sick and tired of swabbing it.

Paul immediately regretted his decision to throw away the meat, when he realized there was now nothing in his hand to eat. Instead of digging for another piece of pork, he decided to drink more rum. He licked the salt off of his fingers while making his way over to the other barrel. Before he could stick his head into it, a small gust of wind coming from the back of the room blew against his face. On the wind, a voice was carried, the voice of the woman lying atop the barrels.

"Looooooook ooooooooout..." The voice was soft, dragging out as though she were calling to him from the other side of a long tunnel.

Paul heard a loud thudding noise coming from the top of the stairs directly behind him. Whatever the object was, it was rolling down the stairs towards him with heavy thuds.

Paul's reactions time had been slowed, in no small part to his inebriation, but thanks to the woman's warning there was enough time to realize what was happening. Paul didn't have enough room where he was standing to dive out of harm's way, so instead, he tried to squeeze his body on top of the nearest barrel. His foot barely pulled up in time before the object made a final, loud crash onto the floor and colliding with the lantern on its descent. The lantern's glass housing shattered, blowing out the flame and drowning Paul in darkness.

If Paul's eyes hadn't already partially adjusted, it would've been impossible for him to see anything. Having been down there for quite some time in the little space, he also felt confident that he could make his way around in the confines of the room.

"What the 'ell?" Paul mumbled. He didn't quite manage to get his entire body squeezed into the narrow space between the barrel and the ceiling. The majority of his stomach wedged against the barrel he was lying on and his chest.

The object that careened down the stairs sounded to him like a cannonball, even though that seemed unlikely since they were fastened securely on the deck above. He'd seen stranger things happen though, like the shadow woman lying twenty meters or so atop the barrels behind him.

"Th-thanks lady...at coulda done some severe damage if it 'anded on me foot or sometin'..." looking behind, he could see she was still resting motionless on the barrels, but her smile was no less intense.

Getting off the barrel was much easier than getting on top of it. Paul let gravity do most of the work as he fell to the floor. One of his feet landed on the wood and the other got stuck. He flailed his arms to maintain balance while getting his foot free. The flexibility of his legs surprised even him. He managed to shimmy the foot off the barrels and when both feet were firmly on the ground, he took a few moments to regain full balance.

Paul looked at the round shape on the floor. It looked roughly the size of a cannonball, at least compared to every cannonball he'd seen, which was several by this point in his life. The only thing was this cannonball wasn't smooth like it should've been. There were multiple protrusions coming out the sides. He took a few steps closer to it, glass crunched under his feet from the broken lantern, breaking into smaller pieces with each step he took.

"Vury funny boys...!" Paul yelled up to the top of the stairs. "Yu' can come out now...!"

There was no reply.

Paul felt strands of what he could only assume to be rope rubbing against his ankles, from around the cannonball shaped object. He thought the sailors must've wrapped some around it, along with a few other odds and ends to make it appear startling.

"Vury convincin' fellas. Makin it looks like..." Paul's voice cut out as he picked it up.

The strands seemed to mimic rope, but they were everywhere. They were all around the surface of the cannonball, as if the strands were coming out of it and not wrapped around. Also, the texture was wrong. The ball wasn't smooth and hard like he was expecting. He felt a couple flaps protruding on opposite sides of it. His brain might've slowed from the rum, but it was currently working overtime to try and figure out what he was holding.

The sensations of dread and disbelief fought for control in his mind. Dread won over in the end, as he realized it wasn't a trick of the dim light or the other sailors trying to mess with him. Paul was holding a severed head in his hands. What he couldn't figure out was who it may have belonged to. It seemed irrelevant at the time, but it was easier for Paul to try and figure that out, or else he'd lose his collective sanity. He tried to study the features and discern anything he could from the contours of the face. Looking to find some clue as to who the owner might be. It was difficult down here in the dark, especially now that his only source of light had vanished. Based on feeling alone, all the features of the head appeared to be in the right place, but some of them seemed...off.

A stiff wave knocked against the side of the Anne-Marie. All the wood down below began to creak and bend. The crates and barrels rubbed against each other trying to break free of their rope bonds. The groaning of wood echoed throughout the room. Paul dropped the head in surprise, grabbing the nearest barrel to maintain his footing. The head rolled away from him into a corner of the room underneath the stairs.

Even after the ship steadied itself, the sounds remained. The creaking continued to grow louder. The barrels towards the back sounded as if they were under some kind of massive strain. Even the stairs were groaning, aching to move.

Paul had slid down to his knees from the shock of the wave that hit the side of the ship. That's where he stayed, holding tightly to one of the barrels and waiting for the noises to cease. He was too drunk; the sounds were pounding in his head and every rapid beat of his heart sent another wave of pressure careening through his skull. For the first time in his life, Paul didn't want any more pork or rum. All he wanted was to be back on the main deck in the protective glow of the moonlight.

Despite his best efforts, the noises refused to settle. The loudest offenders were coming from the other end of the ship, towards him. With both meaty hands Paul covered each of his ears, but it seemed ineffective against the torrent of creaks. As they reached a crescendo of moaning, they suddenly stopped.

Paul cautiously lowered his hands, ready to throw them up again at the first sign of creaking planks. When covering his ears, he'd instinctively closed his eyes as well. He opened them slowly, one at a time. The room was still dark and having open eyes wasn't much different from closed ones. That was until he started to look around. When he did, his pupils met with a different pair of eyes that were blacker than the night sky and deeper than any ocean. The irises swirled around in their cosmic sockets like a vortex of water. He could sense them looking *through* him rather than looking *at* him. Surrounded by a head of hair that floated around them like packs of seaweed on the ocean floor.

Paul mustered the strongest scream he could manage, but it came out no louder than the squeak of a mouse. The last thing Paul remembered was the vortexes of eyes growing to the size of the room and the sensation of falling into them, as though the entire floor had disappeared. There was no wind, no air, no spray of sea water, merely emptiness. The last few seconds felt like an eternity before he lost consciousness.

4

Mathias Crane

What...?

"I don't know..." Mathias grumbled aloud in his sleep.

What are you...

The voice swirled in his head, mixing with fevered dreams.

Mathias was rocking back and forth in his hammock inside the captain's cabin. The sea was calm, gently nudging him back and forth making it difficult to stay asleep or wake up.

What are you..

"I'm...the captain...captain of the Anne-Marie." Mathias answered the voice as best he could, but his responses were incoherent to anyone that may have been in the room. Images and scenes of vast emptiness kept swallowing him every time he almost reached a light. He'd get close enough to reach out to it, to fully awaken, only for the dream to throw him back into the abyss again.

What are you gonna do...

"Complete...the voyage...first voyage...must finish, no matter what." The light was in reach again, but the smooth swinging of the hammock sucked him away from it every time.

...drunken sailor.

"*What? I'm not...who's drunk?*" In his dream Mathias was reaching out for the light, but in the cabin, he was swatting at invisible insects hanging over his face.

What are you gonna do...with a drunken sailor?

"*Punish...punish if necessary...*" Mathias' fingers reached out and finally managed to touch the light with their tips. The light pulled him forward, swallowing him in a bright glow, throwing him out of his sleep and back into the world, awake. His head shot up from the hammock, but once he realized that he'd startled awake, he carefully laid back down, focusing on the sensation of rocking with the ocean waves.

Lucy was asleep on his chest, purring away, chasing ship rats in her dreams no doubt. When she woke up, she'd probably do the same thing, chase some ship rats for a nice morning breakfast. Mathias stroked her fur, and Lucy began to purr louder, stretching out one paw revealing claws, like little needles. Perfect killing weapons against rodents.

It would've been easy for Mathias to fall back asleep with the swaying of the ship and Lucy lying comfortably on his chest like a small fur blanket. The only problem was, directly outside the cabin door, many of the other men were loudly singing. He could make out a verse or two each time they chanted a new line.

"What are you gonna do..." was the first line he heard. Then it got quieter, then picking up again by "...with a drunken sailor."

His dream made more sense now.

"The voice wasn't so mysterious after all, huh girl." Mathias scratched behind Lucy's ears, but the cat didn't stir. "It was just men on deck singing songs. Not the song I'd want to hear them singing this early in the morning, but not much we can do about that now is there?"

Lucy opened her eyes to look at Mathias.

"I guess you're right. Better go take a look and see what's got them all in a commotion." Lucy was about to close her eyes again and fall back asleep, but Mathias was rolling out of the hammock. He swung his feet out and they landed on the deck, with Lucy landing a step or so beside him. She meowed disapprovingly, upset that she'd lost her bed. She'd have to go find a new one if she wanted to go back to sleep.

Mathias was already half dressed. He only had to put on a pair of boots and the larger of his outer coats in order to be presentable to the men. He didn't care much for nicer clothing like naval officers, but they did help to assert a level of authority. Sailors respected the finer things and those individuals that owned them, to some degree. He had to show his aptitude in other realms of leadership, but right now he needed all of the assistance he could get to garner some respect.

Mathias left the cabin. Lucy stayed where she'd jumped down, now cleaning herself and debating whether she wanted to go back to sleep or chase down a meal. She looked around the now empty cabin, first at the hammock and then at the crate filled with hay below it. Both looked comfortable and inviting, but after a nice stretch, she decided that food would come first.

The scene outside of the cabin was a gathering not commonly seen after a night like the men had. Mathias assumed the majority of sailors would still be sleeping off the celebration. The rest who was awake would only be the essential crewmembers on deck, keeping the lines and sails in check. Instead, he encountered a whole slew of sailors all joined together in a circle around someone. Mathias could hear one of the men near the center of the gaggle, playing a violin while all those gathered around chanted, "Drunken Sailor."

What do you do with a drunken sailor.

What do you do with a drunken sailor.
What do you do with a drunken sailor.
Early in the mornin'.
Shave his belly with a rusty razor.
Shave his belly with a rusty razor.
Shave his belly with a rusty razor.
Early in the mornin'.
Way hay and up she rises.
Way hay and up she rises.
Way hay and up she rises.
Early in the mornin'.
Throw him in the lock-up 'til he's sober.
Throw him in the lock-up 'til he's sober.
Throw him in the lockup 'til he's sober.
Early in the mornin'.
Way hay and up she rises.
Way hay and up she rises.
Way hay and up she rises.
EARLY IN THE MORNIN'!

The violinist finished with a flurry of hands and fingers. The rest of the men standing around all cheered. Some of them tried to strike up the chorus again, while others made jokes and laughed their hearts out.

Mathias pushed his way through the crowd as best he could, shouting at the entire group so they'd let him pass.

"Captain coming through! Get out of the way you mangy sea dogs! Let me pass!" Mathias wasn't holding back, but his voice had a minor impact against the boisterous wailing of the men around him. Only those that were directly next to him, as he pushed his way through, listened and got out of the way. They tried to tell others and get them to step aside as well, but so tightly packed together, they all but ignored the requests.

As he made slow progress towards the middle, Mister Howser spotted Mathias within the crowd, trying to make his way through. Frederick clambered on top of the crate he was standing next to and shouted. "Shut it! Your capn's tryin' to get through! Move out o' the way!"

This caused some of the men next to Mathias to realize who was trying so hard to shove them. When they realized, they did their best to get others next to them to realize it too.

"Yes, 'at means you lot!" Frederick pointed at a group straight in line with the direction of the captain's quarters. The crowd was more receptive now. The merry cheering stopped abruptly, and a tunnel opened in the crowd so that Mathias could get through without having to shove anyone else aside.

Mathias fixed his clothing that'd wrinkled and had nearly pulled off a couple of times fighting his way through the crowd. Once his coat straightened out and his boots seated properly on his feet once more, he made his way to the center of the gathering. He spotted a main tied up against the main mast, his head slouched down, almost far enough to reach his stomach. Both of his hands were bound and pulled taut around the mast, as though he were giving it a backwards hug.

"Good morrow gentlemen!" Mathias shouted to the crowd.

"Mornin' capn'!" They all replied.

"What's all this then?" Mathias asked, directing their attention to the tied-up man. "Ya'll act like you've never gotten drunk before. As a matter of fact, I would wager that was the vast majority of you last night." Many of them looked away, a little embarrassed. Some of them not even knowing what was going on since they'd become a part of the group only because of the singing.

"Aye that be true Capn'." Unsurprisingly, it was Frederick who'd responded. Mathias had hoped someone else would come forward, but alas, he still had to rely on his first mate to get any information.

"So, what is it then?" Once again, Mathias directed everyone's attention to the man sitting on the deck. The sailor was unconscious, having no idea that any of this was even happening around him.

"He was on duty last night, assigned to the watch as I'm sure ye remember." Frederick answered.

Mathias thought back to the day before, remembering the two men assigned the first night watch of the voyage. He walked over and squatted down next to the man. It should've been obvious from the rotund stomach that it was the fat one who'd forgotten his name. He lifted the man's head to make sure. The sailor's eyes didn't open, and his head flopped back down as soon as Mathias let go of it. "Aye so it is. That explains it well enough. Someone, fetch me a bucket of water."

"Sir!" Someone called out from the crowd. A couple of men ran over to the railing of the ship with a bucket. They tied the end of a rope to it and dropped it into the water. Once it was full to the brim, they hoisted it up. The rest of the men moved out of the way so the pair could bring it to the center of the circle. Mathias took the bucket from them and flung half the water onto Paul Steiner's face. He jerked awake.

Mathias poured the remaining water over the top of Paul's head for good measure before dropping the bucket on the deck. He knelt down in front of Paul, who managed to get his head up and rest it against the mast.

"Good morrow sailor. Want to explain your drunkenness on duty last night and hangover this morning?" It took a few moments for Paul to understand what was happening and who was talking to him. Everyone in the crowd looked blurry, partly from his hungover state and partly from the salt water that was now stinging his eyes. Mathias gently slapped him on the cheeks with an open palm. "Come on now, wake up. Explain yourself."

Still half unconscious Paul tried to speak. "I…I…there…down below…somethin'."

Mathias looked around at the crowd. "Aye sailor, there are many things down below. You might be one of those things yourself if I don't start getting some better answers." He tapped him on the cheek again. Mathias knew this was one of those golden opportunities to show that he could be a fair, but strict leader. There was a sizable crowd looking on and his actions now would resonate for the rest of the voyage. He never liked harsh punishments, but he knew that starting out strict and brutal while softening up over time was much more effective than starting off soft, and then trying to be tough later on.

"You dunt…understand. There's somethin'…somethin' evil on this ship. She…she…" Paul did his best to recollect what happened the night before, but the light from the morning sun was making his head throb. His stomach roiled and grumbled as he spoke too. Each word was difficult and almost painful to get out. "She was…" Before he could get any more words through, Paul threw his head to the side, vomiting what felt like half the meat he'd eaten last night, onto the deck.

A few of the men tried to jump out of the way to avoid having their feet covered in a disgusting mixture of rum, pork, and bile. Except it didn't look like any of those things and instead resembled a pink and green mixture of gruel.

Mathias stood up, moving away from Paul. He had no intention of being projectile vomited upon, not by the likes of Paul

Steiner. Instead, he turned his attention to Frederick for his line of inquiry.

"Who found him this morning?" Mathias asked.

"That would be the other watchman, sir." Frederick responded.

"That's good, at least one of them decided to do their job last night. Who was it again, James?" Mathias snapped his fingers a couple times, trying to rack his brain to remember the last name.

"Corty, sir."

"Ahh yes, James Corty. Where is he?"

"Oy, James Corty. Present yourself! Capn's got some questions for ye!"

Mathias kept his attention fixed on Paul, trying to determine what an appropriate level of punishment would be, based on what he currently assumed had happened. He wouldn't be able to decide until he knew the whole story, or at least a version of it.

"Movin' sir." A voice called out from the middle of the crowd.

Men were less inclined to move out of the way for James than they'd been for the captain. James had to force his way through the other men to get to the front. Some of them grunted, actively trying to impede his progress. They no doubt believed he was probably as guilty as the man tied to the mast and perhaps, they should've tied him to it as well. James could feel their stares and judgements but did his best to ignore them. When he managed to make it to the front, he stood facing the captain with all the bravery he could muster.

"Mr. James Corty?" Mathias confirmed.

"Yes sir!" James replied.

"What happened last night?"

The question was obvious, and James knew that the captain would ask it when he got there, but it still somehow caught him off guard. The strong front he intended to put on, with his arms behind him and his chest puffed out, had completely deflated after four simple words. "Well, I…he…we were…" This was much harder than he would've imagined. After all, he was innocent of any wrongdoing, but somehow, he felt as though he was guilty by association.

"Let's start with something easier. Where did you find Mr. Steiner?"

"On the storage deck…sir."

"Very good. Now, when did you find him?"

That one was harder to answer. James didn't want to admit that it'd taken him almost the entire night to notice the man was missing. He would've found him much sooner had he been more diligent in his duties.

"I…umm…this mornin', 'bout an hour 'fore first light." James prematurely winced, ready to receive a verbal lashing. A punishment that would make the one he'd gotten the day before look like a pleasant chat among friends.

"Why you…!" Frederick was prepared to give James a strike he'd never forget, but Mathias stopped him before he could get the hit off.

"It's alright. I want to get to the bottom of everything before we start dishing out punishments unjustly. That means hearing the whole story from both sides." Mathias cocked his head to check on Paul's status. The tied-up sailor looked as though he was more prepared to produce another torrent of vomit than provide his testimony.

"We'll get back to that." Mathias said under his breath, before bringing his attention back to James. "Did you hear Mr. Steiner's ramblings a few moments ago?"

"A little bit of it sir…but not much. Couldn't hear much from where I was standing."

"That's fine. He says there was something down in the storage deck. You see anything unusual when you found Paul there?"

"N...no sir. Nothing out of the ordinary. The only thing I saw was his lantern that he'd managed to break, at the bottom of the stairs. Hell, he might have just missed a step and fallen down, breaking the lantern in the process, and knocking himself unconscious. Even this mornin' it was incredibly dark down there. No tellin' what he might o' saw. I found him lyin' up against some o' the barrels, passed out. I couldn't wake him or move 'im myself, so I got some help to get him up here."

"Why did it take you so long to find him? Surely you went looking for him when you hadn't seen him for hours?"

James knew he'd have to be careful now. The next few sentences could mean a light talking to, a harsh beating, or worse. He didn't want to think about that though. His throat was thick and dry. He managed to swallow and clear it before answering. "I...uhh..." There was no point in lying. James knew he wasn't the brightest star in the sky, and the captain catching him in a lie would almost certainly be as bad as any other crime he'd committed. "I never went below deck to do my rounds. I s...stayed on the top side the whole night. Paul had gone down, and I assumed he was doing rounds down there and hadn't come back up. It wasn't till twilight when I remembered that I hadn't seen him in a while and went searching. I checked everywhere until I found him in the lowest room."

After James finished his story, there were stirrings in the crowd. Men grumbled and groaned, while others called out what they considered to be fair punishments for both men. Ten to twenty lashes, before a week in the brig, was the popular opinion. The more extreme sailors called for a hanging the next time the ship made port.

"That's enough! I'll make the decisions here!" Mathias yelled. "I appreciate your honesty Mr. Corty, and your punishment will reflect as much."

James swallowed, hard. He knew that even light punishments could lead you permanently scarred, depending on the cruelty of the punisher. He'd seen light punishment as either a man forced to do more night watches for a week or five lashings of the whip. Clearly, they are severely different punishments, yet to some captain's they were essentially the same. "Aye sir."

Mathias returned to interrogating Paul, who continued to look as though hell itself was disgusted by the man and had spat him back out onto the deck when it'd grown tired of him. Mathias was beginning to tire of him as well.

"You have one minute to provide me with an explanation, or I'll have to assume you decided that last night you were going to skip your duties to get drunk instead. I'll tell you right now, those punishments the men were singing about will sound like frivolities compared to what I'm going to put you through."

Paul's face twisted and contorted. It was clear he was trying to form the words and struggling even harder to get them out without mumbling, stuttering, or sounding like a hungover moron. "Sir...I, you...don' understand. There' things down there."

"What things? You have yet to describe *anything* so far."

Paul blubbered and stumbled over the next few words. He was shaking his head back and forth trying to come out with it, but the only thing that wanted to come out would end up on the deck in a pool next to the other upchucks, and that wouldn't help his case in the slightest. "Woman...shadow woman, black as night. Swallow' me whole. Or at least that what it felt like..."

Some men in the crowd chuckled. Mathias laughed a little at this too, trying to keep his face stern at the same time.

"Sorry to tell you Paul, but there's definitely no women aboard this ship. Especially none that could uhh, manage to swallow *you* whole. I think all of those women are in Barbados." Everyone in the crowd roared with laughter, even Frederick cracked a smile. Mathias waited for Paul to say more, but it looked like that was everything he was going to get out of him for now. "If that's it, then I'm afraid, I don't have much choice in the matter." He motioned at a few of the closest sailors. "Grab a length of rope...long enough to circumvent the ship."

"Aye Cap'n!" Five men ran off to complete the task.

"Wai...wait...no, no there was, there was a severed head too!"

Mathias felt a frigid chill run up his spine and he glared at Paul. "The hell did you say sailor?"

Paul spotted the concern on the captain's face. He'd struck a chord and hoped it might save him. "It was a...head that came down and broke the lantern. I saw it right before the darkness came for me. It wasn't normal either. There was somethin' very wrong about it, besides bein' a severed head and all."

"Where?! Where did you see it?" Mathias asked, flustered.

"Oy Cap'n, you're not seriously listenin' to 'is nonsense." Frederick clapped Mathias on the shoulder with one of his hands, trying to push Mathias away so that he could be the one to deal with Paul. Frederick saw no reason for the captain to have to waste his time with Paul's pathetic excuses and ravings.

Mathias didn't budge. "I'm not done with him." he brushed off Frederick's hand without taking his eyes off of Paul. "Where did you see it?"

"L...lowest deck. Where the shipment's stored. At the base of the stairs."

"Mr. Howser, please keep an eye on everything up here. I'll be back momentarily."

"Uhh, aye, sir."

Mathias left for the stairs leading down into the ship.

"Make way for the captain!" Frederick called out to the crowd.

The men moved aside, making a tunnel for Mathias to pass through unabated. He wasted no time in making his way down to the bottom of the ship. As he descended, Mathias caught glimpses of sailors still sleeping in their hammocks or sprawled out on the floor. This was more than what he expected to see that morning, rather than the spectacle taking place on deck. He'd have preferred it that way, but unfortunately being in charge meant he didn't get to pick and choose the issues he'd have to deal with. He had to manage them as best he could without making more trouble for himself in the future. Listening to what Paul said and going down to investigate was a bad idea and he knew that. The men were going to be questioning his judgement, but it was more important to verify if what Paul said had been true. The head was the only thing he couldn't find the morning before when cleaning up that grisly scene. If there was a chance that he could go down and get rid of it once and for all, they'd all be better off for it, especially him.

On his way down, Mathias walked past the main mast where the woman had been pinned to it. The tip of the blade that'd broken off still lodged deep into the wood, and the splintering of the wood was still there too, but it was hard to see unless you knew where to look. He didn't waste much time looking at it and continued his descent down the next two sets of stairs to the storage deck.

Upon first inspection, everything Paul had stated checked out. The broken lantern at the bottom of the stairs, possibly smashed through by a rolling head, or perhaps knocked over in a drunken stupor. One of the opened barrels of pork and its contents poured out onto the floor. Another barrel, this one containing rum, left open and sitting upright. Mathias put the lid back on both barrels after picking the pork one up off the floor. He searched the area for any sign of the head.

There was almost no space to maneuver down there. Mathias searched every square centimeter of the floor. He even looked around and behind the stairs, but there was no sign of the monstrous head. There was nowhere else it could've rolled to, unless. *I hope no one grabbed it.* He thought to himself.

The ship jerked hard, and the wood began to creak. The sound grew louder until it seemed as though the entire room was shouting at him, like every crate, barrel and board were moaning. That's when the disembodied voice rang in his head again.

Don't be stupid! No one came down here and picked up a head. You would have known about it. Everyone would have known by now. Obviously that man was lying and got lucky in his stupid story to say something that made you believe him for a second. Now get back up there and punish him the way he deserves punishment.

There were waves of pain swirling around his skull, this time the pressure was more aggressive than the last. Mathias gripped the sides of his head, pushing inward as hard as he could. It didn't help with the pain, but it felt necessary to keep the pressure from building up to a point where it might explode outward if he didn't try to contain it.

"Fine, fine. There's no head. I see that, let's go." A thought flashed through his mind. It only lasted a moment, like a fleeting emotion. He'd talked in plural as if the other voice wasn't his own. At the time he didn't give it much thought, but the sensation of knowing he'd done it was there, eating away in his subconscious.

Mathias ascended one set of stairs, then another, not even pausing this time to look at the main mast as he glided past it, and up the last set to the top deck.

Up top, the situation hadn't changed. Everyone was still standing (or sitting, in Paul Steiner's case), where they'd been when he'd left. Some of the men were attempting to revitalize the chorus from earlier while others hooted and hollered at the two men who were about to be punished. They called out all sorts of different penalties for falling asleep on night watch.

Mathias overheard one man say something he didn't care for. "You're fortunate this captain's a softy. Probably won't even punish you at all. Now if I were in charge, I'd have him flogged to damn near death, but that's me."

Mathias pushed past him. The man clamped his jaws shut immediately. The sailor attempted, without much success, to recapture the words and put them back in his mouth. As the captain continued on without saying a word to him, the sailor thought the captain may not have heard him at all.

It wasn't that Mathias didn't care what the man thought. To the contrary, he cared a lot about what the men thought of him at the moment. That was half the driving force behind the decision he was about to make with Paul Steiner. He'd shown mercy with James, who'd been honest and forthright in his admittance of negligence of his duties. Now it was time to lay down the hammer on the one that hadn't been so forthcoming.

When Mathias reached the middle of the circle, the little rumblings and stirrings ceased as a hush fell over the crowd. Everyone turned their focus to what the captain had to say. Mathias looked down at Paul who'd recently finished adding another, smaller puddle of vomit onto the deck. Paul's head was slumped against his right shoulder, almost falling asleep again. Mathias kicked the bare bottom of Paul's feet to wake him up. Paul was slow to react but was able to get his head up enough to pay attention.

Frederick was also intrigued to hear what his captain had to say. "Ya find anythin' sir?" he asked curiously. Frederick was confident that he already knew the answer but didn't dare make assumptions when the man was hell bent on looking for himself. The captain must've known something he was unaware of.

"No, nothing. I couldn't find anything down there out of the ordinary, except for the broken lamp of a drunken sailor." Mathias replied.

Paul's face had fallen towards the deck while the captain spoke. He didn't try to lift it again to combat Mathias' statement. He didn't have the fortitude for either and was ready to accept whatever fate was awaiting him. He knew the truth, but that meant little to everyone else on board. That was painfully clear.

"What are you gonna do with a drunken sailor..." some men in the crowd whispered, but enough of them said it so the sound came out louder than they'd planned.

"Shut it!" Mathias demanded. "I won't be having any more of that rabble this morning. The offenses committed by this man last night can amount to treason in the eyes of the law. Failure to conduct night watch duties puts everyone on the ship at risk, from storms, privateers, and God knows what else. I know you all understand that, but clearly a lot of you need a stiff reminder. I didn't think it would come to this on the second day of our voyage, but it has, and the punishment will fit the crime accordingly. Let it be a warning to the rest of you and when everyone else wakes up, be sure to let them know what happens when you fail in your responsibilities." He expected a lot more of the faces in the crowd to be solemn and sad. Instead, they were all steadfast in agreement with what he was saying. After all, it was their lives put at risk by the negligence. When out at sea, the only things you can rely on are yourself and your crewmates. If you lose faith in either, it can spell disaster for everyone. "Mr. Steiner." Mathias continued.

Paul found the strength to lift his head and meet eye to eye with the captain. "Aye…Sir."

"I find you guilty of failing to perform the requirements of a watchmen during the night. Your lack of motivation in your duties placed everyone on the Anne-Marie at grave risk. I will record your crimes in the manifest and report them to the company upon our return. Seeing as we are only two days into our journey, I don't want to take up space in the brig where you can sleep and be lazy for the duration. Instead, we will keelhaul you and demote you to the lowest position on the ship. You'll do chores with the rest of the cabin boys for the remainder of the voyage." Mathias finished his sentencing of Paul to the approval of the crowd.

"Here, here!" The crowd around him shouted in agreement, but Paul's face turned ghastly pale. There were few fates worse than keelhauling. The thought of barnacles tearing through his flesh as salt water forced its way down his throat from dragging beneath the belly of the ship, made another spot of pork and rum want to make its way up and out of him.

"We need 100 lengths of rope. Run it across the underside and have five men ready to pull." Mathias ordered. Then he pointed at Paul. "Get him tied up to the other end and let's get this over with."

For the first time, Paul pulled against his restraints. He used every ounce of remaining strength he could muster to resist what felt like half the ship's men grabbing at him. The crew pinned Paul down to make sure he didn't go anywhere, while others untied the rope keeping him against the mast.

Frederick tapped Mathias on the shoulder. "Sir, this doesn' seem like enough. There are hardly any barnacles underneath at this point. We only been at sea for a day ya know."

"I know. It's not meant to permanently maim the man. I want him to sober up and maybe learn a lesson. That's why I added the demotion on top of it. There's no point nearly killing a man this early on. I'm not a tyrant. Everyone else seemed satisfied with the decision as well, so I feel that it is the right course of action." Mathias responded.

"Aye they do. It's not bad, just burns my soul when sailors fail at the simplest tasks. Especially one so important. I don't think this man deserves any mercy from you but that's my opinion."

"And I appreciate your input. I hope you continue to offer it freely and I am glad to hear you out, but I will not have that much blood on my hands before we've barely even gotten started. I know it's selfish, but I would say it's more for my sake than for his."

"Aye sir. As you wish."

A group of sailors grabbed the required length of rope and ran to the bow. They handed off one of the ends underneath the figurehead to another group and guided it beneath the ship. They continued feeding it into the water as necessary to get the appropriate amount of slack. They worked together to shimmy the rope under the Anne-Marie towards the main mast where everyone else was waiting. Once they reached it, the men holding down Mr. Steiner tied the end to his hands, bounding them tightly. They gave the end a few solid tugs, pulling Paul around and having some laughs while doing so. Mathias noticed and put it to an end.

"That's enough. Men are you ready?" Mathias asked the five who'd volunteered to be the rope pullers. They were the ones that were responsible for dragging Paul beneath the bottom of the ship and over to the other side.

"Aye Capn'!" The men replied enthusiastically.

"Very well." Mathias stared Paul down. "In accordance with the punishment I have laid out, we are keelhauling you. Afterwards,

Frederick will put you to work scrubbing the decks and then you'll work under the supervision of the cabin master." There was no emotion in Paul's face. His features were expressionless and vapid. All color had drained from his cheeks, and he looked more like the shell of a man, than a man himself. Mathias wasn't surprised, but he was also not remorseful. If anything, it was a light punishment compared to what he should've given Paul.

"Are you ready sir?" One of the men holding Paul asked.

The captain nodded for them to begin.

The group holding Paul picked him up, using every available part of his limbs, and hoisted him into the air. "Start pullin"!" One of them shouted to the five holding the other end of the rope. They obeyed and the slack began to disappear. Once the line was tight the men threw Paul overboard. The five picked up speed to reel in the slack that was quickly overtaking them as Paul plummeted towards the surface of the water. The rope got tight again after a few seconds of pulling. The five men continued to haul rope behind them, working in unison and calling out "HEAVE!" with each tug.

Everyone on deck watched them work.

"Heave!" A length of rope landed in the pile.

"Heave!" Another length of rope landed in the pile.

"Heave!" The pile continued to grow.

All the sailors watching could only imagine what Paul was going through underneath their feet. Best case scenario, he was holding his breath well, and not choking on too much sea water. The wood on the bottom should still be smooth and the damage to his back would be minimal, but the sensation of dragging against it while feeling as though you were drowning would be a miserable experience for anyone to endure.

"Heave!" No rope added onto the pile.

"Heave!" Again, the men pulled but no rope came out on the other end.

Whispers and murmurs passed through the crowd.

The ship began to creak and moan. The wood screamed against waves that weren't there. It was a sound only heard during the worst of storms, when every board and nail pushed to their limits to stay held together. The massive strain on the ship was undeniable, but the sea was calm.

"The hell is going on?!" Mathias demanded an answer from the five men.

"Don't know sir!" One of them replied, still pulling on the rope.

"Heave!" They yelled, but still no rope came up.

"Hea-" This time they lost some ground. All five of them slid closer to the railing, the one they were supposed to be pulling away from.

The wood continued to creak as the ship began rocking back and forth.

"Heave!" The men cried out, pulling with all their strength, but again, instead of making progress they slid towards the starboard side railing. It was as if Paul himself was somehow tugging against them under the water. It should've been a one-sided tug of war. Instead, it appeared the other side was somehow winning.

Without thinking, Mathias ran over and grabbed the rope in front of the lead man. He pulled with every muscle in his body, trying to push with his feet against the deck while pulling the line with his arms. It was no use though. It felt like they were trying to pull up the bottom of the ocean itself. There was no progress made as all six jerked closer to the edge of the ship again.

Frederick jumped in to help as well when he saw they were beginning to lose progress.

"Get on the rope ya lazy mongrels!" He yelled out to the crowd. Everyone stood dumbfounded by what was happening. It took them a moment to snap out of the trance, but once they did, every able body was trying to get a claim on the rope.

"Ready now men!" Mathias shouted against the groaning of the ship. "Heave!" Everyone pulled in unison. "Heave!" He called out again and they all pulled. "Heave!" Finally, they managed to pull in some of the line. "Heave!" Again, a few meters gained. *If this takes much longer, Mr. Steiner is sure to drown.* Mathias thought. "Heave damn it all!"

No rope pulled up that time. What little progress they'd made as a group taken away in an instant. The line once again felt as though they were fighting against an immovable object, like an anchor securely planted underneath a reef. The ship's moaning intensified as they all gave the rope a final pull.

One second, they were yanking with all their strength, and the next, they were all laying sprawled out on the deck. The rope had snapped, throwing the extensive line of sailors stretching from one side of the deck nearly to the other onto the floor. They ended up mangled together in a sweaty pile.

Mathias was the first to get his wits about him. He pulled on the rope that now had no tension on it at all. The line moved freely this time, coming up without any resistance. Others that came around him quickly did the same and it wasn't long before they got to the end of the rope.

The end came up empty except for a few frayed strands. There was also a dark tinge roughly four meters from its end. Most of what was left had washed off underneath while they were fighting with it on deck. More importantly, Mr. Steiner was no longer tied to the end. He'd become detached and was likely floating adrift somewhere behind the ship. As a knee jerk reaction more than anything else, Mathias yelled out.

"Man overboard!"

Any sailor still laying down, were back on their feet. The coxswain at the helm began ringing the emergency bell as he tried to stop the ship from its present course, as best he could. Men from below deck that'd still been asleep, were throwing on their shirts, pants, and shoes, if they even bothered with them. Few things got men on their feet and into action more than that bell. Often times it was a harbinger of death.

5

Vincent Carroway

Sailors were lining the circumference of the ship from bow to stern. They all checked the surf for any sign of Paul whether it be flailing or him attempting to tread water. Chances were, he'd be floating unconscious, so any indication of floating objects would help. The surf wasn't rough by any means, and it should have been easy to pick him out in the clear blue water. Some men climbed the rigging to get a better view. Many were already on top of the yard arms, shielding their eyes from the morning sun that was reflecting off the surface of the ocean.

"Capn', I think you should see this!" One of them yelled from the stairs next to the helm.

Mathias was still investigating the end of the rope. He noticed that the fraying wasn't a clean cut like you'd see with a knife or other blades. The strands were all jagged and uneven, like some animal chewed the rope apart, rather than cut it. He'd only seen something like this a couple of times, like when dogs would fight over a length of rope.

When he heard his title called out, he dropped the rope for now. It wasn't going anywhere, at least he hoped not. Besides, the missing man was more important at the moment.

Two other men were nodding and pointing in agreement towards the water. Whatever the first man had seen, the others were seeing it as well. This made others join them too, all pointing and debating about what they saw. They were crowding into the corner of the stern making it difficult for Mathias to push through.

"Move out of the way, damn you!" Mathias shouted.

When Mathias reached the banister at the back of the helm, he pushed against it to see as far out as he could. At first there didn't appear to be anything out of the ordinary. The surf was splashing against the side of the ship, creating small waves, forming foam on top of them that moved swiftly away from the Anne-Marie. He had to look farther out, away from the ship approximately fifty yards. There was a dark trail forming behind the ship. Mathias had seen something similar a few times before, when sharks would follow and feast on fish carcasses thrown overboard. In that moment, Mathias knew Paul Steiner was gone, but that didn't make figuring out how it happened any easier.

The ship's onboard physician, Vincent Carroway, had been able to make his way through the crowd as well. His diagnosis of Paul's fate matched Mathias'.

"I don't think he's still alive down there, sir." Vincent lamented.

Mathias ignored him and pushed back through the crowd to investigate the rope once again.

Frederick already had it in his hands, doing the same.

"This doesn' make any sense sir. I ain't never seen anythin' like this happen with a keel haul before. Them barnacles can be sharp, but not enough to cut straight through a rope this thick, so easily. An' that's after bein' at sea for weeks and months, not one day. You don' think a shark or somethin' mighta." Frederick's words trailed off, horrified at the thought of Paul being torn apart below the ship.

"I don't think so at all." Vincent interjected. "This isn't the work of a shark or any sea creature that I am familiar with. I'll tell you right now, I'm acquainted with many of them."

"Oh, then I suppose Mr. Steiner musta' cut it himself loose then, aye?" Frederick's argued curtly.

Vincent did his best to defuse the situation, instead of giving into the first mate's taunts. "No, I do not believe that Mr. Steiner did this either. His hands were bound and there wasn't a thing but the clothes on his back when he went overboard. There must have been something on the bottom of the ship, sharp enough to cut the rope and probably the poor soul along with it."

"Bah! Look who's speakin' out o' both ends now. There ain't nothin' down there but wood and nails. I say it was a shark. Plenty in these waters. Musta been followin' us for a day or so and took the opportunity when it saw one."

"While there is that possibility, I do not find it probable. It would have to have been waiting at exactly the right spot *and* time to grab him that fast. Besides, I am sure the men holding the rope would be able to attest to whether or not the rope was tugging against them while they were pulling it."

"There was no direct pulling." Mathias interjected. "It was like we were trying to pull the ship itself up, or an anchor stuck on a reef at the bottom. There was no tugging after the rope pulled tight. We would have felt it if there was a shark or fish on the other end jerking it repeatedly, but it didn't feel like that at all. The tension was unwavering."

"You, see? The line must have caught on something and severed it due to the extreme tension placed on the line by all of those men heaving on it at the same time."

"Now you listen-" Vincent and Frederick were face to face. Vincent was a head shorter than Frederick and nowhere near as heavily built, but Vincent stood unwavering against the first mate.

"That's not it either." Mathias interrupted. The two men deflated their chests and gave the captain their attention. "Mr. Howser felt it and everyone on that line felt it as well, including myself. I agree it wasn't a shark, but I also don't agree that it snagged on something either. I have no explanation for what happened, but I *do* know the only way to find out is by going down there and taking a look."

"I highly advise against that sir." Vincent retorted. "If it was a shark-" he shot the first mate a sideways glance that Frederick tried to ignore "and I am not saying it was, but if I am wrong, then whoever goes down there'd be at notable risk. Especially now that there is a clear trail of blood flowing behind the ship. We might as well ring the dinner bell for any sharks within thirty leagues of this area."

"Aye, that I do agree with." Frederick added.

"What do you two suggest then?" Mathias asked.

Neither of them answered straight away. Both kept looking at each other and back at the captain. Mathias had a feeling of what they wanted to say, but neither could bring themselves to say it, and it was ultimately up to him to make the final call. It wasn't their place, and they made it abundantly clear that was the case.

"Very well then, I suppose we'll just have to leave it at that." Mathias was prepared to face the crew and explain what was happening to the best of his abilities, until Vincent chimed in before he could start.

"Nay Captain." Vincent interjected.

"What? Do you have some other suggestion?" Mathias asked.

"Aye sir, I do." Vincent started taking off his clothes. He folded each piece into a neat pile near the mast as he removed them, one by one. "I certainly don't want to do this, but I see no other choice. Even if Mr. Steiner is dead, we should at least attempt to recover the body, if not for a funeral, but for everyone's peace of mind. I think the crew will rest easier knowing what happened."

"I think that's true, but I don't need to be risking the only physician we have on board. If something were to happen to you, we would probably have to turn this tub around and sail back to London." A delicate throbbing started to creep into Mathias' head. He could feel the voice around the corner of his mind, ready to spring out and give his brain a proper pounding.

"That's true, but as the physician it is my duty and responsibility to ensure the health and safety of everyone on board. That includes the almost certainly deceased Mr. Steiner as well. It was the lack of duty that got us in this situation in the first place and I will not accept that I hadn't done my part."

"I see your mind is made up on the matter then."

"Yes, it is."

A smirk crept onto Mathias' face, the corner of his lips curling upwards. He was proud of Vincent's resolve. Frederick had indeed chosen the right man for the job, even though Mathias had his initial reservations. As long as Vincent could keep himself from liquor imbibing, there was a good chance the captain could become solid friends with Vincent.

"You'll be needing a weapon then."

"I already 'ave that covered." Frederick came around the captain and handed Vincent a small knife, along with a half-length wooden spear. "They should do for at least stoppin' a shark or two if you aim for the eyes. I sharpened the knife myself. It should cut through thick rope within a few seconds."

"Thank you, these should suffice. I am certainly hoping I don't need either, but I will be happy to have them, should the occasion arise."

"Get Mr. Carroway tied up in a rope harness! Store all sails and drop anchor! I don't want this ship to move an inch while our physician is down below!"

Some of the sailors scrambled to get Vincent tied up in a rope harness. They made a few loops at the ends of a line. Vincent slipped his arms through the holes like the sleeves of a shirt. Then they wrapped a few laps of rope around his chest and threw the other end onto a pulley, so he could retrieve him from the water if necessary.

Men sitting atop the yard arms worked on the sails. They pulled the lines closest to them, closing up the fabric of the sails to help keep the ship from moving. Instead of large, cream-colored canvases covering up the morning's blue sky, the sun penetrated past the masts and down to the deck. The stowing of the sails alone almost brought the ship to a halt. The only movement was the synchronous bobbing up and down with the waves that passed by underneath the Anne-Marie. The anchor dropped and the rope attached to it screamed out of the hole in the bow where it hung when not in use. The anchor's line ran through almost the entire length of rope before catching a boulder on the bottom, locking the ship in place.

"All set Captain. The ship's not goin' anywhere!" The coxswain at the helm called out to Mathias.

"Very good, thank you Mr. Baley!" Mathias yelled back.

Mr. Baley threw the captain a half-hearted salute before locking the wheel into place.

"Are you sure about this?" Mathias asked, looking at Vincent with genuine concern.

"If I'm being honest, not anymore, but it needs to be done." Vincent put a belt on merely for the sake of holding the knife. He tucked the knife into the loop and held the spear with both hands. With the rope harness around his arms and chest, he felt a little ridiculous but knew it would function well for what he was about to do. "I am as ready as I will ever be."

"Not to worry. The ship is in place. She won't go anywhere; I can promise you that. You should have no trouble while down below." Mathias assured him.

"Alright. I think it best that we get on with it then."

The crew gathered on the starboard side railing of the Anne-Marie. Even though Mathias hadn't asked them to, a few of the men had prepared a seat and pully, along with the one attached to Mr. Carroway to lower him down easier into the water. Vincent was appreciative of that since the rope was already digging into his skin in irritating ways. Red rings formed around his shoulders and armpits. He slid onto the makeshift seat and pushed off from the railing with his bare feet.

"If I tug three times in quick succession, then pull me up." Vincent was speaking to the men holding the harness line but was looking at Mathias.

"Don't make me come down there and get you myself." Mathias said.

"Hopefully, that will not be necessary sir. Alright men, lower me down." Vincent commanded, one hand on the pully rope, the other firmly gripping the spear.

The sailors holding the pully line slid the rope out slowly through their hands, letting it slide against their palms, the weight of the physician doing most of the work. Vincent descended down past the railing, as though he was sinking but through air instead of water. Once his head passed the point where they could see it through the railing, Mathias and Frederick leaned over the side to look down. Everyone that could find room along the edge of the ship was looking as well.

Vincent continued using his legs to push off the side of the ship as he lowered. This kept him from rubbing up against the side and preventing any nasty splinters from catching his skin or shirt. Progress was slow, but he wasn't in a major hurry to get to the water either. He knew the chances of sharks being involved, or in the vicinity were slim, but that did little to comfort him. In fact, it was because he couldn't think of what might have happened that scared him the most. It was one of those instances where he wasn't certain if he really wanted to know the truth, knowledge and curiosity be damned. One of the reasons for him volunteering, that he failed to share with the first mate or the captain, was that he wanted to satisfy his own curiosity. He passed the last row of port holes, and behind them sat the ship's cannons. The next stop was the storage deck, and then the water. The lines got tight a couple of times as the men on deck adjusted their hand positions to help provide a smooth descent. For the most part, they did a respectable job lowering the ropes in even intervals, so Vincent wasn't hanging by the harness more than by the seat. When his feet touched the water they recoiled to his chest, the surf was colder than he'd expected.

"I'm at the bottom! Give me plenty of slack on the harness line." Mr. Carroway couldn't see or hear the men he was yelling to on deck, but the rope around his chest loosened and began pooling next to him in the water. The fibers absorbed some of the water, sinking down beside him. The water was clear, and he didn't see any obvious signs of sea life, either malicious or benign. He took a quick look around, even sticking his head under the surface a couple of times for a better look, but there wasn't anything to see. All he could see was open water and sun rays penetrating the ocean's blue-green surface in long streaks. He took a deep breath, diving headfirst into the blue abyss.

There was no sound beneath the Anne-Marie other than the slow, methodical creaking of the ship as it rocked with the waves. Had it not been for the task he was performing; it might have been soothing for Vincent. He had a job to do though. He kicked his legs while pulling himself along the bottom of the ship with one hand. The wood was barren of any foreign debris including barnacles that would undoubtedly encompass the bottom of the ship by the end of their voyage. This made it easy to maneuver towards the keel line, where Paul's body should've been waiting.

When Vincent reached what appeared to be the middle of the hull, he was frustrated and confused. The long piece of wood that ran from the helm to the rudder like a spine was the point where Paul would've gotten snagged or hung up, but there was nothing there. He expected to see a loose nail, board, or anything that would have kept the man from moving smoothly across the bottom of the ship. The keel line and hull were both as smooth as the day the Anne-Marie set sail. There was no indication of a body either. The man would have been easy to find if he was down there.

Vincent's eye caught one detail though. Directly on the other side of the running board, was a bit of rope, about the same thickness as the one that made up the harness he was wearing. It was sticking out the bottom of the hull, in a narrow corner where the hull line and the hull properly met. He ran a couple fingers over the end of the bit of rope. He tugged on it, trying to pull it free of the wood but the line wouldn't budge.

A black shape flashed by his peripheral. Even though he only saw it out of the corner of his eye, it was enough to give him pause. Whether he saw something or not, it made him want to be on the ship again, rather than under it. He maneuvered back to the wooden seat that was still floating on the surface, patiently waiting for his return. Vincent broke the surface of the water, taking a deep breath of air along with a mouthful of seawater. He wanted to call up but was choking and coughing too much to do so. Instead, he pulled any remaining slack in the rope harness around his chest and tugged on it.

The men holding his harness line were overzealous. When they felt the tugs, they didn't only pull on the line, they ran to the opposite side of the ship. The loops around Vincent's chest and arms synched down around him aggressively, digging deep into his skin forming rope burns the likes of which he'd never experienced before.

The sailors with the seat line reeled theirs in as well when they realized what was happening, but it was much slower than the other group. They were unable to keep up, so Vincent was flying upwards, rubbing against the side of the ship instead of riding leisurely on the seat.

Upon reaching the top, Vincent flopped onto the deck like a fresh catch of fish. He landed with a hard thud, trying to catch himself with his arms and feet, but failing miserably. The tightness of the rope around his chest made him cough even harder than the water he'd swallowed, but all that came out was a bit of air and a torrent of sea water.

Two of the closest sailors helped the physician to his feet, while he was still in the throes of a coughing fit. They each had an arm under one pit, waiting patiently for the hacking to end and for Vincent to catch his breath. It would be a lie to say they were not as interested as everyone else on deck about what happened, only thirty feet below them.

When more air managed to get inside Vincent than was leaving him, he raised his hands to inform the sailors flanking him on each side that he was all right and that they could let him go. The sailors released their grips slowly, ensuring their physician was stable enough to stand on his own without assistance.

Frederick brought Vincent his clothes. Vincent took them from him but had no intention of putting them on right away. He wanted to wait until he'd dried off a bit first. He nodded to Frederick in appreciation anyway. The first mate nodded back and moved to stand next to Mathias so he could have some space.

Vincent tried to clear his throat. The taste of seawater lingered there, which dried it out along with the rest of his mouth, making it difficult to speak. "I...I..." nothing else would come out. He hacked and coughed, begging for his mouth to cooperate so he could get the words out. All eyes were on him, and this made him even more uncomfortable. He was never a fan of large crowds and even less so of crowds directed towards himself. Everyone on deck was looking at him anxiously. Many of them had their own ideas about what took place under the hull of the ship. Regardless of their opinions, most of them would take what the physician said happened as gospel, knowing full well his deductive abilities far surpassed their own. "Ahem...sorry. Based on what I saw, there is little evidence to suggest that this was the act of some animal, like a shark or other sea creature." Whispers stirred amongst the crowd. Several of the onlookers' personal theories were proven wrong, to their disappointment. Vincent waited a few moments for the rumblings to subside before continuing. "However, having said that. There is also no sign to indicate something sharp cut the rope. To me this can only indicate one thing. The knot loosened at some point and Mr. Steiner slipped out, he was most likely unable to swim out from underneath the hull and drowned. Another possibility is that a blow to the head knocked him unconscious, also causing drowning or a similar fate." As more stirrings broke out among the crew, Vincent started believing the story himself. He might've ignored everything he'd seen down below, but the mind has a way of distorting facts to fit truths.

"Wha' 'out the 'ullin'?!" One sailor called out. All heads on deck turned towards the source of the outburst. The yeller was a skinny, older man with most of his teeth missing. What little hair he had left was a dirty gray. A lifetime at sea hadn't been kind to him, but what he lacked in appearance he made up for in tenacity.

"I beg your pardon?" Vincent replied, slightly taken aback.

"I 'ays, wha' a'out the 'ullin'?"

The doctor was still confused, mainly because he didn't fully understand what the man was saying. "I don't understand what you mean."

"Me's an' the o'her men who was 'ullin' 'he rope wi' 'im tied up. When we's 'ullin' some'n was 'ulling back." The old man mimicked the action of pulling on the rope during the keelhauling.

"Aye" some of the men grumbled. These men agreed with what the man was saying, at least the ones that could understand the old man's speech.

"Are you suggesting that something was at the other end of the rope, pulling against you in some kind of tugging match?" Vincent gave the sailor a quizzical look while asking.

"'at wha' I'm 'ayin'." Replied the old man.

"Could it not have simply been the current underneath working against you?"

"Coul'a been. Don' 'ink so 'ough. Kee' hau'ed 'ough men 'o knows 'e difference."

Sweat formed on Vincent's brow. The little saltwater droplets ran down the sides of his face, mixing with the salty water of the sea.

"W-well you certainly bring up a good point. I can only go off of what I know and saw when I was underneath the ship though. Unfortunately, I cannot attest to what happened during the event itself, in terms of those pulling on the rope that is."

The old sailor shot him with a distrustful look, as though he was accusing him of something. Vincent picked up on this and tried to correct it.

"That's not to say it didn't happen. I fully support all of your takes on the events. Based on the evidence that I personally saw firsthand, I can only say that it didn't look as though the line was cut from an animal or something sticking out of the hull. That's all."

The captain could sense the tension building between the old sailor and Vincent. Mathias decided to interject before the discussion became heated.

"Based on the accounts and what the doctor has seen, currently I think it's safe to say that there is no obvious explanation for what's happened. For those who just joined us this morning, other crew members caught Paul Steiner passed out below deck. Mr. Steiner was as drunk as any man I'd ever seen before. He was supposed to be on duty last night as a watchman, but he failed in his responsibilities, putting everyone at risk. I made the decision to punish him with one trip around the bottom of the ship and a demotion to cabin boy for the remainder of the voyage. Somehow during the keelhauling, the line cut, or the knot slipped, and Mr. Steiner disappeared. A few of you, including myself, saw the blood trail in the water. Our onboard physician, Mr. Carroway, confirms that even if we did find him, there'd be little he or anyone else could do to help the man. Therefore, it's deemed that the sea has claimed him, and that the sea will keep him. The manifest stands at 124 souls. Dismissed."

At first, no one moved. There were small patches of rumblings in the crowd, but for the most part the ship was quiet. Some of the men thought there was more that needed said, but when nothing additional came from the captain or the first mate, they weren't sure what else to do besides talk about it.

"What are ya doin' you lazy bastards! Don't you 'ave work to do?! The captain declared *dismissed,* so dismiss yourselves and get out o' me sight!" Mr. Howser's shouting got men moving and ended most of the discussions that were cropping up. "I said I want to see some movement!" Half the men stayed on deck, while the other half went below to get more sleep, but most were too awake to even try dozing off again.

Mathias was the only one who didn't move. He stood on deck trying to wrap his head around everything that'd happened, finding difficulty in validating what he'd seen.

Vincent was dry enough to put his clothes back on. He slipped on his shirt and was working on the pants when he noticed the captain lost in thought. After buttoning the trousers, he joined Mathias. He'd hoped that he could console, or at the very least, provide an attentive ear for him. When Mathias didn't speak, Vincent tried to start the conversation.

"I know it was a hard decision sir. We are only one day in, and we have already lost someone. It is never easy, especially for a man in your position, but you know as well as I do that these things happen. To make a voyage without losing anyone is extremely difficult and there wasn't anything you did that directly caused it."

"I declared the punishment though. Regardless of how it happened, it was my direct order that sent him under the ship, and ultimately to his death."

"Yes, while that all might be true, the punishment was light by everyone's standard. Despite that, every sailor in attendance seemed to be more or less in agreement with it. I want you to know that I think this does not reflect poorly on your leadership." Vincent tried to get Mathias to turn and look at him. Mathias, consumed by his own thoughts, refused to meet the physician's eyes. "I will investigate further and see if I can find anything else, but there was no way you could've known what would happen. Regardless of whether I find something or not, I want you to understand that this isn't your fault."

"I'm the *captain,* Mr. Carroway...everything is my fault." Mathias turned away from the physician, walking over to the starboard railing, leaving Vincent alone in the center of the deck.

Frederick had listened in on the conversation from a safe distance. When it appeared that Vincent had failed to lighten the burden of the situation, he joined Mathias by the railing to give it a try.

"Aye it's true that yer the captain, but we're only a day out. We can always go back. We'll lose a couple days sure but" Frederick's words cut out as he failed to make a convincing argument.

Mathias didn't hear another word as his skull filled with dull pain, like a headache moving around the inside of his head from the back to the front. After a few laps around his head the voice that sounded like his own rose up from somewhere inside his subconscious.

To hell with that! There's no going back now. We can only move forward do you hear me? If you go back now, there's no telling what might happen. The company could very well replace the useless cap-

tain that put one man's life before the success of their well-funded expedition. You don't want that to happen, I know it. Don't you dare consider doing anything other than pressing on!

"I know...I know." Mathias mumbled, pressing on the sides of his head, trying to alleviate some of the pressure that was attempting to escape. When the voice seemed satisfied with its host's answer, it backed off.

The voice faded, sinking back down to where it'd originated from, but leaving behind the throbbing. The thumping slowed its movement around Mathias' head, subsiding until it was little more than an afterthought.

"Captain, are ya alright?" Frederick had been snapping his fingers next to Mathias' face after the captain started grabbing onto the sides of his head.

Mathias only noticed the click of fingers after the majority of the pain was gone.

"Yea, yea I'm fine." Mathias pushed Frederick's hand away and rubbed both sides of his head with the palms of his hands. Putting inward pressure on the skull helped the pain alleviate faster and that's all he wanted to do. The choice not to go back was already one he was planning on making, but the thought of that agony coming back again cemented the decision. "We're going to press on. It's too late to turn back now and I know it's inappropriate to say but...Mr. Steiner no longer being with us is no great loss."

Vincent had joined them, standing a couple paces away from the pair, listening in on the conversation. He didn't care for how the captain had phrased his last statement, but the sentiment was something all three of them, and surely the rest of the crew could agree on. Regardless of a man's status or rank, they all had value onboard a ship, whether the crew was large or small.

"The least we could do is have a memorial service this evening to honor his memory." Vincent suggested.

"Aye, we can do that." Mathias replied. "A lost soul is a lost soul, no matter the value of it, and losing a sailor doesn't make the voyage any easier either." Mathias walked back over to the railing. He looked over into the water for any signs of life, but there wasn't anything to see. Even the streak of blood that was drifting away from the ship was gone, carried off by the current. The water was pure and blue once again. "Mr. Howser, can you make the preparations and arrangements for this evening?" Mathias asked without looking away from the ocean.

Frederick was standing next to him, but he was looking at the horizon more than the ocean. "Aye sir. It will be a simple service but should suffice."

"Very well, spread the word that we encourage everyone to attend. However, no one is forcing them to come if they don't want to."

Frederick was surprised at the decision but decided not to inquire about it further. "Aye capn'." He left to begin preparations for that evening. The deck needed scrubbing, lanterns needed put out in abundance, and a sendoff package needed to be prepared due to lack of a body.

As the sun finished descending below the edge of the horizon, the deck filled with crew members. Mathias was at the helm, watching as all the empty spaces below him closed up. It was a different sight compared to the evening before. The air was void of songs and celebrations. Now the only sounds were those of shuffling feet, boards creaking as the ship pushed against the tide, and the splashing of the surf as it forced its way around the bow.

Lanterns lined the edges of the ship. They formed an elliptical ring around it and Mathias imagined how it must have looked from the crow's nest. The setup was the best he could do for Mr. Steiner's sendoff. He wished there was more they could provide but when out to sea, ceremonies had severe limitations.

When it appeared that the majority of the crew was present, Mathias looked for Mr. Howser. He found him moving about the deck, ensuring proper final preparations. He was easy to pick out from the crowd since his stature was greater than that of most everyone around him. Their eyes met and Frederick gave him a nod, indicating they were ready to proceed.

Mathias stepped forward, pressing his waist against the railing positioned next to the wheel.

"Good evening gentleman." Mathias called out, waiting a few moments for everyone's attention to come to him. "It is with great sorrow and deep remorse that I have called all of us together like this. We set sail less than 48 hours ago...and already we've lost a sailor. I can't speak about the man's life, as I didn't know him personally. However, I'm sure that some of you knew him quite well. For you, I have the utmost remorse. Despite the actions leading to his punishment, *we* carried it out; he didn't deserve such a fate. It was never meant to be a death sentence, as you all well know. My only hope, is that he is now resting peacefully with the sea."

There was no reaction. The crew stared on, taking in the words, some processing them internally while others only listened. "Does anyone have anything they would like to add before we commence?" None of the crew stepped forward or appeared to have another word to append. Mathias took their silence as affirmation. "Very well. Whoever has Mr. Steiner's affects, please step forward."

"Here sir!" One of the men held up a wooden box containing the rest of Paul's clothing, along with any other personal objects he brought aboard.

Mathias maneuvered down the stairs and through the crowd to meet him. When they met, the man handed the small, rectangular wooden box to his captain. "It's all in there, sir."

"Very good, thank you sailor." The man nodded in response, taking a step back.

Mathias walked to the edge of the ship and looked over the side. The blue water from earlier that day was gone, replaced by a black abyss that was ready to accept Paul's belongings, after having already claimed the man himself.

"We surrender Mr. Steiner's possessions to the sea, in the hopes that they reunite on the other side. May he not suffer there, as he had here." Mathias tossed the box, watching it sail through the air before hitting the water and sending a splash up around where it landed. He watched the wood bob up and down as the current carried it away. Once it was no longer visible, having drifted far enough behind the Anne-Marie to no longer be discernable with the water surrounding it, he turned around. "That concludes the ceremony. Good night gentlemen. Hopefully, this will be the last time we meet under these circumstances."

The following week, there were no other major events of note. It was the usual seven days of sailor life, monotony aboard the Anne-Marie. Every crew member in the trade ship performed their duties to the standard expected of them.

Mathias spent the majority of this time in his cabin, reviewing charts, maps, and overall trying to keep busy. Every so often he'd have to make calculations and pass on corrections to the coxswain in order to keep the ship on course towards their final destination. He'd suffered a few headaches that week. Each one growing heavier and more pronounced than the last, but this week none of headaches had the voice that usually accompanied them. He was grateful for that. It was bad enough that he was unable to think when they came about. It was even worse when his thoughts were intermingled with those of another. The voice always sounded like his, but he knew deep down it was coming from somewhere or someone else. He did his best not to think about it too hard and to keep his attention to what mattered most, the successful completion of the voyage.

Mathias spent the entire day after Mr. Steiner's death in his cabin. He needed to adjust the manifest and write letters to anyone who might've cared about the man. The trade company would also want a formal write-up of events that took place leading up to the death of one of their sailors, regardless of the man's position on the ship. The only source of outside information that came into the cabin was from Mr. Howser's bi-daily reports, most of which were uneventful. The first mate recounted a couple of fights that'd broken out, a drunken brawl here, and a name calling there. They were paltry matters. Mathias knew the first mate was able to handle those instances without interjection from himself. Frederick informed Mathias that the other sailors mostly stopped the scraps before they'd the chance of becoming a full-on fist fight anyway.

Vincent had stopped by a couple of times to check up on Mathias as well. He conducted routine physicals, ensuring that the captain was eating enough, but Mathias was convinced the man was more interested in his mental state than his physical one. Several times throughout the examinations, the physician asked how he was handling everything. Mathias assumed he meant about Mr. Steiner, to which he only replied "I'm fine. This is hardly the first time I've been aboard a ship where we lost someone." That was the truth. Death was hardly an outlier among sailors, especially on longer voyages. He'd found out at an early age that death is an expectation at sea. Often times the longer the voyage, the greater chance of death and disease setting in. If the starvation and lack of fresh water didn't get to the men first, then scurvy and madness surely would. Vincent knew that wasn't the only thing bothering Mathias. He didn't want to push the issue though, so he finished the routine physical, then left to check on the rest of the crew.

At the end of his weeklong solitude, Mathias noticed that Lucy hadn't come to visit him. He decided it was time to take a long walk around the ship and check up on the crew and cargo. In the meantime, he could look for his missing furry companion. Before heading out, he looked out the back window and noticed that they'd run into a stint of fog. Although dangerous, the sight was a pleasant change of pace from the endless blue they'd seen that week. He put on a pair of boots and his jacket, leaving the room for what felt like the first time in a month.

The back window didn't do justice to the level of fog that settled on the deck of the Anne-Marie. It was gravely thicker than Mathias had originally imagined. The ship was cutting through the gray wall of moisture, leaving behind an empty space that slowly closed around it over time.

The deck was barren of men, except for two cabin boys on their hands and knees scrubbing the deck, one on each side of the ship. Both had a bucket next to them that they used to dip their scrub brushes in. They had their sleeves and pants rolled up as far as they could go, trying their best to not get them wet, though it was a futile effort. For a minute, the boys were in perfect sync. They pushed on their brushes with both hands, using their entire body in a forward and back motion. Mathias heard the *swish* of their bristles scraping against the wood.

Mathias started walking toward the bow as the ship entered a thick patch of mist. The two boys, who were faintly visible a second ago, disappeared entirely, swallowed whole by the fog. Only the sounds of their scrubbing remained in a hauntingly rhythmic sync.

Instead of continuing forward, Mathias changed course, up the stairs on his left to the helm. The man in front of the wheel was Norman Bailey's counterpart and secondary coxswain, Jonathan Crenshaw. He looked almost identical to Norman, like they could've been twins in another life. They were so close in appearance that Mathias could only tell the two apart up close. Jonathan had piercing blue eyes, where Norman's were a deep brown.

Jonathan locked eyes with Mathias as the captain finished climbing to the top of the stairs. "Mornin' sir." Jonathan greeted him.

"Good morning Mr. Crenshaw. I'm sure you've been keeping a keen eye on our headings, given the fog." Jonathan didn't take offense at the line of inquiry, as any good sailor would've been extra cautious given the conditions. Instead, he nodded and pointed a finger at the map and compass sitting on a crate next to him.

"Aye, been keepin' a real close eye on it. Luck has it we ain't goin' too fast, which helps. Anythin' that might show up, we at least have a little time to maneuver 'round it." Jonathan glanced down at the compass. He made some slight adjustments to the wheel until the needle of the compass shifted to point directly in line with the 'S' stamped at the bottom.

"Is anyone manning the nest?"

"There's someone up there. Not sure who though. Saw them climbin' up to replace the other sailor 'bout an hour or so ago. Can't imagine they doin' much more'n sleepin' through this thick grog." Jonathan chuckled. "In fact, they probably seein' even less than we are."

Both of them looked up towards where the crow's nest should've been plainly visible, but they could see nothing past the first yard arm. Even the base of the mast and the web of ropes strutting off the ends towards either side of the ship, looked like mere hallucinations among the gray.

"I see none of the lanterns have been lit." Mathias mentioned. It sounded like a passive-aggressive statement when it came out, but he only meant it as an observation. He was curious about Mr. Howser's decision to keep them doused.

"Yessir, I asked the first mate 'bout it. Based on where we're at, we both thought it better to navigate through without them. We're already south enough to be at risk of another vessel comin' along and takin' advantage of us in the fog. They could see the light, slip right up next to us and damn near climb aboard 'fore we even knew what was happenin'. Seen it before myself, wish I hadn't though. Didn't end well for us, I can tell you that much."

"No, I imagine it would not. Very well, let's try and keep her under ten knots for the time being. Anything faster and rogue ships attacking us will be the least of our worries."

"We's goin' about eight last time I had the boys down there, check." Jonathan motioned to the two cabin boys on deck that Mathias spotted scrubbing on his way out of the cabin. "Good, safe, even speed sir."

"You're more outspoken than I originally thought Mr. Crenshaw, no offense."

Jonathan's eyes grew bigger. Mathias could see every part of the pupils, like two big circles of crystal-clear water nestled within rings of white.

"No offens' taken sir!" Jonathan bellowed with laughter. "That probably the nicest thin' anyone said to me. No offens', no offens' taken at all. It's true us coxswains aren't the most social types."

Mathias smiled. "Good, good. You haven't seen Mr. Howser or Lucy running around here anywhere, have you?"

"The first mate was makin' rounds last I saw him, so probly' below deck somewhere. As for your Lucy, I ain't seen her in a couple days at least. Musta' found a nice den o' rats or somethin' down below." Jonathan made another slight correction to the wheel.

"Thanks, I'll take a look around for them. Keep an eye out though, will you?"

"Oh, aye sir, both eyes." Jonathan scanned the deck with a hand over his eyes in an exaggerated manner, moving his head back and forth in a large sweeping motion.

"Good man, carry on."

Jonathan chuckled again. "I always do. These ladies love me." Jonathan tapped one spoke of the wheel.

Not this lady, Mathias thought. The thought was fleeting but a flash of rage shot through him after Jonathan smacked the wheel. Mathias only hoped the sensation didn't start becoming a recurring theme like the headaches. He could only handle one senile issue at a time.

Hoping to clear his head before searching for Frederick and Lucy, Mathias walked to the stern of the ship. Through a small gap in the wood, the air appeared almost clear as though there was no fog at all. The gray clouds were still, and the Anne-Marie cut through them so deliberately that it left a void behind her. In that void, the water swirled and twisted from the resistance of the rudder. With no sun, the surf looked like a dark pool with harshly contrasting white bubbles floating on top of it.

There was something else floating on top of the shallow waves, a circular object he wasn't able to quite make out at a distance. It was too large to be one of the fruits they had on board, and it didn't have the right consistency. This sphere looked deformed in places, not a perfect sphere or cylinder at all. The longer he stood there, with his face pressed against the wood and his eye partially bulging from their sockets the more his head began piecing together what it might be. The thought was terrifying enough to tear his gaze away. His heart started to race, and new unexplained emotions started to creep up. Through sheer will, he forced away these feelings, refusing to acknowledge them.

Jonathan had turned around at some point and was watching Mathias.

"Are you a'right sir?" Jonathan looked concerned, raising an eyebrow at the captain kneeling on the deck, clutching his chest. The coxswain was unattuned to the intricacies of medicine, but it was never a good sign when a man was gripping his shirt near their heart and sweating.

Mathias stood, correcting himself, and loosening the death grip on his overcoat. With his other hand Mathias smoothed out his hair. "I'm fine. Something spooked me in the fog is all." Mathias rushed past Jonathan, flying down the stairs. He needed to talk to the only man that would listen to what he had to say without thinking him mad.

As Mathias reached the staircase leading down to the first deck, he looked for the two boys who were scrubbing minutes earlier. The same rhythmic *swish* of their brushes was still audible, but neither of them were visible still. It seemed strange how they could stay in perfect unison for so long and it felt like they' hadn't moved since he'd stepped outside his cabin.

You are just adding more and more cargo to your problems...you have more than enough of that already. Let it go.

The voice was a familiar one that always existed in his head. The sensible, logical one, that always made the right call. He followed its advice to ignore the nagging sensation and descended the stairs to the next lower deck.

Everyone had claimed their little area of the ship by that point in the voyage. Hammocks hung on every post and those that had men sleeping in them, swung haphazardly with the rocking of the ship. Those that were empty, hardly swayed at all, and only added to the web of dirty white cloth that filled the room like a spider's web.

A group of sailors sitting on crates had made a makeshift table out of a barrel. The word 'POWDER' painted in black on the side of it. Three men sat around the powder keg, one on each available side. They'd reserved the fourth seat for what tiny light made it through the porthole they positioned the keg underneath. A set of dice sat on top of the barrel in the middle. Each man sitting around it was eyeing the dice, carefully calculating their next move.

"Good morning gentlemen." Mathias nonchalantly called out.

The sailor sitting farthest away from Mathias was the first to break his concentration to see who was interrupting their close scoring game. He nearly moved the crate a foot with his knees as he stood upright. The two others grabbed the crate to keep it from shifting the position of the dice. Each of them was about to give the standing man an earful, until they realized he was standing at attention. The sailor sitting directly across from the first one to stand, ended up moving the crate back into its original position with his own knees as he stood, wheeling around to face who he knew was either the first mate or the captain.

"Good morning, sir!" They replied loudly.

"No need to be so loud, don't want to wake anyone sleeping do we?" Mathias asked, raising his hands up and down in a quieting motion.

"Aye sir. S'pose your right." The first man to stand answered back, this time he was whispering.

"Do any of you happen to know where Mr. Howser is?"

"Oh aye, he went by here probably around ten minutes or so. Saw him makin' his way to the other side o' this deck. Think he descended when he got to the other set of stairs on the end. Can't say for sure where he gone off to after that though."

Mathias clapped the man on the shoulder with a firm smack of his hand. "Very good, thank you. Please, continue your game." Mathias motioned towards the dice on the barrel.

As he walked away, the three men took turns looking at each other. They slowly descended back down onto their respective crates; they struggled to remember who'd rolled the dice last, deciding instead to reset the round. The second one to stand looked over the shoulder of the sailor sitting closest to the walking path, to make sure Mathias was gone before turning his attention back to the other two.

"Not many Capn's nowadays doesn' care about men playin' dice below deck." He spoke.

"Think maybe he's one of them what you call…uhh…" The man sitting across from him struggled to find the words, tapping his forehead with one of the dice that he'd picked up while sitting down. "Pro, progres've, types."

"I know what you mean. If you ask me, he too young to be in that position, but if Mr. Howser swear by 'im I guess he must know his stuff." The other two grumbled in agreement. "We's know better than to play for money anyhow, no good come out of it anyway, only trouble."

"That probably why the first mate doesn't care much either. They know we don' 'ave two silver pieces to rub together anyhow." They all chuckled softly.

"We might not be playin' for keeps but don' go thinkin' you can cheat ya octopus suckin' troglodyte!" The remark directed towards the first man to stand.

When he realized he'd been tapping his forehead with the dice, the other man's accusation made a lot of sense. He threw it back down, trying to rotate the die back into the position he remembered it being in before the captain had interrupted them.

"No, no, no it wasn' like that. Here I think it was a six..."

"Not on yer life it was a six!" The middleman protested. "It was a three!"

"Wasn't either ya cheatin' sea dogs it was a two. Who you tryin' ta fool?"

Mathias moved to the other end of the ship. He walked alongside an extended string of hammocks wrapped around support beams and hull ties across the deck. It was almost deafening the amount of noise an entire deck of sleeping sailors could make by only *breathing*. He was sure it drove some men insane when trying to sleep. Many would rather find a place on the floor, a deck below or above, then have to deal with the incessant groaning of their neighbor. This thought reflected on the next deck down. Amongst all of the crates and barrels, men splayed out in random arrays of bodies. If he hadn't known any better, it looked like a massacre had taken place. Some men were laying over the tops of cannons like a bundle of rope, while others sprawled out on the floor like human starfish. With the thick fog outside and a dismal amount of light making its way into the ship, most of the men didn't realize it'd been morning for hours.

It was difficult to tell, but Mathias did his best to take a mental roster of all the men he saw. It was hard to imagine over a hundred men were aboard the Anne-Marie, but when they were all spread throughout the decks like this, it became more believable. He made his way as best he could through the sea of bodies.

Mathias did well to not step on anyone, until the end, where a few men were all laying so close together, there was no open wood to step on. He attempted to place one foot down in between a pair of hips where a small gap presented itself. He was able to get the foot in, but when taking the second large step to move across them, it caught on one of their shirts, causing him to stumble. He was close to the hull wall, so when he fell it was only a short way. His hands caught the hull framing to prevent himself from falling over. The man he kicked woke with a start but went immediately back to sleep after rolling onto their side. After making it past this cluster of limbs, he was free to descend the last set of stairs.

Mathias could barely see the first mate's silhouette on the deck below. The storage area was much darker than the rest of the ship since the area had no windows.

The first mate was standing next to the closest row of barrels and crates with a hand on each hip, staring at the cargo. He heard Mathias descending the stairs, which turned his attention away from the task at hand.

"Mornin' sir." Was all Frederick said before continuing to look at the barrels and crates.

"Good morning. What brings you down here at this hour? You're a surprisingly hard man to find, given the circumstances." Mathias meant his comment as a joke, but the first mate seemed to take it more to heart than he'd intended.

"Aye, apologies. This whole mess with Mr. Steiner has left a bad taste in my mouth. I can't shake the feelin' that there's more to it than what he claims. This part is certain I know." Mr. Howser used his foot to push salt around in an arcing motion on the floor. "The man certainly helped himself to a nice meal of meat and alcohol. But to start ramblin' on about shadow women and severed heads rollin' about, jus' didn't sit right with me."

Mathias' stomach churned at the mention of the head. He could never fathom telling Frederick the truth, or anyone else for that matter, even though he knew it would probably come out eventually. The head was the only part he couldn't seem to get rid of when tossing the grisly evidence overboard. It would've seemed paranoid to believe that it was still rolling around the ship though, scaring sailors, while mocking him at the same time by disappearing again and again.

"You know better than anyone how these sailors get when they're drunk. He probably saw a rat or something. The man is clumsy enough without a bit of drink in him. I can only imagine what he was like down here in the dark all by himself shoveling food into his mouth." Mathias tried to sound confident in this explanation of events, but it only served to make the first mate more unsure than ever.

"Aye sir…" Frederick replied, but he wasn't believing it for a second. Mathias never lied to him in the past and wasn't sure why he'd start now. The captain's face screamed something was wrong. Frederick knelt down, plucking a shimmering piece of glass from between two boards of the deck. He placed it in an open palm and stared at it, hoping it would reveal clues, even answers to what happened down there. The fragment failed to enlighten the first mate; however, it did cause him to notice something between his fingers. There was a long strand of black hair pinched between them. It was much too long to belong to the captain's furry friend or anyone else on board.

"Sir, this wouldn' belong to your Lucy, would it?" Frederick held up the strand so Mathias could take a closer look.

Mathias gave it a cursory glance before dismissing it. "No, it's much too long to be from Lucy. Speaking of which, I haven't seen her this week either and that's not like her." He started to look around the small clearing himself, but instead of searching for evidence of the events that took place, he was now looking for the black cat that'd failed to visit him during his week-long reprieve.

Frederick peered back at the boards where he'd plucked the glass shard from. His heart rate began to speed up as he noticed a few more strands of the black hair he was holding. There was a dozen or so, caught between the boards in a messy knot. He reached out, pinching them between his fingers, trying to pull them away from the wood. They became taut as he tugged. He was about to put more strength into ripping them out when the emergency bell rang out topside.

"That's the crow's bell. On deck Mr. Howser!" Mathias left the first mate who still sat in a squatting stance looking at the space between the boards.

Frederick upended his hand, dropping the glass piece and single strand of hair onto the floor. He stood and headed towards the stairs. He took them two at a time, bellowing orders before his head had even broken the opening of the cargo hold. "Get up ya lazy birds! Didn' ya hear the bell, I know ye ain't deaf! If I don't see every lily-livered soul movin', I'll make it my personal mission to upend ya!"

Frederick was no longer the detective that he was a minute ago, he was once again the first mate. He was gone before the hair floated to the floor and made contact with the wood. Once it touched, the strand started to disappear from one end, running to the other, like the burning wick of a cannon. A stream of black smoke rose up as the hair disintegrated, but that too dissipated, leaving nothing behind on the cargo deck but specks of ash.

Mathias was already up the stairs and halfway through the deck directly above the cargo hold before the men on the same floor were even awake. He'd thrown caution to the wind, stepping on no less than three hands and feet on his way to the other side of the ship. All around him, sailors were awakening, scrambling to throw shoes and shirts on. Some were already preparing powder and wicks for the cannons. The captain's only goal was to get topside as fast as possible.

On the deck above the cannon line, most of the men had already dressed and were either tying down loose barrels or sprinting to the main deck to prep rigging for whatever was about to happen. This made it easy for Mathias to cross to the other side and ascend the last set of stairs.

The first thing he witnessed was the sun as it blinded his ascent to the main deck. The orange ball no longer hid behind a thick veil of gray mist, but instead stood out proudly, beating down upon Anne-Marie. Mathias had to shield his eyes with a forearm for a few seconds while he finished his climb up the stairs.

Above him, the bell was ringing out with an intensity that could only mean one of two things. Either the ship heading directly into a storm, or an unidentified ship spotted on the horizon. Based on the intense brightness of the sun, Mathias felt safe in assuming it was the latter.

Once he was fully out of the ship's interior, Mathias moved to the port side, where men lined up across the entire length of the railing.

"Move aside!" Mathias commanded.

Four men scuddled out of his way to attend to their duties.

Mathias looked over the starboard side of the Anne-Marie to witness something he'd never seen before in all his years at sea. The mist they'd come out of looked like the face of a cliff. It stretched for kilometers, straight up into the sky and spanning across the horizon in both directions, as if cutting the world in half. Little puffs of misty fog managed to pull away from the greater mass, disappearing a second or two later.

Roughly half a league or so down the misty wall, another ship had exited the fog. It was impossible to see only a few minutes ago, but now it was as clear as the sky above.

Mathias wheeled around, calling up to the man atop the main mast. "What is it?!" Mathias yelled up to him, as if shouting to the sky itself.

"Hard to say for sure Cap'n. I cannot see their colors fully but based off the rough pattern I'd say she's a French vessel."

"Damn it all." Mathias cursed, moving with haste towards the helm.

Jonathan Crenshaw was keeping the Anne-Marie steady, waiting for instructions from either the first mate or the captain. Mathias was now present at the wheel and more than ready to provide them.

"How close are we to the Western coast Mr. Crenshaw?" Mathias asked.

"Last I checked sir, we were about thirty kilom'ters away, but that was 'fore we ran into the blasted fog. There's no tellin' if I was able to keep 'er straight and true the whole time. We coulda popped out anywhere."

"No, I'm sure you did fine. We need to try and hug the coast. Maybe we've been lucky, and they haven't spotted us yet, or perhaps they have no desire to engage with us at all."

On the starboard side of the ship, a splash of water exploded into the air, creating a fine mist across the deck. A couple of men working on the rigging got wet but continued on as if nothing had happened.

"I think you 'ave your answer, sir." Jonathan joked.

"We do. The plan remains the same, however. Bring her about hard due East, we'll try to run alongside the fog for as long as we can and we'll either reach the coast or dip back inside the mist if necessary."

"Setting course due East." Jonathan threw the wheel around in a counterclockwise direction. The rudder turned hard against the water and the ship began to creak against the strain of the resisting water. Large waves crashed against the port side, splashing over the handrails, and soaking anyone unlucky enough to find themselves caught under the spray.

"Run up all auxiliary sails Mr. Howser!" Mathias yelled out. His first mate was nowhere in sight, but he knew the man would hear him regardless.

An unembodied shout echoed in reply "Get out those side sails men! We need to get this wooden mistress a movin'!"

"Aye aye!" Answered the crew.

Two more pillars of water formed somewhere behind the ship. Mathias was unable to see them, but he heard the residual rain of sea spray hitting the surface of the ocean. The distant boom of the cannons chased each splash, catching up to the Anne-Marie a few seconds later.

"Keep her steady and true to heading, Mr. Crenshaw." Mathias ordered.

"Yessir." Replied Jonathan.

Mathias checked the map and compass sitting atop the crate nearby. The red needlepoint sat unwaveringly atop the 'E'. He knew that as long as they could outrun the other ship, they would be able to break away clear without so much as a scratch.

"Captain!" A voice called out from the crow's nest above the helm. "They've changed course and are making chase towards us! No idea if they have a long nine, but I'm sure we'll find out soon!"

"Can you confirm their colors!?" Mathias asked them.

"She's French alrigh', the privateerin' vultures!" The second part he didn't mean to say out loud, but it came out anyway.

"Any confirmation on the bow cannon?!"

"Aye ther' looks to be one!" As if to confirm his statement, a splash rose up behind the Anne-Marie, this one smaller than the others, but much closer.

This is what they're out here for. No ship has a bow cannon that's not looking for a fight. They won't give up this chase. Mathias thought. "All we can do is hope that we're faster." He said to the coxswain who knew the Anne-Marie's purpose didn't constitute speed nor maneuverability.

There was another splash from behind, followed by the trailing *boom* of a cannon. This time it sounded closer than the last shot. The time between the ball hitting the water and the sound of the cannon continued to shrink.

"I knew outrunning them was too good to be true. This ship has a big stern and stocked to the brim." Mathias pounded a fist on the railing. "We have to go back in. Take us north into the fog Mr. Crenshaw."

"Movin' Nor-" Jonathan's words cut out while he struggled to turn the wheel.

Mathias was looking at the wall of fog unaware of the coxswain' abrupt cutoff. When they continued moving parallel to the gray cliff face instead of steering directly towards it, he became frustrated. "I said North Mr. Cr-!" His words cut out too as he looked at Jonathan.

The coxswain' arms stretched to their limit as he tried to turn the wheel. Veins stood out on his arms and forehead; from the immense effort he was putting into turning the wheel, but it wasn't budging. His feet firmly planted, putting legs, arms, back, neck, every muscle he had into trying to turn the wheel. He gave it one more aggressive push. His rear foot slipped out from underneath him, and the wooden handles began to spin wildly around in the opposite direction. The ship swung violently to the side, knocking everyone aboard, off balance. Cannonballs fell to the floor like dead weights, each one making a *thump* so loud every deck heard it. Sailors cried out their frustration and irritations, which everyone else ignored.

Mathias nearly fell off his feet as well. Had his grip not been true around the railing, he would've fallen over like everyone else. Quickly realizing what was happening, he pivoted in place to address the wheel. The angle of the ship was becoming more extreme by the second. Mathias released his grip on the wooden beam and slid towards the wheel, reaching out with both hands. Two of the spokes smacked his forearms, forming red marks that would turn into purple bruises by nightfall, but he hardly gave them any notice. He was finally able to grab the handles and stop the wheel from spinning but was unable to make any progress in turning it clockwise. He put every ounce of strength into trying to turn the wheel, but it refused to budge. For the time being, the Anne-Marie started to straighten out again, leveling the deck.

Jonathan regained his footing and joined Mathias in trying to turn the wheel and move the ship back into the mist.

"Is the rudder stuck Mr. Crenshaw!?" Mathias asked.

"Nay sir! It was perfectly fine a minute ago! There's nothin' out here to catch on anyhow!" Jonathan replied, becoming flustered as much as Mathias.

It took all of their energy to prevent the ship from turning in the wrong direction. They were no longer maneuvering towards their pursuers, but they were also now moving away from the fog, their only chance for escape slipping away behind them.

While Mathias and Jonathan struggled at the helm, the French schooner had closed the distance. A column of water exploded only meters away from the port side of the Anne-Marie, drenching several sailors in the resulting sea spray. A few of them realized that if the cannon ball landed any closer, that pillar of clear water would've been an eruption of broken wood, flesh, and bone.

Mathias was able to witness the latest impact in the water between two rods of the helm railing. He knew the next shot would most likely land a direct hit on the deck. If their trajectory remained the same, it could even impact the main mast, and they would be stuck floating in place, easily picked off at the schooner's leisure.

"Move away Mr. Crenshaw!" Mathias commanded.

"Say again sir!? You can' hold it on your own!"

"I know, I don't intend to. I'm going to release it after you, but I need you to get clear of it first."

Jonathan looked at the captain, perplexed. He knew better than to argue though, so when he was certain that Mathias had a good footing, he released the wheel and leaped backwards. The wooden spokes spun around, blurring together like an unwinding top. The ship lurched to the side and Mathias fell onto the deck, along with half the crew on the main deck and other sailors down below.

The initial intended effect was successful. The Anne-Marie straightened out and was moving at a decent clip away from the French schooner. More water exploded where the ship had been only moments prior. Disaster avoided for the moment, but they were once again in a precarious position without having the fog to retreat into. The wall of gray was well behind them. Even if they tried to break for it, the schooner would be upon them before they could maneuver inside. Especially since they would have to move against the tide to get there.

"Mr. Howser, are we set for a direct confrontation?!" Mathias yelled down towards the main deck. His first mate's reply came from directly below.

"Aye sir. Cannons rolled out and locked in place. Blades and muskets set out too. They might try to keep us at range though, take out the mast before moving in."

"True, but they won't be able to do much with just the front gun. They can't risk sinking us either, or else they'll lose everything."

"We're ready for them either way, cap'n!"

The Anne-Marie and the schooner were on a collision course facing bow to bow. They sped towards each other over the next several minutes. Water continued to splash onto the deck of the Anne-Marie from cannonball impacts against the ocean's surface. The ship continued to avoid any direct hits, but it was only a matter of time before the French schooner got lucky. Mathias saw all the men on the main deck, waiting to engage. They'd managed to stick to their posts for the moment, but there was no telling how they would react when fellow sailors started getting torn apart by musket and cannon fire.

"Steady men! Stick to your posts, we're beginning to move into range now!" Mathias could see they were growing nervous. The crow's nest continued to call out distances between the two ships, while a cabin boy called out the Anne-Marie's speed in knots.

"We're at twelve knots sir and gaining speed." One boy said.

"Very good, this'll help keep them from zoning in on our position. Hopefully, they continue to miss until we're right on top of them." Mathias turned his attention back to the coxswain. "Any luck shifting the heading, Mr. Crenshaw?"

Jonathan was still fighting with the wheel, trying to change the course of the ship, but with little to no success. Mathias could see the struggle and fight the man was putting in against the wheel.

"No. She won' budge in the direction that I want her to. She's adjusting beautifully against the current though. It's like she knows what to do, without me having to do anything at all."

You may be more correct about that than you know. Mathias thought to himself. He was expecting the headache and voice to chime in any second, but luckily there was silence. He was grateful for it, although at the same time, it concerned him. *Perhaps I'm doing what it wants me to do. Maybe it only calls out when I don't agree with its next course of action.* Mathias wanted to almost test the theory, but felt it wasn't the appropriate time. There was a chance that a higher power was at work, one he couldn't fully understand. So far it hadn't led them completely astray, so there may be some merit to following its direction for the time being.

"Keep trying Mr. Crenshaw. Let me know if it gives up control at any point. We may get an opportunity for some quick maneuvering if it does." Mathias ordered.

Jonathan didn't reply, he continued to grunt in an ill-fated attempt to force the wheel in either direction.

The enemy schooner drew close. Mathias saw a flash of light from the front of the schooner as the French long nine bow cannon fired another round. The explosion, followed by a loud *boom* of black powder and a splash in the water nearby rocked the Anne-Marie.

"Make ready the guns! Two more minutes and we'll broadside them!" Mathias' command was out before the first direct hit against his ship scattered planks onto her deck. Wood exploded beneath the helm and a sizable hole formed in the main deck as a cannonball ripped through to the lower levels. There was no telling where the final trajectory of the ball went, but there was a good chance that down below some men had lost their lives.

The nerves of the men tested against the enemy's. The vast majority of Anne-Marie's sailors stood their ground, getting ready to return fire at the first possible opportunity. Some of the sailors had never been in direct confrontation with an aggressive, privateering ship such as the one they were. Luckily, those that were willing to stand their ground, grabbed hold of the wavering men by the arm or neck to convince them to stay in their respective positions.

Some of the sailor's strengthened by fear, were able to break free from the hands that grabbed them. Mathias only saw the glimpse of a body plummeting towards the water. The man next to them cried out "Man overboard!"

Mathias was about to call out, but Frederick beat him to it.

"Leave 'im! Deserters get no quarter, nor remorse! Cowards get you killed! Belay that command and any other given by the captain or myself!" Frederick had come up from the floor below after the cannonball punched through the surface of the deck.

"Mr. Howser! What is the damage below from that hit we took?" Mathias asked.

"Minimal sir. It went right through the top and bounced out the side. Nothing to be concerned about for now and luckily no casualties far as I can tell."

"Very good. Get back down below and manage things there, I'll handle the main deck."

"On my way." Frederick disappeared into the dark of the hatch; his commands echoed out of the hole as he descended. To Mathias it sounded like the ship itself was speaking, with the hatch acting as the mouth.

Everyone who could see it was staring at the schooner. The French colors were in full view for everyone to see. The schooner's sailors were maneuvering around their deck, keeping their ship on course towards the Anne-Marie. This was in stark contrast to Mathias' own ship that refused to take any commands from them, regardless of wheel or sail position. All they could do was sit and wait, hoping beyond all hope that they'd be able to turn in time to gain a successful broadside position. At the current rate though, they were going to ram head on into the French schooner. That form of collision wasn't something the Anne-Marie was built to withstand, at least not without grave damage to the hull and keel.

Mathias could see the captain of the opposing vessel yelling out orders and waving his hands. Mathias almost made out what the man was saying. The enemy leader stopped for a moment, locking eyes with Mathias, and if Mathias didn't know any better, it appeared as though an arrogant smirk broke across their face. The French captain became obscured by the smoke of his cannon fire. Once the black mist had cleared, the man was gone.

Wood exploded from the bow of the Anne-Marie. The resulting shrapnel flew across the deck, impaling sailors with small wooden shards without discretion. Men screamed as their skin and clothing were torn to shreds. The impact rocked anyone close enough to feel it yet lucky enough to escape unscathed.

"Any luck on the wheel?" Mathias asked Jonathan.

"No luck at all sir. She won't budge."

Mathias took a deep breath and exhaled. "So be it..."

"Sir?!" Jonathan asked, fearing he'd missed an order among the noise.

"Brace for impact!" Mathias yelled to the crew.

Another direct hit rattled Anne-Marie's bow. This one impacted much lower on the hull than the last. Shards exploded outward from the front of the Anne-Marie in a vomit of wooden chips. Mathias was unaware, but they'd been fortunate that the enemy schooner was on the frontside peak of a wave which pointed the bow of their cannon downwards, and away from their intended target. Had the enemy ship been on a level plane, it would have taken out Anne-Marie's main mast, leaving them dead in the water with no ability to maneuver.

That was the last shot before the enemy turned their bow away from the Anne-Marie. Their cannons were prepping for a decidedly, one-sided broadside assault. The French captain waited until their port side had at least three cannons in line with their prey, before shouting the command to fire.

The port side of the schooner's enveloped itself in smoke from its cannon fire. Multiple balls ripped through the sides of the Anne-Marie, going straight through from one side to the other. Frederick was doing his best to reorganize the men and keep them at their stations to prepare for their own broadside, but he was concerned it might be too late. No less than six sailors had blown away from their positions. Two of their cannons had gotten hit directly, forcibly ripped off their anchors and tumbled through the air shortly after. One cannon landed on a man who was unfortunate enough to have fallen down directly in its path. The cannon crushed him, killing the man on impact.

Rifle fire peppered the side of the Anne-Marie. The indents looked like mere mosquito bites compared to the massive holes created by the main cannons. None of the small shots hit their targets, as everyone protected themselves with the wooden beams and railings of their ship.

It was the only broadside volley the schooner was able to fire. The Anne-Marie hadn't slowed down at all during the head on collision course she'd been charting for the past half-hour. If anything, she'd picked up additional speed. She also turned in the direction of the port side of the schooner, knocking her sailors off balance again.

Mathias held onto the helm railing with all his strength, in preparation for the impact. He never expected what happened instead.

As if a massive wave pushed itself under the bow of the Anne-Marie, her bow began tilting upwards, ascending towards the sky. It was fortuitous that everyone on deck already braced and held on tight to either rope or railing. They were able to hang on, while their feet began to slip out from under them due to the extreme angle.

There was a long pause as the front end of the Anne-Marie hung in the air. Water fell from the hull like hundreds of rivulets, showering the deck and sailors of the French schooner with seawater. A multitude of screams and French curse words bellowed from their deck. Men abandoned the ship in droves, jumping in any direction that might save them from the Anne-Marie crushing them between her hull and their own deck.

An ear numbing wail came from the Anne-Marie as she descended with her full weight. If they hadn't been holding on for their lives, every sailor on board would've had to cover their ears. The creaking wail reached its peak directly before the hull of the Anne-Marie connected with the main deck of her prey.

The screams of sailors broke through as the Anne-Marie crushed the schooner in half. The French captain was no longer smirking. He witnessed their easy prize come alive, breaching the surface of the water like a whale, and crashing down onto his beloved ship. Being on the far end of the schooner near the helm, he catapulted into the air on impact. He flailed his arms, reaching for rope or anything else to grab hold of. The yard arm of the main mast of the schooner came between him and his path to the water. His back collided with the rounded post of the beam. The last thing he heard was his own scream mixed with the screams of his men, before the shattering of his spine killed him.

Mathias witnessed the enemy captain's death in slow motion. He wasn't able to decide if it was the satisfying snap of the captain's back, or the French ship breaking in two that sent an orgasmic wave of satisfaction throughout his body. With a single hand still on the railing trying to keep him up, he fell to his knees, shaking uncontrollably.

While Mathias tried to catch his breath, there was cheering on the deck below. Sailors threw out curse words at the drowning French privateers while they basked in the suffering of their enemies. Screams of sailors in the water mixed in as well, creating a salty sweet atmosphere of emotions. Most of the men who didn't know how to swim were already drowning. It was only the ones that knew how to stay afloat that begged for mercy from those standing above them on the Anne-Marie.

Mathias felt a hand on his shoulder. He whipped around to see the coxswain Jonathan, standing over him and offering a hand to assist the captain into a standing position.

"A'right there sir?" Jonathan asked.

"Yes, yes, fine thank you." Mathias graciously took the hand and stood up. He would've been lying if he said the scene laid out before him wasn't, in many ways, satisfying. The French schooner was in shambles, its main mast broken into thousands of tiny wooden pieces, and the body of the ship broken in twain. The larger sections were quickly beginning to sink below the surface of the water. Smaller pieces like cargo, crates, barrels, and pieces of broken shrapnel floated away haphazardly with the tide. Of course, there were also a few survivors treading water.

Mathias saw a man floating atop a large piece of wood on the starboard side of his ship. The name 'LOUISE' etched into the wood that the sailor was holding onto.

"Bring me four survivors from the wreck. The rest can sink or swim, whatever their creator dictates for them." Mathias gave this command to no one in particular. Enough men heard it though and began throwing lifelines of rope out to those struggling to tread water near the ship.

The survivors were more than happy to grab hold, willing to take their chances with their captors than to potentially float for days on end only to die of starvation, or more likely of thirst, within a couple of days. There was also the insanity and mental anguish as well, drinking sea water out of sheer desperation, which would only serve to make their thirst worse, and in some cases, cause agonizing stomach cramps. The French sailors desiring neither outcome, allowed themselves to sink into the sea. They gulped as much water as they could manage until their lungs filled with it, letting unconsciousness take them to the other side.

"I don' know how sir, but we have control again..." Jonathan freely moved the wheel of the ship, clockwise and then counterclockwise in full rotations.

Mathias thought he knew why, but again, it wasn't the proper time to attempt unwrapping those mysteries. "Put us back on course, South by Southeast. Get us out of this area as fast as you can." Mathias ordered.

"Aye sir." Jonathan threw the wheel counterclockwise, aligning the needle of the compass between the 'E' and the 'S'.

Meanwhile, sailors dragged four survivors onto the deck. The French privateers' soaking wet clothing drenched the wood as they coughed up seawater trapped in their mouths. Mathias left the helm to look them in the eyes. They all refused to look at him when he came down, except for one.

The defiant sailor was younger than the rest, no older than 20 by the looks of him. There was a fiery, defiant glare when eyeing Mathias. They stared each other down for a few moments, neither succumbing to the other's gaze. Brave men were notoriously bad talkers in Mathias' experience, so he decided to let him go.

"I asked for only *three* survivors." Mathias said. There was no malice or aggression in his words. He stated it as a basic fact, one that had grave repercussions for the intended recipient.

Two sets of arms grabbed the defiant prisoner by his shoulders and under his armpits. They hauled him to the nearest railing to dump him over the side. The whole time he thrashed and spewed curses Mathias didn't understand, nor cared to. He screamed as his body fell overboard. The yelling ceased shortly after an audible splash. The screams replaced with gargled noises of someone choking on water while franticly flailing in an attempt to stay afloat with bound hands.

Mathias made sure to let the other prisoners hear the fate of their companion, hoping it might loosen their tongues in the process. He approached the first man, the one closest to the bow; the sailor was shaking with fear. Small droplets of water ran down the side of his face, mixing with drool from his mouth, and creating a steady flow that dripped from his chin onto the deck.

"What's your name?" Mathias asked.

"Q-q-quoi?" The prisoner was genuinely confused by the question. He didn't speak a lick of English, and it showed on his face.

"Very well, let's try this again. Comment t'appelles-tu?"

The prisoner's confusion amplified, surprised at the quality of the enemy captain's French.

"J-j-jean." Was all the man managed to mutter.

"Jean...parles-tu Anglais?"

The man shook his head vigorously, repeating "non, non, non" with each rotation. Some of the drooly saltwater splashed onto the companion sitting next to him. He didn't notice and neither did they.

"Non." Mathias repeated. He asked the question to the other two prisoners. Both shook their heads as well. He motioned for Frederick to join him.

"Aye sir?" Frederick asked.

"Do we have anyone fluent in French?"

The first mate was surprised at the question. "Ya sounded pretty fluent there, sir. What you need an interpre'er fer?"

"I'm afraid that was the extent of my linguistic skills when it comes to French."

"Ahh."

They both chuckled and looked at the three men still on their knees. The laughing made each of them tremble nervously.

"Lock them up until I can figure out what questions we need to ask. It doesn't look like there were any other ships in the area, which is a good sign. We should be safe for now."

"Agreed, but are we goin' to ignore what happened with the ship?"

"Happened? The only thing that happened was, we easily defeated our aggressors and are no worse for wear, at least until we get a full report from Mr. Carroway."

"Sir..." Frederick wasn't satisfied with that answer. The events of late have been anything *but* normal, and he didn't like the idea of his captain ignoring them.

"Leave it alone." Mathias commanded, seeing the disappointment in Frederick's expression. "At least for now. We have other things to worry about at the moment, wouldn't you agree?"

Reluctantly Frederick dropped it. "Aye, for now."

"Good." Mathias agreed.

Several sailors took the three prisoners below and placed them into individual cells. There were only three cages on the ship, which was convenient, so long as no one else needed added. If that happened, they'd have to merge them, or the number of prisoners would need to be reduced. The cells themselves were empty for the most part. There wasn't a chair or bench to sit on, only a bucket. The prisoners could use the bucket for a seat, but only until they needed to use it for other necessities. Each prisoner elected to sit on the floor. They said nothing to each other until they were alone.

Mathias waited in his cabin, fingering through a book of rough translations of English to French. He was looking for questions that would be the most beneficial to ask the men they'd captured. Mathias had decided none of the phrases in his small book seemed to fit well enough, when a knock came from the door.

"Enter." Mathis ordered.

Vincent opened the door to Mathias' quarters, covered in blood from head to toe. His sleeves rolled up to the elbows, which seemed pointless given the current state of his clothes.

"I'm ready to give my report sir, if you're ready to hear it." Vincent began.

"Of course." Mathias waved him in, placing the small book he was holding onto his desk in the process. "What's the damage?"

"We have five dead, three severely wounded, and one who's not in the right state of mind."

"So, nine casualties in all." Mathias lowered his head, pinching the bridge of his nose.

"That's correct." Vincent was cautious to enter the room, not wanting to track any blood into the captain's cabin.

"Could've been much worse given the circumstances."

"Aye sir, I agree. However, no amount is a good amount when it comes to casualties."

"Of course not. Thank you for your efforts. I know you'll do everything you can for those three grievously injured."

"I will. It doesn't look too good for them though. They'll most likely need an amputation at some point. Needless to say, they'll never be the same again after this."

Mathias picked up his head and nodded. "That's true enough."

"One more thing sir..." The physician looked at Mathias nervously, trying to find the right words.

"What is it?"

"The men...they've started talking."

"Talking? Seems hardly noteworthy. I imagine there's a lot to talk about after today."

"That's true, but it's *what* they're talking about that concerns me."

Mathias was getting frustrated with the roundabout nature of the discussion.

"Well out with it then, be frank. Speak freely Mr. Carroway."

"Very well. Based on the events that took place with Mr. Steiner, the fog, and now the French privateer vessel. They're beginning to think that this voyage is, cursed."

"Hardly!" Mathias harshly cut Vincent off. "Don't tell me you of all people are becoming superstitious."

"Of course not, you and Frederick know me better than that. Regardless of what I believe though, the men think there's something *unnatural* occurring. You can't deny that what's been happening isn't strange. I'm afraid it will only be a matter of time before they start losing faith...and loyalties begin to waver."

Mathias thought about it for a moment. He knew the best thing to do when spirits were down was to find a way to bring them back up again. When it came to long trips at sea, there were few options other than extra food and drink. To his advantage, they'd recently subdued a French vessel. The Louise was certain to be full of provisions and alcohol. The sailors should've nearly finished collecting the barrels and crates as they floated up from the sinking ship.

"If you run into Mr. Howser before I do, have him tell the crew that they can have as many of the provisions from the wreck as they want tonight. Drink, food, whatever they can find."

"Aye Sir. I agree that it will help in the short term, but I honestly think you need to start finding a way to turn the fortunes of this excursion around. Boring voyages can be miserable in their own right, but this is getting out of hand."

"That it is." Mathias silently dismissed the doctor by grabbing the small translation guide he'd placed on the desk and opening it, separating the two of them between a couple hundred pages.

Vincent took the hint and left, not fully convinced that his captain saw things the same way he did. Of course, Mathias wasn't among the men as often as himself, so he expected it. He only wished the captain would take his advice to heart and stop the misfortune that seemed to be plaguing the Anne-Marie.

When news of Mathias' orders spread around the ship, there was an immediate shift in the attitude of the crew. The loss of their fellow sailors, along with the suffering of those down below of agonizing injuries, were now far in the back of their minds. The main thought going through their heads was whether they should eat until they threw up or drink themselves under the table. For most, it was the latter.

6

Vincent Carroway

Vincent didn't partake in the festivities, neither did captain Mathias, nor the first mate Frederick. None of them felt much like celebrating that evening. Their minds and emotions were not so fickle. Each of them continued doing what they considered was necessary at the time, coping in their own ways.

Vincent was two decks down from the main deck, tending to the three critically injured men. The worst off was a cabin boy, no older than twelve from what the physician knew about him. A large chunk of flesh on the back of the boy's thighs was taken out by one of the schooner's cannons. That, in conjunction with the few dozen large pieces of wooden shrapnel that'd peppered the rest of the boy's body, made it somewhat apparent as to what caused the damage. After cleaning and bandaging the gaping leg wound, to the point where it stopped bleeding through the bandages, Vincent then spent the next few hours painstakingly removing each of the splinters one at a time. The lack of lighting in the room made the operation even more difficult. Some sun rays made it through the small portholes, but the majority of light came from several dimly glowing lanterns set out in a ring around the boy's body.

The physician was beginning to feel like he was trying to sacrifice the boy more than attempting to heal him.

The other two physically maimed sailors were not as bad off. They had some deep gouges taken out across multiple limbs, but so long as the wounds didn't become infected, they would make full recoveries within a couple of months. Both of them were sleeping blissfully a few meters away from where Vincent was working. A couple cups of gin were enough to sedate them in order to bandage their wounds.

After finishing, Vincent would have to go take a look at the prisoners. Mathias wanted a full physical done and wanted them kept healthy, at least until their usefulness had run its course. Vincent knew he'd have to take care of them until port and then have them shipped off to a prison when possible. It was not a requirement for merchant ships to show leniency towards prisoners, but if the roles were reversed, they would want to be shown the same courtesy.

Before leaving the underbelly of the Anne-Marie, Vincent checked up on the last man, who by all accounts, seemed to have a mental breakdown at some point during the conflict. He failed to acknowledge the physician's approach and refused to look him in the eye, even when their faces were mere centimeters apart. The lantern the physician was holding to inspect the patient didn't faze him either. The mentally unstable man sat in a quasi-fetal position, leaning up against a wooden beam, staring off into nothing. His eyes dilated when introduced to the light, which was a good sign at least.

Vincent checked the man's vitals, but could find nothing wrong, apart from a dirty physical appearance, and a beard that'd grown a few weeks too long. Ailments of the mind were never an easy ailment to diagnose or cure, and it was certainly not in the main wheelhouse of what Vincent was used to dealing with. Unfortunately for the sailor, the physician could do nothing but try to keep the man fed and hydrated, until he either broke through this phase, or became enough of a problem that he'd needed detained for the remainder of the voyage.

As he'd mentioned to the captain, fear could destroy a crew from within, and there were few things as fear inducing as a man gone mad, raving about creatures or spirits that weren't there. At best no one believes them, at worst everyone's incited into a riotous frenzy.

Vincent stood and walked back to the critically injured boy. He took one last look at the bandages, which appeared to be staving off the flow of blood, at least for the time being. As he turned away and headed towards the stairs leading up to the next deck, he heard a faint whisper.

"Wooo-man".

It was almost inaudible, but he thought he heard it come from the man whose mind had slipped away. Vincent whipped around with the lantern, shining it towards him. The man hadn't moved and none of his limbs so much as twitched. Vincent couldn't be sure he was the one who'd spoken. The other men were still unconscious, but perhaps they could be talking in their sleep, he thought.

As he turned away once more toward the stairs, the same whisper brushed against his ear. This time he chose to ignore it completely and raced up the stairs, feeling a bit childish, but unable to ignore the chill shooting up his spine all the same.

7

Frederick Howser

While Vincent was below with his patients, Frederick was busy keeping the crew in line. It was difficult, seeing how they were all drunk even before the order given by the captain had reached every sailor on board. He planned on partaking in a little drinking himself when the time came. It'd been a long time since he'd drunk himself into a stupor, but there were few things he enjoyed more than a stiff swig and meal in peace on the main deck. He fancied watching the waves flow by, the stars above reflected in the water like sparkling sea creatures. Unfortunately, he'd have to wait a while longer before enjoying a drink. At the moment, Frederick had the task of breaking up an argument between two men over who could outdrink the other.

"What's going on here?!" Frederick demanded, placing himself in-between the two men who were preparing to trade blows.

"This tosse- tink -e can best me a d-ink." The overly confident sailor was a man of short stature, only weighing 100 pounds soaking wet. Frederick gave him a confusing look, sizing him up against the man he claimed to be able to put under the table. A man three times his weight and almost twice as tall.

"Why -ou -ittle" The larger man started charging the smaller one, but Frederick shoved him back far enough to be able to get a word in.

"That's enough now the both o' ya. Now we all know there ain't a man aboard who can outdrink *me*. So, there be no use arguin' about it with yourselves. Now shake hands, make up, move along, and be merry."

Both of the men looked drunkenly at the first mate, neither one ready to concede. They looked back at each other and refused to budge.

"I mean *now*! Unless you want to risk the same fate as Mr. Steiner."

That got their attention, breaking through their drunkenness more than any other threat could've ever accomplished. The two of them shook hands, each missing the others, but making the effort was good enough for the first mate. They went their separate ways, continuing to drink and looking to pick fights with someone else.

"Is goin' to be a long night for sure." Frederick mumbled under his breath. "Hey you! I know you know better!" He chased after another group of sailors, who looked like they wanted to head below to start some mischief.

8

Mathias Crane

While the doctor was down below tending to his patients and the first mate was running around the rest of the ship trying to maintain some semblance of order, the captain remained in his quarters. He was busy skimming through the English to French translation book, but not paying much attention to its contents.

Despite Mathias' best efforts, the Vincent's words kept coming back to him. He knew the voyage wasn't progressing well on his maiden voyage, but at the same time there was little he could do about it. It wasn't his fault that Mr. Steiner decided to skip the shift and gorge himself on meat and alcohol. Just as it wasn't his fault the man somehow ended up dead underneath the hull of the ship. Mathias had only done what everyone expected of him.

Then there was the fog. Albeit the weather was a little strange, they didn't seriously expect him to be able to predict or have control over the weather. *Control,* that was something that seemed to keep slipping away more each day. He lost control of the ship when it refused to turn. He'd lost control when it rammed a French privateering vessel. He was beginning to lose control of the loyalty of his crew. He was feeling that he was losing control of his mind, thanks in no small part to the events leading up to the Anne-Marie setting sail, and the stories told around the ship ever since then.

Mathias threw the book down on his desk before falling into his hammock. The ship rocked him back and forth as he stared at the wooden frame above. The swaying was enough to put him to sleep, if it wasn't for all of the thoughts racing through his head. What he needed was a short break, anything to get his spirits up so he could forget about all the current issues, if only for a few hours.

That was when he remembered Lucy. He'd forgotten he was looking for her before the run-in with the schooner. She still hadn't come to see him, which was strange. He decided once it got dark and most of the men were asleep, he'd go look for her again. Mathias really needed a friend. One that would lay on his stomach and listen to what he had to say without judgement.

There was a lot he needed to get off his chest. If he could say it all to Lucy, he might be able to regain some semblance of control over the situations unfurling aboard the Anne-Marie. None of it made much sense and he was too seasoned of a sailor to be surprised by much at that point. Boring voyages were irritating in their own right, but excessive surprises were downright dangerous if not handled properly.

At some point, while deciding what to divulge to his feline companion, Mathias drifted off to sleep. The rocking ship, the humming of voices outside on the deck, and the gentle swaying of the hammock all gave a feeling of comfort and security, if only for a couple of hours.

9

Lucy

Lucy had spent the past couple of days in the lower parts of the ship. She ran around, chasing some of the smaller mice that'd managed to elude her that far into the voyage. All of the larger, less agile rats she'd picked off already, dispatching them with the lethal precision of an apex predator in the wild. In a world where every other creature was larger than herself, it was comforting to know there were smaller ones on the ship that she could exert power upon. There was no pride in the task of keeping the ship clean from the disease-ridden vermin. However, the hunt was more than satisfying enough to keep her at it until the ship docked again, where more prey was guaranteed to come aboard.

Lucy sat perched atop a wooden beam running along the top edge of the storage deck. Her body pressed firmly into a corner so dark that the contours of her form were indiscernible from the darkness surrounding her. Her tail hung down, flipping lazily back and forth like the loose end of an unproperly tied off rope. Her two emerald eyes reflected what tiny light existed within the space. They didn't move like the tail though. Each one sat still, floating in the darkness of the corner, watching vigilantly at the floor below.

A small form flickered into view. Untrained eyes could've mistaken it for dust, and most wouldn't spend the effort to verify otherwise. Not Lucy's eyes though, standing guard like a sentry. They knew what they were looking for and after a few hours of waiting, they'd finally found it.

The shape skittered across the floor, moving from one barrel to the next. It never moved without having its next objective picked out beforehand. When it *did* move, the tiny shape shot to its next hiding spot with speed and precision. There was no wasted movement in its actions. Any mistake could spell disaster for its already short, fear filled life. It'd already made the gravest of mistakes without even knowing it. Getting aboard the Anne-Marie where Lucy lay waiting, had sealed its fate.

Lucy didn't move from the corner until after the tiny shadow stopped darting back and forth. She recognized the size and the way it moved as a mouse, likely the one she'd been chasing for the last day or so. The little mouse had found a large piece of hard tack that'd broken off from a sailor's snack earlier. It was holding the crumb with both paws, gnawing away at the edges, breaking off tiny pieces, and swallowing them.

While the mouse took its time with the hard tack, the watchful eyes disappeared and the shadow in the corner shrunk.

Lucy hopped down as far away from the target as she could, while still maintaining line of sight on the mouse. She kept her body close to the floor, her stomach nearly scraping the wood as she crept closer. Mimicking how the mouse had moved before, Lucy darted between crates, making her way closer. She only moved when the mouse was in the middle of a bite, or when it was cleaning the residue from its whiskers. Once she reached a distance to where she could pounce on it, she stopped.

The mouse paused from eating. Its nose twitched in the air. The scent of something familiar, yet strange, had wafted across its whiskers. Instinctively, the mouse knew that it should give up on the current meal and come back again for it later when the surroundings appeared safer. The allure of the food was overpowering though, coupled with the near silent surroundings made it a hard decision. It thought a few more bites would be safe enough to take, before scampering back to the nice hole it'd found beneath a pile of rope next to a support beam. It was unable to get in three more bites before knowing it'd made the wrong choice.

Lucy was midair the second the mouse had started eating again. She descended on it without hesitation. Both paws made contact with the rodent's furry neck. Lucy could feel the faintest snapping sensation beneath her paws and knew the prey was dead. She gingerly picked the mouse up by the torso and carried it off.

The mouse blinded its senses with the food it ate. Lucy made the mistake of allowing herself to be distracted by her hunt too much to notice that she was being stalked in turn.

The massless form had witnessed the entire chase take place, from Lucy patiently waiting in the corner, to the mouse discovering its last meal. It had followed Lucy step by step up until the cat attacked the mouse, where it stopped to watch. The form allowed Lucy to revel in the kill for a few moments. As the cat strutted away, arrogant in her own power, the shadow pounced.

Lucy neither heard nor felt the presence of what killed her. All she knew at the time of death was that she'd made a mistake. The same mistake she took advantage of with her own kill. That feeling of surprise and understanding was all she had time to experience before plummeting into permanent darkness.

10

Mathias Crane

Mathias awoke in a cold sweat. He felt something terrible had happened. Looking around the cabin, everything was exactly how he'd left it before drifting off to sleep. The humdrum outside on the deck was all but nonexistent. Only the snores of inebriated sailors managed to make their way through the walls. With how suddenly he'd woken up, Mathias expected the emergency bell to be ringing, or signs of some distress. Instead, there was silence. He was ready to lie back down and fall asleep again when a scratching noise came from the door.

That's right, Lucy. I was going to look for her. He thought. Still half asleep, Mathias swung out of the hammock, nearly falling over as he hopped down.

More scratching at the door. This time a soft *meow* accompanied it.

"I'm coming girl, hang on." Mathias reached the door, unlocked the bolt, and swung it half-way open. Normally Lucy would come trotting in like she owned the room and take up whatever flat surface she felt like. When she didn't enter the room, he opened the door the rest of the way. "What's going on with you?" Mathias heard Lucy cry again. He saw a small, black shape darting away from him, heading towards the hold. The last thing Mathias wanted to do was chase her down, but he'd already made the decision earlier that he'd look for her, and perhaps there was something she was trying to tell him.

"Hang on, I'm coming. This better not be about a mouse..." Mathias mumbled, grabbing the lantern hanging on a hook next to his cabin door.

It was dark still, the sun's light not even remotely breaking over the horizon. The main deck looked about how he expected it to at that hour. There was food, empty cups, and bottles strewn across the deck. Frederick was going to have a heart attack seeing the top deck in such a state, but the first mate would have it cleaned up before the sun finished rising the next morning.

The Lucy shape hopped down the top step, disappearing below and crying out as she went. "Lucy, wait!" Mathias called out, in a loud whisper. The only reply was another *meow,* this time echoing from the darkness of the hold. He tried running quietly, but each footfall sounded like cannon fire on an otherwise quiet night. After reaching the stairs leading down, Mathias tried to shine the lantern into the hole. He looked for Lucy's shape but couldn't see anything beyond the first couple of steps. He used the dim light to guide his way down the stairs.

It was colder than expected for only being one floor down. His breath wasn't visible, but he still looked for it, convinced small white puffs would start coming out. Every sailor unlucky enough to find themselves without a hammock wrapped their arms around themselves while pressing their backs against the sides of the ship. Mathias was unable to fathom how they could sleep like that. Even as drunk as they were, the chilly air would keep most people awake.

Lucy purred behind him. Mathias' ankles tingled as she pressed against each leg, working her way in a circle around him. It wasn't the warm and comforting sensation Mathias used to feel though. Her fur felt like ice crystals rubbing against his calves. The sounds of her cries were wrong too. They sounded distant somehow, even though they were coming from only a meter or so away. He looked down, but Lucy was already gone.

"Lucy?" Mathias spun around in a circle, looking frantically for his companion who was there only a second ago.

Another *meow* echoed from the other end of the ship. He knew that even Lucy wouldn't have been able to reach the other side of the ship that quickly. He'd seen the cat do a full sprint from one end to the other chasing mice, and even that took more than a few seconds. The time between his ankles rubbed with ice and him spinning in place, to the callout from the opposite side was nearly instantaneous.

You're not Lucy. I don't know what's going on, but I'm getting to the bottom of it tonight. Mathias held the lantern out like a shield, steeling himself against the chill running through his body.

The cat cried out again as a taunt. Mathias crossed the ship to the next set of stairs and descended without hesitation. It was even colder on the next level down. The temperature change wasn't as dramatic as the main deck to the first floor, but there was an obvious decrease all the same. Small whisps of white mist appeared when exhaling.

"It went that way." A hollow voice directed him.

Mathias whipped around, raising his arms up to defend himself. Against what, he didn't know. The voice didn't sound familiar, and it carried a French accent.

"Come again?" Mathias asked, realizing he was standing next to one of Anne-Marie's three prison cells.

"I said, it went that way." A scrawny, pale arm stretched out from between the cell bars, pointing in the only direction Mathias could go.

"Obviously she…hold on." Mathias' mind flickered to his cabin for a second where he remembered scouring through the translation guide in preparation for this very conversation.

"Yes, I speak Eng'ish. Per'aps you should 'ave spent more time learning my language, so we could 'ave had a better conversation before now. That time has passed 'owever, and it is neither 'ere nor there." The bony arm retracted back into the cell.

Mathias held the lantern up to the bars, not willing to get any closer than he needed to. Especially not close enough to be within reach of the prisoner's hands. All three cells were pitch black, even with the light of the lantern shining on them. The small flame did nothing to break the blackness between him and the back of the cell. He couldn't discern the arm from the body it belonged to, no matter how hard his eyes tried. Based on the arm's appearance it was better that way.

"You weren't like this before, what happened to you?" Mathias asked.

"*She* 'appened to me." The Frenchman replied, his voice raspy and weak.

"She?"

"Oui, she."

"Who are you referring to? There is no *she* aboard this ship. We would've found any stowaways by now."

"Oui, if she was 'nly a person to be found, you would 'ave."

"If she isn't a person then what is she?"

"I 'annot say. I thought since you 'ave been on this ship for so long, you would know more than I. It appears that is not the case. You must be quite the capitan." The Frenchman laughed. His chortles were hollow, choppy, almost like he was choking on smoke as he spoke.

"Quiet now, before you say something you'll regret." Mathias threatened.

The prisoner cackled again, louder this time. His bones rattled with each laugh, like his skin and muscles were no longer able to hold them in place.

"There is no time left 'or me to regret much. Not much time left 'or you or anyone else on this ship for that matter." Bony fingers poked out from between two of the bars and slowly curled around one of them in a death grip.

"Tell me what you know and maybe you can pass on with a clear conscious." Mathias grew agitated. There was more bone rattling as the man laughed again.

"All I know is what I saw. I 'ssume it started only a few hours ago. Is hard to tell much in terms of time down 'ere. Your *celebration* of our ship and crew's demise was in full swing. The other cell mates and I were conversing when one of your men came down. He taunted us with food and drink, waving both in front of the bars barely out of our reach. None of us stood or cared much, we tried to wait for 'im to leave. However, our lack of reaction made him more frustrated. He started bangin' on the bars with a leg of meat and splashed 'is drink on me. When I refused to react to 'is taunts, he was ready to leave." The prisoner's grip on the bars loosened slightly, before clenching down even harder. The finger bones cracked, snapping in a few places. "That' when we saw her. The silhouette was dark, darker than the deepest recesses of this room. We would 'ave ignored it completely, but it was *moving*. We looked at each other, confirming we were all seeing the same thing. Our mouths must have been agape because your man quickly changed his tune. *Well thas' more like it.* That was all he said before the shape ate him whole. There were no screams, and he'd no time to struggle. The shadow had crept up behind him without making a sound, its mouth, or at least what I assume was its mouth, opened wide, stretching down to the deck. A moment later the man was gone along with the shadow. No blood, no mess."

Mathias thought he was beginning to understand what was happening, but he wanted to find some proof, any proof to the contrary ideally.

"You mentioned it was a woman, but how do you know? You said it was completely dark and a shadow attacked him. Surely you wouldn't be able to tell specific features based on that alone."

Bones were now protruding from the Frenchman's fingers, breaking through the skin like splinters of wood sticking out of a board. There was no blood dripping to the floor, instead small whisps of black smoke seeped out, quickly dissipating when coming in contact with the outside air.

"I see why she's gotten so powerful. I'm sure you 'ave chosen to ignore all of the signs up until now and I wonder how much longer you'll manage to keep ignoring them. I would 'ave turned this ship around and sent it to the crushing depths had I seen half of the things I know you've seen." The man's voice was losing any clarity it had left. Each word sounded like they took a massive amount of effort to say. The man was fading, and he'd soon take all of the answers to Mathias' questions with him.

"You didn't answer the question. How did you know it was a woman?" Mathias asked again, shaking the lantern in a futile attempt to coax the answers out of his prisoner.

Several more whisps of black smoke joined the few from before on the prisoner's thumb. The Frenchman's entire hand was dissolving into nothing. The bones of his fingers were completely exposed to the outside as the skin receded and evaporated.

"She spoke to us, of course, but in our minds, not out loud. Hard to misinterpret that isn't it? The sweet, melodic sound of a woman's voice after months at sea softens even the hardest sailor's heart. It would 'ave been pleasant if not for the head splitting pain that came before and after." The prisoner saw Mathias wince as he said this. "I know she speaks to you too. Only I chose to listen, and you've chosen to ignore."

"What did she tell you? I need to know!" Mathias was angry, his grip on the handle of lantern matching that of the Frenchman's grip on the bars of his cell.

"Then you need to listen. All I know is that she's in pain, but soon that pain will pass, and she'll have gotten what she needs."

"What does she need? What's she trying to do?!"

There was no response. Mathias noticed the man's hands were no longer around the bars of his cell. He was sure they'd not moved back inside. They evaporated into nothing before his very eyes, likely with the rest of the man's body, but the captain couldn't have known for sure without opening up the cage.

Meow, Lucy cried out from across the room.

"You're not Lucy, are you?" Mathias asked, turning towards the cry.

In response, the Lucy impersonator called out again. This time a splitting headache accompanied the call. It crept around from the back of his head to the front like all the other times when the voice was about to speak.

"What have you done to my Lucy?" Mathias didn't get a verbal answer, instead the headache exploded into a mind-numbing throb. It continued to grow worse until reaching a peak that brought him to his knees. The pressure behind his eyes was the worst internal pain he'd ever experienced. He wanted to listen for the voice, but he was too angry, trying to fight through the pain. *I swear if you hurt her...!*

I would never dream of it. The voice responded.

The pain subsided, but only enough for the voice to come through. What it didn't allow was room for Mathias to think clearly.

Then where is she? Mathias asked desperately.

She's here, with me now. I'm looking after your precious Lucy.

Mathias began to understand what the prisoner had been saying. The voice inside his head had always been hers, from the very moment they set sail she'd been talking to him. He'd refused to listen. He did everything he could to convince himself that it was his own voice and thoughts driving his actions, but he knew better now.

What do you want? Mathias' thoughts sounded more pleading than he' would've liked. It was hard trying to act tough when his brain felt like it smashed into a wall repeatedly.

I want what's denied to me, I want what's owed.

I'll give you whatever you want, you name it. Mathias pressed both palms on either side of his head, trying to counteract the pressure that tried to force its way out from within.

You can't give it to me now, not yet. Soon though, you'll be able to. You've all given me so much already, but I need more, much more.

More? You need more what? The pain began to subside. There was room to think, but all Mathias could feel was rage. *Where are you going? What happened to Lucy? What do you need more of? Answer me!* Mathias demanded.

A hand reached out and grabbed Mathias' shoulder. He wheeled around, ready to attack the woman. Instead of a shadowy face, he met the light of a lantern; the dim glow almost bright enough to blind him momentarily. Vincent's face stood out against the light.

"Are you alright?" Vincent asked him.

"What? Yes, fine." Mathias lied. The throbbing in his skull was dissolving, but the anger and frustration remained. He understood the physician's concern. He'd have reacted the same if he'd found Vincent on the floor in a fetal position, yelling at nothing. "Did you see anything?" Mathias asked.

"Anything? Like what, exactly?" Vincent swung the lantern around, looking for something out of the ordinary.

"Right now, as you came walking over here, did you see anything? Strange shadows, Lucy, anything?"

Vincent raised the lantern again, rotating his body in a sweeping motion. "No, nothing that I'd considered strange or concerning. I was checking in on the injured and saw no sign of Lucy on the way here. I thought I caught a whiff of something like rotting flesh on my way up, but it wouldn't surprise me one bit. The men I've been treating aren't faring well to say the least."

"Fine, don't worry about it then." Mathias wanted Vincent to check and see if the three prisoners were still in their cells. "Can you shine your light in the cells?"

"What for?"

"I need to confirm something."

Vincent released his hold on Mathias' shoulder and walked up to the first cell. The light was dim, so he needed to stick his arm halfway in for it to reach the back wall. After the first one, he quickly moved to the second and then the third.

"They're all gone!" Vincent yelled in surprise. "Everything but their clothes."

Mathias felt relieved and dreadful at the same time. It confirmed that he was sane, but that did little to soothe him, knowing the growing threat was real as well. At the moment, insanity seemed preferable.

"We need to ring the bell; they could be wreaking havoc all over the ship!" Vincent was sprinting to the stairs. Mathias grabbed his arm as he passed by.

"Don't bother." Mathias ordered.

"Sir?!" His captain's lack of concern made Vincent recoil.

"I said don't bother. They're not here anymore. They're dead, gone, poof."

"What do you mean they're not here? As in they're not on the ship?"

"I didn't say that. I don't know where they are, but they're not here."

"You're not making any sense."

"I'm well aware it doesn't make any sense. All I know is, you could search the entire Anne-Marie from top to bottom and you wouldn't find a single trace of them. They're gone and that's all you need to know for now." Mathias' anger had subsided, replaced with solemn acceptance and fear.

"I disagree. I think I need to know a lot more than what you've told me up until now. There's clearly events out of your control taking place. Everyone can feel it and it's only a matter of time before men get restless. They'll start demanding answers, or worse, your head."

Mathias never thought mutiny would be a problem until then. The physician was right. It was only a matter of time, but what was he supposed to do? There were forces at work far outside the reaches of his control. The only thing he knew how to do was try and keep the peace while convincing everyone to carry on like nothing out of the ordinary was occurring.

"I need you to trust me, Vincent. You, Frederick, and I will look for answers tomorrow. I don't think we can accomplish much else tonight."

Vincent didn't like the idea of ignoring three missing prisoners potentially running around free on the ship. The amount of damage they could cause unchecked would be devastating, but the captain was wholly convinced they were no longer present or a threat. It was clear he'd not get any answers that night, but he'd be demanding them from Mathias in the morning.

"Tomorrow then." Vincent begrudgingly agreed.

11

Vincent Carroway

Vincent grabbed Mathias below the elbow and helped him to stand. They walked together back up onto the main deck before walking into the captain's cabin. Once inside, Vincent deposited the captain into his hammock and left. He paused once outside the door, having closed it on his way out, and looked up at the night sky. There were a few stray clouds floating effortlessly against the black backdrop, the light of the moon highlighting their edges. It was going to be light in a couple of hours so the decisions of whether or not to try and get some sleep weighed heavily on his mind. After recent events, he thought it would be nearly impossible to lay down and subdue his thoughts enough to fall asleep. So instead, he decided to return to his patients to keep an eye on them. Plus, he wanted to take a closer look at the cells where the three men had disappeared.

Two levels down, Vincent raised the light towards the lock of each cell. There was no apparent damage or attempts at forced entry from what he could tell. Vincent raised and lowered the lantern against each bar too, searching for signs of rubbing, damage, breaking, or anything at all that would indicate affliction or tampering of any sort. He couldn't find traces of breaking or tampering with the locks, as the captain had said. As a man of science, he readily refuted the ridiculousness of the situation, assuming there had to be a logical explanation, but this was only one of several events that he couldn't rationalize. A man's mind can only deny so much before he has to start asking himself fundamental questions about his range of knowledge and understanding. Vincent gave up on the cells for the moment but would return first thing in the morning with better light to make a more thorough examination. He descended another floor, to where he'd left the three men to rest and heal.

The lantern nearly dropped from his hands as we watched the unthinkable happen right in front of him. Both men who'd been lying on the floor had disappeared, all except for their clothing. The bloodstains from their wounds, that'd marked the floor, were gone as well. The boy on the table had almost dissipated entirely too. The doctor only saw the last traces of his form melding with the table, before it vanished in a whisp of black smoke.

Sprinting over, Vincent tried to grab onto any last trace of the boy, but all he managed to grab was the tattered shirt the boy had been wearing only hours ago.

"What in the hell...?" Vincent scoured the area for signs of the other two men, but it was the same result. Their bodies were gone along with any signs of their injuries, except of course, for their clothes.

As he searched, Vincent started getting a nagging feeling that someone was watching him. His stomach began to turn, and he no longer wished to be alone down in the hold. Without a second thought, he raced for the stairs, climbing two at a time towards the main deck. As he ascended there was a whispering voice following behind him, but he refused to listen to what it had to say, focusing instead on not tripping over every sailor laying on the floor in front of him.

"Got to find Mr. Howser." Saying the words didn't align with his actions, as he barreled through the decks only half searching for the first mate's bulky frame. He was on the last set of stairs, about to break through the hull, and back onto the main deck. A large figure was about to come down the same set of stairs, completely blocking his path. The physician was ready to yell at the man to move aside when Vincent noticed the man blocking his path was the one he'd been looking for.

Frederick was equally surprised to see Vincent running into him, out of breath no less.

"Woah, where's the fire?" Frederick asked.

"Not fire, worse than fire…I think? Not worse? Different, weird, strange? I don't even know what word to use anymore." Vincent's mind churned faster than his mouth could keep up.

"Slow down, what are you on about?"

"I, I, them, they are below. Gone! The men I was treating are gone and the captives along with them."

The last part struck a chord with Frederick, and he ignored everything Vincent had said prior. "You mean the privateers escaped?!" He tried to push past the physician, but Vincent blocked his path.

"Yes, but no. Listen to me, you don't understand."

"You're not making it easy. In fact, yer not makin' any sense at all."

"I know, but please let me try." Vincent looked down behind him, he didn't think the voice had followed him all the way up there, but he wasn't about to take any chances.

"What are you looking for?" Frederick asked, looking over Vincent's shoulder to see what the man was searching for.

"You won't believe me. At least not until I tell you the rest. Can we get up on deck and off these stairs? I don't exactly feel comfortable in this area."

"You're one to talk but yea, come on up."

Frederick turned around and Vincent followed him up and over to the port side railing on the main deck. Both looked around them, but for distinct reasons. Vincent, still spooked by the voice. Frederick was concerned someone would see their physician acting like a loon which would do grave damage to morale on top of all the other recent events.

"What's going on Vincent?" Frederick's question was cold and direct. With how the captain, the other men, and now the physician had been acting, the first mate was past courtesies and wanted answers.

"You know as well as I do that this ship isn't right. I don't know how long it's been this way, but my guess would be as soon as this voyage began. We've been in trouble from the start, but the cause is completely unknown to me." Frederick was still not getting any answers, but he wanted his friend to at least have a chance to try and explain himself, even if the explanation only managed to frustrate him further. "I didn't think much of it at first. The incident with Mr. Steiner and Mr. Corty. Seemed a pretty straight forward case of belligerence and a spot of bad luck on Paul's part, but when I went underneath the ship..."

Vincent covered his face with one hand. He was trying to remember the events as best he could, without missing out on a lot of detail, but it was hard recollecting exactly what he saw.

Frederick clapped him on the back, trying to be supportive.

"I know it wasn't easy but try to explain. At least describe it as best you can." Without moving his hand away, the physician continued.

"The rope attached to Mr. Steiner was *inside* the ship. I tried to pull it out, but it wouldn't budge. It was as if the ship itself had swallowed the man whole. I also thought I saw a shadow shoot past me while I was inspecting the rope, but I can't be sure. That's when I came back up. I had no idea what the shadow might've been, but I wasn't about to stick around and find out."

"How come you didn't bring this up to me earlier? We go way back Vincent; you should've told me."

"No, I couldn't. I needed to try to understand it for myself. There's plenty of times I've missed vital details during my, *sessions.*" Vincent was referencing his past life before joining Anne-Marie's crew. He'd had a series of unfortunate patients die by his hand while intoxicated.

"Aye but that wasn't one of those times, I hope. You promised me you were square."

"Doesn't matter. What's important is I believe what I saw now. After the fog, the French privateers, my patients, and now the voice; I believe almost anything anyone told me."

"Wha' voice you talkin' about?" Frederick removed his hand from Vincent's back, as if the physician's mental condition could somehow infect him too.

"Before I ran into you, I heard a woman call out to me, right after seeing the injured lad disappear. It wasn't sweet or sultry, but ominous. Almost like a siren's call if you believe such a thing. You haven't heard anything like that, have you?"

"Not on this trip, naye, but in the past. Heard plenty o' stories about hearin' women's voices callin' out to them but thas' common enough among men who ain't even seen a woman in months, let alone talked with one."

"That's true. I know you're not an overly superstitious man and you've known me long enough to understand I keep both feet solidly grounded in the realm of logic and reason. I also know there are many things that aren't explainable either. I hadn't run into any before this voyage, but I'm starting to believe in them now."

Frederick let Vincent pause for a minute, so he could process the information. He agreed with everything he'd said about the occurrences, but there were more questions than answers popping up, and answers were the whole point of the conversation.

"So, what *do* you think happened to them all? The missing men, that is."

Vincent uncovered his face to meet Frederick's eyes.

"They're gone. That's all I can say for certain. I have little doubt they're still alive. I can't confirm that, since I haven't seen any bodies, but I can feel it. They're well and dead. The real question is, what happened to their remains? Based on what happened to Mr. Steiner I'd wager they're on the ship. Not *on* the ship per se, but now part of it. More like *in* the ship, the essence of the ship itself, fused with it somehow."

Frederick wanted to pass off Vincent's words as rubbish, but he couldn't. He said he'd believe what Vincent told him and, in a way, he did. He'd certainly heard some wild tales and stories in his years, but this one beat them all. The main issue was, enough of the information had merit to convince him.

"What do you think we should do about it? Have you told the captain yet?"

"Not yet, the man needs sleep. He's seen some things today too, and I also think he knows more than he's letting on. I only hope he's not keeping anything from us on purpose, or with ill intent."

Frederick raised a firm finger and pointed it at Victor like a loaded pistol. "Careful now, those are soundin' like whispers of a mutineer, and I'll do what I 'ave to do to protect that boy."

Vincent knew the first mate's reaction was reasonable, but he'd not intended the comment to come off as confrontational. "Never Frederick, however I've seen what happens when a man's mind comes undone. It's not a pretty sight and can look a hell of a lot worse for those caught up around them. We need to be cautious is all, while keeping an eye on him."

"Aye we do. What say we wait 'till he awakens and then we'll look for evidence of those missing sailors? If we can at least find some remnants we might have a better chance at understanding the bigger picture." Frederick suggested.

"That sounds like a plan. I expected a more hot-blooded reaction from you to be honest."

"Just because I ain't a man of science doesn't mean I can't be a man o' reason."

Frederick slammed Vincent heartily on the back, nearly sending the man over the rail and into the water. He walked off, leaving the physician alone with his thoughts. The sun was beginning to rise and there were duties as the first mate that he needed to perform before the bulk of the men woke up.

Now that his patients were gone, Vincent didn't have much else to do besides watch the sun slowly rise over the horizon, spilling yellow light into the water, flooding its reflective plain with orange light.

12

Mathias Crane

A harsh banging on the cabin door woke Mathias. He took his time getting out of the hammock before shuffling over to it. A sailor, whom he didn't quite remember the name of, was on the other side after he opened it. The man's face twisted with fear and anxiety. He was breathing heavily as if he'd run all the way down to the lowest deck and back up again several times.

"Sir! The Frenchmen have escaped! I tried to find Mr. Howser, but he was nowhere to be seen, so I came to you. Should I sound the bell?!"

"No sailor, stand down." Mathias tried to stifle a yawn, but it managed to eke out anyway. "They're gone. *Dead* and gone if we're lucky."

"But-"

"Go find Mr. Howser and Mr. Carroway if you can. We'll begin the search for their bodies, but I doubt we'll turn up much." Mathias didn't wait for the man's reply. He closed the door to the man's confused face and turned around to search the interior of the cabin for his effects. The clothes he'd been wearing the night before were in a pile next to his hammock. He put them on, pausing to look at the empty crate where Lucy used to lay. His heart was solemn as he forced himself out of the cabin and onto the main deck.

A couple of sailors were organizing rope outside. They were more focused on their conversation though, their hands simply working from memory as they whispered about the sailor who'd run up the stairs and started banging on the captain's door.

Mathias tried to ignore them as he walked by. Hair stood up on the back of his neck. He could feel their icy stare follow him as he went down to the lower deck that held the cells. Unsurprisingly, Vincent and Frederick were already standing in front of the iron cages. There was enough light coming in through the portholes to illuminate each of them completely.

"Still missing?" Mathias asked rhetorically.

The two of them looked at their captain. They gave each other a sideways glance, not sure who should speak up first.

"Aye." Started Frederick. "We were checkin' to see if there were any signs of forced entry or exit. Nothin' from what we can tell and you're the only one with the key 'sides me." He grabbed a small iron ring from the side of his pants and held it up. The keys on the ring jingled as he found the one that opened the cells. He inserted it into each hole unlocking the cells, opening them, then closing and locking them again to confirm they functionality. All three passed the basic test, showing that they were operating properly. "Checks out, like we thought it would. The only thing left of the prisoners is their garments. Either they're gone or they runnin' 'round naked somewhere." He eyed Vincent. "You gonna tell 'im?"

Mathias looked over at Vincent. "Tell me what?"

"These weren't the only men to disappear last night..."

Vincent was concerned with the captain's lack of surprise, but if his hunch about Mathias knowing more than he was letting on was correct, then it made sense.

"Well, who else has gone missing?" Mathias asked.

"Three of the men I was caring for in the lower deck. They're all gone too. After I helped you to your cabin last night, I went back to tend them, knowing I wouldn't be able to go back to sleep after what you'd told me. As I was coming down the last step, I could see the last of the boy, Johnson, vanishing in a whisp of black smoke."

"That's the same thing that I saw with the prisoners." Mathias added.

"There's more." Vincent continued.

Mathias looked at Vincent with morbid curiosity. The physician explained everything he'd told Frederick about the night before. Vincent failed to catch the captain unawares by any of the information. It all made sense, in the current situation where nothing made sense, pretty much anything Vincent told him, he'd believe.

"Now it's your turn sir." Frederick motioned towards Mathias. "What do you know that you haven' told us already?"

Mathias was hesitant to answer truthfully, but he needed allies. There was little chance that he'd be able to uncover the secrets of what was happening alone, and with Lucy gone he needed a pillar of support more than ever. He told them everything, except for the part about his headaches that had been growing steadily worse with each passing day. He also left out the part with the voice talking directly to him inside his own head but had admitted to hearing the voice in general. When the part about Lucy came up, the other two looked worried. They both knew the significance of what the feline meant to the captain, and both felt that she'd been almost as much of a crewmember as any of the other sailors on board.

"So, we agree that the bodies are all gone, and we don't know where they went. I think we can all assume they're dead as well, but we don't know for sure. I'm open for suggestions on where we go from here." Mathias concluded.

"Vincent brought up a good point las' night. We can't explain exactly what happened to them, but we should look for any remains. Anything we can find other than clothing." Frederick suggested.

Mathias took a minute to think it through. There were over 150 sets of eyes on the ship. It was hard to believe that no one had noticed *something.*

"Frederick, get everyone onto the main deck. We're going to search this ship top to bottom. Every crate, every pile of rope from the crow's nest to the underbelly of the ship. I want every board, every porthole, inspected for evidence of what happened to the missing men."

"Aye sir!" Frederick was happy to see that the captain appeared to have some of his fervor back. A level head and strong commands gave him a new sense of confidence.

"Vincent, you're with me. Let's go take a look at where your patients disappeared. We may find a clue or indicator that you missed last night in the dark." Mathias commanded.

"To be honest I didn't stick around long enough to look at anything." Vincent couldn't help feeling a little foolish saying it out loud.

"Probably a good thing you didn't. I don't think you'd be standing here talking to me if you had."

Vincent hadn't considered that possibility until now. The three injured men were easy targets, since they couldn't fight back against anything larger than a mouse. He was uninjured but being alone down in the hold certainly made him vulnerable.

"I think you might be right sir."

The two of them headed off towards the lower deck, waking any sailor they came across along the way that wasn't already awake and heading up to the main deck. Most of the sailors asked what was going on, but the captain and physician ignored them. Instead, the sailors met with commands to get up so that the captain could explain topside.

Descending the last flight of stairs, Mathias and Vincent began searching around the area where Vincent treated the injured men. All the lanterns the physician had lit the night before had burned through their oil reserves. They did an exemplary job of showcasing where the bodies had once been though. For each patient, Vincent had at least two lanterns placed next to them, one at the head and one at the feet, so that he could keep a better eye on them. The men's clothes were also still laying where the bodies had once been, like deflated silhouettes.

Mathias inspected the floor near the leg of a pair of pants that were crusty with dried blood. The wood was dry and there were no signs of blood or any other residue for that matter, even though Vincent mentioned that while operating on him there'd been a significant pool of it on the floor. He was looking at the areas around the lanterns themselves when Vincent called out to him.

"You should take a look at this."

Mathias joined him at the table where the youngest and most grievously injured patient had been laying. On the table was what he'd expected to see on the floor. A massive spot of dark burgundy covered the surface. Vincent had pulled the clothes away from the center, placing them in a pile at the corner of the table. There were only a few spots spared of blood where the wood showed through cleanly.

"Blood." Mathias ran his fingers across the tabletop and scraped some of the dried material off with a fingernail.

"There wasn't any over there where you were looking though, was there?" Vincent asked.

"No, there wasn't."

"What do you think that means?"

The captain scraped a bit more off with his finger. "I'm not sure." He flicked the dried flakes off of the fingernail and knelt down to look at the underside. It looked how he'd expected as well. Small stalactites of blood had formed underneath where it was dripping down and had hardened over time. His eyes tracked the invisible path that the drops would have followed as they fell to the floor. The boards were free of stains and appeared normal, no traces of blood, dried or otherwise. As he inspected the area beneath the table, he realized that the legs of the table weren't nailed down.

"This table was originally against the wall, wasn't it?"

"Yes, secured like the others, but I needed to be able to operate on the boy while keeping an eye on the other men, so I had it moved. Why?" Vincent bent down across the table from Mathias and looked at the floor. "Ahh, I see- That's indeed strange."

"You find anything else?" Mathias asked.

"Nothing of note. The man having the mental breakdown is gone too though. I don't see his clothes where he'd been sitting, so hopefully he's alright."

"Then we best head up to the main deck then and see how Mr. Howser is getting along with the orders." The alarm bell began chiming, its ringing deafened by the multiple decks between them and the main one, but the sound was unmistakable. "And quickly it seems."

As the two men poised themselves to ascend, a strong odor wafted across their noses. They both recognized the scent as rotten fruit. It seemed to originate from the open hatch at the other end of the ship. That hatch led down to the storage deck where Mr. Steiner was found drunk, passed out either from overconsumption, or now more likely, from something more nefarious. There'd be time to investigate it more thoroughly, but for the time being they subconsciously agreed to leave it alone.

The thunder of feet all across the ship made the Anne-Marie feel more alive than she had in days. The jovial celebration the night before made plenty of noise in its own right, but when every able-bodied man was moving around simultaneously, it felt like she had a heartbeat, and the men were the blood in her veins. There were a few stragglers attempting to shake off their inebriation and gain a footing as they fell off their hammocks. Mathias called out to them before they were far enough away to not hear or care.

"Sailor, who sounded the alarm?" Mathias asked them.

A half awake, still partly drunken sailor turned to answer. A line of drool was making its way down the corner of his mouth, almost having reached his chin before he could answer.

"Dunno, 'ust woke up." He hadn't realized who'd asked the question and didn't seem to care much either. He shambled across the deck towards the stairs, one of his legs seeming to still be half asleep as it dragged behind him with each labored step.

Mathias and Vincent ran by the man and up the stairs. They raced across each floor until they were atop the main deck. The clanging of the emergency bell was ear piercing now. There was yelling and cursing from all directions as crowds of men shouted at the first mate. Mathias was having trouble discerning any single question or comment out of the flood of words the sailors were producing. He spotted Frederick at the helm, yelling right back at the crowd as if trying to push back against a torrential wave without much luck.

The two men forced their way through the crowd towards the helm. The stairs leading up were mostly clear, so once they were able to break through the throng of sailors the climb to the top was easy.

Frederick was yelling and raising his arms up and down to sedate the crowd. Mathias was impressed by how well the man was keeping his composure and professionalism given the circumstances, but it didn't last long. Frederick's aggravation reached fever pitch as he bellowed.

"Ya stupid bastard's, shut the hell up for one bloomin' second!" The emergency bell felt like nails hammering into his head. "And stop ringing the damn bell, if they're not up here by now they're probably dead!" A few of the men subsided their shouting. Others only grew louder, and this made the quieter ones erupt once again with increased fervor. Frederick dropped his arms, giving up entirely. Mathias grabbed him by the shoulder. Frederick wheeled around and breathed a sigh of relief.

"Everyone, please listen!" Mathias yelled. The loudest sailors in the crowd settled down a bit, but there was still a general buzz of comments and questions that made their way through the congregation. "Who rang the bell?"

Heads turned towards each other asking their neighbor if they were the one or if they knew who was.

A voice called out from the crow's nest. "I did sir!"

Everyone looked up to the top of the main mast. The man was already scuttling down the rigging towards the deck.

"I saw the prisoners had escaped and I couldn' find Mr. Howser, though I see he's here now." The man finished climbing down the last bit of rope ladder and hopped off. The crowd parted so he could make his way through to the stern of the ship. He stopped a few paces before the captain's cabin door and looked up to address the men up top. "I was doing my morning rounds when I noticed they were missing. Seemed the right thing to do was to sound the bell."

"Aye, right you are. We know they're missing, but we're quite sure they're dead." Mathias answered.

"Dead?" The buzzing echoed through the crowd again. "Dead how? The hells goin' on?" They asked.

"Well…" Mathias looked towards Frederick and Vincent who were standing on either side of him. They both nodded. They knew they couldn't hide it from the crew any longer. "We don't exactly know."

"You don' know? How could you not know? How do you know they're dead then?" One sailor asked.

"Yea! How ya know?!" Others added on, yelling for answers.

"What' he sayin?" Another man asked.

"Who killed 'em?"

The questions started coming rapidly as fear and confusion quickly engulfed the sailors.

Mathias waved his hands to hush the crowd. "Please listen to me. We don't know how they died; we also don't know where they went. They disappeared sometime last night but we don't know exactly how or why."

"What about the dingey's? They woulda taken one of 'em if they'd escaped."

Another wave of shouting and questions erupted from the men. They began to split into two groups, one heading towards the port side and the other heading towards the starboard. They were looking for any missing lifeboats, but it was clear once the sailors accounted for them that they weren't the answer.

"They' all 'ere." One man said to another.

"Aye all here." Confirmed another.

When each side was convinced that there wasn't anything amiss, they looked across at each other. They confirmed the same and the gap they'd created filled back in like water filling in the empty spaces of a bowl.

"Maybe they swam for it?" Someone suggested.

"Not likely, we're at least thirty kilometers offshore." Replied another. More theories and questions were being thrown around and then shot down by others. Mathias let them take a minute to figure out they didn't have any answers and were willing to once again listen to what he had to say.

"Look, they're not on the ship from what we can tell. Mr. Carroway, Mr. Howser, and I, are convinced they're dead. The patients the physician was working with yesterday are gone as well. We don't know where they went, and we've been trying to find answers all morning."

"An' what you find so far?" Multiple men asked in unison.

The captain was hesitant to reply. "Not much unfortunately, only their clothes."

There was a general grumble of discontent among the sailors.

"So, what' the plan then?" The man who rang the emergency bell was the one to ask the question.

"We're going to look for them. We will scour the ship from top to bottom looking for any evidence we can find."

"But you said they weren't on the ship anymore." An older sailor mentioned.

"We don' know that for certain." Frederick interjected. "Just cause we 'avent found anythin' yet doesn' mean there's nothin' to find."

More questions and concerns mumbled aloud, none of them discernable enough to reply to. There seemed to be a general consensus of discontent.

"We're going to start in the storage hold. There's something Mr. Carroway and I want to investigate first. We want all of you to search for any sign of the prisoners or the wounded sailors. If you find anything at all, wait for us at the helm and we'll take a look at it when we come back up." Mathias ordered.

"What are we lookin' for?" An indiscernible voice cried out.

"Anything. Anything at all that seems evenly remotely strange, different, or may be evidence of those missing. Travel in groups and if the prisoners somehow did escape you can assume they'll be hostile." Mathias added.

No one moved. They had too many questions and almost no answers. To most it seemed a pointless waste of time and effort. The ship was big, but not so large that six full grown men and one boy could disappear without a trace.

"You heard the captain; you have your orders. Get a move on!" Frederick commanded.

Small patches of men began to break off from the main group. Most of the small contingents were hesitant to go below the main deck. A few souls decided to venture down and soon, others followed. Mathias turned to address the coxswain. It was Jonathan Crenshaw on duty again at the helm.

"Mr. Crenshaw, start moving us towards the mainland. I want us traveling as close to the shore as we can manage without running aground." Mathias ordered.

"Aye sir." Was all Jonathan said before turning the wheel in an easterly heading.

"Let's go take a look down below and see what we can find." Mathias motioned for Vincent and Frederick to follow him.

"Aye sir, settin' an example is what we should be doing." Said Frederick.

Vincent nodded in agreement without saying anything else.

There was still a large crowd on deck. Many of the men didn't know where to start. The last thing they remember was the entire crew in a good mood partying the night before and enjoying their well-deserved victory. Now all of a sudden, their lives were in danger by some unknown force on the ship, one that half of them were not fully convinced even existed. The other half were scared enough to not want to go below deck. They may not have understood what was happening, but they were superstitious enough to believe anything.

Mathias pushed his way through with the first mate and physician in tow. Everyone in their way was more than happy to let them pass through. As they disappeared below deck, more of the men topside were inclined to follow behind them. So long as they weren't the first ones to go down, they were more willing to traverse below.

A scent hit the three men's nostrils before they even made it down two more decks. It was the same acrid stench Mathias and Vincent had smelled when they left the second to lowest deck earlier. Mathias looked to Vincent who nodded him onwards. They pressed forward slowly, afraid of what they might find, but even more terrified of what might happen if they failed to investigate the storage hold.

The three of them reached the deck where Vincent had been attempting to heal the injured men.

"My god!" Frederick exclaimed. He believed what the doctor and captain had said about the men going missing, but he hadn't expected how terrifying it felt witness the scene in person. There wasn't anything left of any of their bodies besides the pool of blood left on the operating table. He thought there'd at least be some remnants of the men, but they were completely gone. "Is this what happened to the prisoners as well?" Frederick directed his question at Mathias, but an answer from Vincent was acceptable too. He'd have taken an explanation from anyone.

"As far as I understand it, yes." Mathias answered. "I watched as one of them disintegrated into nothing before my very eyes. His muscles atrophied and sucked down to the bone, until there was nothing left but black smoke and ash. Seems anyone that's not free to roam about the ship, the Anne-Marie absorbs."

"But how, why?" For the first time Mathias saw fear in Frederick's eyes. He didn't blame the man one bit. This was beginning to move past the realm of superstition and into the world of sheer impossibility.

"I don't know. I wish I knew the answer to that, but after we look for evidence, I think it's time I tell you both everything about what happened before we set sail..." Mathias had been dreading the moment. He'd hoped to keep the events leading up to their departure a secret, but it seemed that was no longer possible.

"You mean you know more about what's going on than you've led us to believe, again?" Vincent confronted Mathias.

"Aye, but it was for everyone's sake, including my own. If I told you the events I was a part of and had witnessed, you'd wish you hadn't heard about them at all. What I know now is that I can't fix this on my own. It involves not only me, but everyone on the ship. All I can ask is that you trust me to tell you in time, after we search through everything thoroughly first."

Vincent gave Mathias a disconcerting look. "I can't say I agree with your judgement. But so long as you promise to tell us absolutely everything, we'll stick with you, for now."

"Aye, for now." Frederick agreed.

"Agreed." Mathias pressed onward. "For starters, let's find the source of that smell."

"I'm not so sure we want to." Vincent countered.

Frederick and Mathias ignored him, climbing down the last set of stairs into the lowest levels of the ship. Down into the very bowels of the Anne-Marie. As they reached the bottom floor the scent was more pungent than ever. It was the familiar scent of rotting fruit. By the strength of the stench, it seemed that all of their reserved stores had spoiled. That would've indeed been a dire situation for all involved. Mathias was now happier than ever that he ordered the coxswain to move the ship towards land. They may need a port to trade with, and fast.

"Look at that!" Vincent directed their attention towards the barrels a few rows back from the front. Their sides were beginning to bulge like festering wounds. The rotted fruit forced its way through the cracks in the boards of the barrels, like pustules on the brink of bursting.

"Help me move these out of the way." Mathias ordered.

Frederick moved to help Mathias shift the first set of barrels out of the way. All of them were full, except for the couple that Mr. Steiner had helped himself to. That night felt like ages ago to them. The evidence of the man's transgressions had been more than washed away at that point. All except for the half empty barrels closest to the stairs. Mr. Steiner had managed to move them by himself, but it took both Mathias and Frederick to move the full ones a couple rows back.

It was a labor-intensive process pushing each one onto the edge of its bottom and rolling it to the side so that they could reach the next one. They created a narrow path, barely wide enough for two men to work their way through towards the opposite end of the floor. Vincent, not being much of a physical laborer himself, watched them struggle from the base of the stairs, offering words of encouragement every time they managed to open up a steps worth of walking space.

When they reached the first barrel of reserved fruit, it was pressing so hard outward from inside, that Mathias was afraid it could explode open any second, covering all three of them in disgusting, rotten fruit. If they didn't know any better, it appeared that the barrel itself was pulsing, pressing apple puss through the narrow gaps created from the pressure.

"We should probably relieve this pressure before we 'ave ourselves a real messy situation to deal with." Frederick suggested.

"Agreed." Mathias replied.

They dug their nails into the open slot near the top of the barrel. With immense effort they were able to tear the lid off. A cloud of rotten smelling gas billowed out, almost as if the barrel was releasing a great sigh of relief. The outward pressure subsided, the planks on the sides of the barrel moved inward as the majority of the gases easily escaped through the top instead of trying to force its way out the sides. They moved the newly depressurized barrel of the way and began working on the others nearby.

Only two more appeared to be near the point of failure. Frederick and Mathias focused their efforts on those two but noticed that a few others were beginning to reach the same level of danger. Once they took care of the extreme cases, Vincent decided to join them.

"Have either of you ever seen anything like this before?" Vincent's look of concern was mutual among the other two.

"Nothin' like this. I've seen cases of maybe one barrel doin' somethin' like it, but never multiple at the same time. If I didn't know any better, I'd say it was intentional. You saw how much effort we put into getting' to these ones and openin' them up. I can't imagine why anyone would do this on purpose, especially since it would only mean dooming themselves in the process." Frederick looked towards Mathias.

The look of grave concern on the first mate's face told Mathias it was time for him to explain everything that'd led up to then. So, he started from the beginning, before he'd arrived at the Anne-Marie the morning of their departure.

"The ship's tryin' to kill us. Is that what you're sayin'?" Frederick's question was blunt and direct, but he didn't have a more articulate way to express how he felt.

"In some ways yes, in other ways no. If it only wanted all of us dead, it would've probably killed us already, but it hasn't. That leads me to believe that it needs something from us. Maybe it's absorbing the men like some kind of nutritional source or something, I don't really know." Mathias tried his best to cover all of Frederick's questions.

Frederick threw up his hands. "I don' know if I can accept tha' sir. This is beyond anythin' I'm willin' to accept." He turned his attention to Vincent. "What do you think 'bout all this? Are you willin' to accept a ship gone sentient and homicidal all of a sudden?"

Vincent took a minute to respond. He appeared lost his own train of thought, working his way through the tale spun by the captain.

"I admit the series of events are indeed strange. I can't logically explain any of them away. Everything he's said so far fits what has happened. But like you said Frederick, it does not explain what the end goal is. As the captain succinctly put it, the ship could most likely kill us all if it desired, but it has chosen not to. Instead, it picks us off when we're weak or when we're alone or isolated. At the very least it appears to not pick its victims at random, which is good news for us."

"Now you're starting to sound as crazy as him?" Frederick was ready to leave the two of them down in the hold alone with their crackpot theories. He was halfway up the stairs when Mathias called out.

"Fred..." Mathias called out pleadingly. The inflection in the captain's voice stopped the first mate in his tracks. "Please, we need your help. I've been completely honest with you now. There's nothing left to hide. That poor murdered woman has taken hold of this ship, *is* the ship, I don't know. All I know is that she's already killed at least nine men, probably more...and Lucy. We have to stop her."

Frederick heaved a sigh of frustration. He turned back around to face Mathias. "An' how exactly do you plan on doin' that?"

Mathias smirked. "I was hoping *you* had some ideas."

"Well, not leaving anyone alone seems like a good start to me. Good call, having everyone search the ship in pairs. I don' see much point in anyone looking for evidence of those that have already died though. If we didn't see anythin' on our entire way down here, there most likely isn't much to find."

"We realize it was more to keep the men busy and distracted while we looked for real answers." Vincent interjected. "With the fruit rotting away, we aren't going to have a good chance of fighting off scurvy. The direct attack on the French vessel could've been much more disastrous than it was. We were fortunate to come out as unscathed as we did. This leads me to believe that she's trying to reduce our numbers as much as possible. Captain, you said that the ship was uncontrollable during that encounter with the schooner?"

"Correct, even with me and the helmsman, we couldn't move the wheel. Even when both of us were trying to turn it with everything we had. However, as soon as the other ship sunk, we were able to regain control."

"So, we know that it can take control when it wants to but decides not to intervene unless it has a specific objective in mind."

"Aye, but to what end?" asked Frederick.

"That part I'm still trying to figure out. There must be something we're still missing. Assuming it thinks the way we believe she does." Mathias added.

"It's certainly smart enough to know what targets to go after. Those that are too weak to defend themselves for instance." Mathias thought about the poor men who'd been lying injured and vulnerable, taken before their time. Including a young boy, a fate he didn't rightly deserve.

"Not necessarily...if we think of the ship as a living organism, it may simply be absorbing the weakest willed among us, almost like digesting food. It's not something we do consciously, it happens naturally, organically." Vincent countered. "That doesn't explain the stories of the men attacked by a shadow figure. Those men were more than capable of defending themselves. Clearly not against this, but overall, yes. It seems she only takes a physical form when attacking those that aren't weak. I'm sure it is out of necessity though. If we assume she caused the fruit to rot, then she's either trying to weaken us to make us more susceptible to attack, or assimilation. *Or* she used the nutrients of the food to directly nurture herself."

"I feel like we're making a lot of assumptions here." Frederick kept looking between Vincent and Mathias, still struggling to accept the rabbit hole of logic they both seemed to be taking each other down.

Vincent chuckled. "That's not even the half of it. We don't have enough time to go through all of the theories I have running through my mind right now. I'm only giving the two of you the highlights. Leaving its intent and purpose aside, we need to get off this ship, plain and simple."

"I think we can all agree with that." Mathias said.

"CAPTAIN!" A voice screamed from the deck above them. They looked up, their ears following the loud thudding of footsteps all the way to the top of the stairs, where a distraught sailor stopped to look down at the three of them.

"What's wrong?" Mathias called out.

"The ship's not turning again. The coxswain told me to tell you right away. He said it's happened before and to let you know immediately." The sailor was out of breath. He was panting, making it difficult to fully understand what he was saying, but they comprehended most of it.

"We're on our way up." Mathias informed him. The sailor ran off, not waiting for them to make it up to his level.

As they raced to the main deck, Mathias was pleased to see more men had dared to venture deeper into the ship. It was clear their hearts were not in the search of evidence of the missing sailors, but it was better than them being too cowardly to even walk below the main deck.

The situation Mathias found himself in was eerily similar to the one that occurred during the battle with the French privateers.

Jonathan was at the helm still, pushing on the wheel with all of his might, but it was refusing to budge. He looked up as the captain made it to the helm and began pushing on the wheel alongside him.

"She not goin' sir. Can' make her turn no matter how hard I try. We're in open water there nothin' to catch on the rudder. It's like that other time…" Mathias continued to push as hard as he could while Jonathan pulled on the spokes of the wheel on the other side.

"When did it start?" Mathias asked.

"Not too long after you went below. I knew somethin' was off when I started headin' more east than south. She let me for a few minutes, but it wasn' long before I couldn' get it to turn more than a couple degrees. All of a sudden it started turnin' west and I haven' been able to turn her back since."

"She's movin' us to open water…" Vincent's words trailed off. The realization of what they meant dawned on Frederick and Mathias.

"Mr. Howser, we need the sails up. Get all of them furled *now*, and I mean *right* now!" Mathias commanded.

"Aye sir. Listen up you lot!" Frederick was yelling down towards every able-bodied soul on the main deck of the ship. "Get everyone up from down below. Get 'em up here and furl the sails, then strap 'em down. Don' all go down below neither, some of you stay up here and start on 'em, but we need everyone on deck gettin' the riggin' in order!"

With familiar orders they could understand and follow, the sailors sprang into action. A dozen were already scaling the rope ladders towards the yard arms. They crawled across the beams towards the ends, untying the knots holding the sails in place before pulling them up and tying them once again to secure them in an upright position. Sailors were billowing out from below deck like a disturbed ant hill. The drastic change in speed from having all of the sails down catching wind to having them all up, caused the ship to buck forward as it stopped.

"All sails secured sir, we shouldn' be able to get anywhere, at least not fast anyway." Frederick informed the captain.

"Good, that should at least buy us some time." Mathias didn't intend to say it as loud as he did.

Jonathan stared at him, confused. "Time for what exactly?" He was holding onto the wheel, more out of habit than anything else as the ship wasn't moving with any great speed due to the current tide. The wheel was completely frozen in place, unaffected by the pressure of the water on the rudder. For the coxswain, there was a sense of comfort holding onto the wheel regardless.

Mathias ignored him. "Mr. Howser, how many paddle boats did you load the morning we set sail?"

"Half a dozen or so, not enough to get everyone off the ship without risking half of them capsizing on us before we make it to shore."

"That's not good, we would need to get everyone off at the same time, otherwise those left behind would be in even greater danger. It will have to be all or nothing. Speaking of shore, how far would you gauge we are away from the nearest one Mr. Crenshaw?"

Mathias' directed the question to Jonathan. The captain's question caught Jonathan off guard. He was more concerned about the lack of the ship's ability to turn than he was about their current position and heading. "It'll take a minute, but I can try to calculate it."

"See that you do."

Jonathan released his death grip on the wheel and moved to the crate with the compass, to determine the Anne-Marie's current position. As he measured out distance on the map, the color began fading from his face. His mind frantically checked and rechecked the coordinates. Without picking his head up to look at the captain, he murmured. "Approximately forty kilometers captain."

"Not close enough for most to swim, and a long trip in the boats as well. She has us right where she wants us." The realization of their dire situation was slowly seeping into Mathias' mind. "The *ship* sailor, the ship!" Repeating it did nothing to clarify to Jonathan what was happening, and the captain didn't expect it too. He knew the man would understand soon enough, if he was lucky to live that long. "Mr. Howser!" Mathias called out again.

"Sir." The first mate replied.

"We still need everyone back up on deck. It's time we learned what they've found if anything. I'm not holding my breath though."

"You're not alone there, sir." Frederick leaned over the railing and called out for all hands to return to the main deck at once. A few minutes passed and he was growing impatient. He ordered the emergency bell to be rung again as it now seemed to be the only way to make the sailors move with a sense of purpose.

Personally, Mathias was getting tired of hearing the ear-piercing clang of that damned bell. It was never a good sign to hear during normal voyages and it certainly wore out its welcome on the current one. The effectiveness was undeniable though, as men began spilling out of every nook and cranny. Men seemed to come out of the woodwork, clambering out of portholes and hull holes. Their search of the vessel appeared to have done little to subside the questions and confusion they'd experienced before beginning their investigations though.

Mathias didn't care. He was about to inform them of the harsh reality of their situation. They would either accept it or they wouldn't. The latter was much more likely than the former. When it seemed the vast majority of the crew arrived topside, he asked the question everyone had at the forefront of their minds.

"Did anyone find anything? If so, please come forward."

No one moved. Every sailor looked at their neighbor, the man standing closest to them on either side and shrugged. There was general chattering among them, but none had cause to claim they found anything of importance. Mathias was unsurprised. There was little to no evidence of those that'd gone missing, and he knew it. He was about to reveal the situation to them when someone stepped forward.

"I might have seen something sir." The voice was quiet. It was barely audible enough to be discernable from the rest of the crowd. Mathias could barely see the hand raised above the shoulders of the men around the origin of the voice.

"Step forward lad, tell us what you know." Mathias ordered.

A man standing directly next to the boy tried to interject. He grabbed the boy's arm, pulling it back down towards his side and muttering in his ear. "It's nothin' boy let it go."

"Belay that sailor!" Mathias yelled. "I want to hear what the lad has to say. Please step forward son and tell us what you found."

"Aye sir!" The boy pushed his way through the sea of bodies. His head barely sat higher than most of their waists. Sailors grumbled while he pushed through them to get closer to the helm. Once he popped out into the open, Mathias was able to get a better look at him. He recognized the boy as one of the two that were scrubbing the deck before they broke through the fog and fought the French vessel.

"What's your name?" Mathias asked.

"J-james sir."

"That's a fine name, strong name. Can you tell us what you found James?"

"Of course, sir. A couple days ago I was sitting on the lift at the stern of the ship. I was scraping barnacles off the hull when I noticed some boards were bulging out from the sides. At first, I wrote it off as normal wood swelling. I focused on the board that was protruding the most, chipping away barnacles one after another. I was almost scraping off pure wood when I got down to the last one. It was a bugger and a half to get off I'll tell you that. Took both my arms to dig under it with the scraper before I could pry it loose. When I finally did manage to break it away, I saw it'd attached and grown on the inside of a knot in the wood. Once it was gone, it revealed a big hole. I thought I could hear something, like a thumping noise or knocking." The ship was silent. The crew all hung onto the boy's every word. The wooden deck creaked as the Anne-Marie bobbed in place. "I tried peeking in, to see what was making the noise, but..." everyone on board took a collective breath. "I couldn't see anything; it was too dark. It was so black inside it looked empty. Ss I was about to move on, I could've sworn I saw something flicker by, but I can't say for certain. It scared me enough to pull myself back up before finishing the work. Took my share of lashings for that, but those were nothing compared to having to go back down there."

"Ehh quiet you." One of the other men tried to push the boy back into the crowd. "Capn' don' have time for your ghost stories sonny."

James protested, trying to push his way past the man's arm in a futile effort.

"But it's true! I saw what I saw and I ain't a liar." The boy argued, standing up on his toes trying to get as close to the man's face as his short, unmatured legs would allow.

"Away with ya." The man was much more forceful this time, shoving James away. The boy was already off balance from leaning forward so the push had enough power to knock him down onto the deck. His back hit hard, forcing the wind out from his lungs. He laid there gasping for breath, a hand to his chest as he tried to force oxygen back inside, but failing miserably.

"That's enough!" Mathias exclaimed. "The boy was only answering the question that I asked of him. For what it's worth...James was it?" James tried to nod his head, but he was still struggling to catch his breath, so his head only lolled back and forth. "Thank you for telling me son. Is there anyone that can corroborate what he's said?" Mathias scanned the crowd, but none came forward. He thought he saw one of the other cabin boys trying to say something, but they remained as silent as the rest. "At the very least it's something we should check out. There's no detail too small."

"But Cap'n..." The shoving man protested.

Mathias ignored him completely. "Is there any easy way to access the area beneath my quarters?" Mathias directed the question at Frederick. He said it loud enough so that anyone who knew could answer as well.

"I'm not entirely sure." Frederick replied.

"There might be aye." A well-built sailor sitting atop the nearest yardarm called out.

"What's your name?" Mathias asked.

"Mitchell sir. I spent a lot of time down in the hold where the boy claims to have found the hole, and I also know quite a bit about the ship's overall structure. There's an empty space back there near the stern directly below your quarters, helps the ship float better and sail smoother, it also increases the overall size of the back end of the ship for ballast. Nothin's stored in there for obvious reasons but it's certainly large enough to house somethin', if there was something livin' inside. Not sayin' there is or not."

Mathias was impressed and curious about the man's knowledge of the area. "How is it you know so much about it? Now that I think about it, I never really knew that myself."

"Aye sir, not to offend, but many don't. I used to work near the docks building these exact style ships years ago. Turns out sailing 'em is easier than building them, go figure. So, I left that life behind and began working on the same ships I helped build."

"Is there an easy way to access that area without having to knock a big hole in the wall or floor?" Mathias continued his line of inquiry.

Mitchell shook his head and sighed. "'Fraid not. We'll have to take a hatchet to it or try to pull the boards away. Neither option will do any significant structural damage, but I would close it up afterwards."

"And why is that?"

"Well, if we were to spring a leak and water filled that empty space, we'd sink faster than that anchor." Mitchell threw a thumb over his shoulder directed at the anchor fastened to the bow.

"Thank you, Mitchell."

The man who knocked Jonathan down looked at the captain, confused and disgusted. "Are we seriously listenin' to this drivel? Men disappearin' in the middle of the night and in broad daylight, on a ship a farthing from the nearest spit of land. Not to mention boys talkin' of haunted holds in the back of the ship?" He turned his back on the helm to address the crowd. "This is bloody ridiculous. I won't stand here and eat up bullshit ghost stories. Will you?"

"How'd you like me to throw you in one of those cells the Frenchman went missing in? Then when you're gone, not only will we be rid of your mutinous arse, but you'll get to reap the rewards of your own stupidity along with it." Frederick threatened.

The first mate could tell the man didn't want to back down, but the punishment for opening his mouth another time wasn't worth the potential repercussions. Instead, he spat on the deck. His spit landed right next to the hand James was using to support himself. He pushed his way through the crowd, mumbling obscenities shoving anyone out of the way that wasn't letting him easily pass by. The man disappeared below deck.

Frederick leaned in, to whisper in Mathias' ear. "He may be the first, but he's certainly not going to be the last. We need a plan, and we need it quick."

"I know, it'll get worse if we do nothing, but what would you have me do? There's no precedence for this." Matters continued to worsen as Mathias was beginning to feel another headache coming on. The thumping in the front of his skull quickened as the waves of pain began crashing back and forth in his head. They'd all been painful, but he knew this time it was going to be more severe than the rest. "I need some time to think." He was already pressing his palms against each temple in a futile effort to stave off the throbbing. "I'll be in my quarters, do whatever it is you need to keep the peace for as long as you can."

"Are you alrigh'?" Frederick asked concerned.

Another crashing wave of pain shot across Mathias' head from the back to the front, pressing with a force so great he felt like doubling over. He managed to keep his footing for the moment, but another throb like that would have him curled up on the deck.

Vincent shot Mathias a concerned look as well. He could tell the man was suffering from severe migraines. He was about to offer a mild sedative that may help alleviate some of the pain. Before he was able to offer, the captain had already shambled away.

Everyone watched Mathias while he descended from the helm to the main deck. Both of his hands pressed on either side of his head. Anyone that was within a few paces away saw his face flushed of color. Mathias could barely keep his eyes open while making his way to his quarters. There was complete silence, until he opened the door and disappeared into his cabin. Then all hell broke loose on deck as sailors began yelling at Frederick, demanding answers. The first mate was unable to tell them any more than they already knew. it did little to stop them from continuing to shout and argue amongst themselves, directing their anger towards the men at the helm.

Inside the captain's quarters, Mathias heard none of the commotion outside. His entire focus was on trying to suppress the pain that continued to flow into his head like torrential waves. He lost his balance, slamming his back into the corner of the room. When the suffering became unbearable, he collapsed onto the floor, his back still against the wall as he sat there in the darkened room, forehead pressed against his knees. Only when the throbbing became too much to bear did the voice finally accompany the pain.

Why do you resist me so? There seemed to be a sense of genuine concern in the question the woman asked. Mathias refused to answer. ***The suffering will only last as long as I'm talking to you. It may be in your best interest to reply.***

What the hell do you want from me? Mathias demanded, answering only in his head. His terror increased when she replied.

All I want is your acceptance.

Acceptance? What are you on about? How can you hear my thoughts to begin with?

I have been able to hear you ever since we set sail weeks ago. Only when I've felt strong enough, have I been able to talk to you directly.

Every time the woman replied, a fresh wave of thumping pressure pushed on the walls of Mathias' skull. If the conversation lasted too long, he was afraid he was going to pass out from the pain. He realized that if she could read his thoughts, then everything he'd done up to that point was likely what she'd wanted. She was leading him and everyone on board by the tail and now they were sitting right where she'd planned for them to be. Before he could think about it much more, a fresh wave of pain came crashing in.

This will only last as long as you allow it to.

You're the one invading my space.

You may not understand this but you're invading mine as well. We're connected, you and I, which is why it is important that you understand and accept me.

But how? I never intended this nor asked for it.

True, but you did intervene at the time of my death. You saved me...well part of me, and unintentionally gave me a second chance.

A second chance at what?

Life, the life I'd always wanted for myself.

So, have you always wanted to be a homicidal bitch? You've killed nine men already. How many more will you take before you're satisfied?

I've told you before, they were necessary sacrifices. The only way I can gain enough strength to create life is to take it from others. I wish no ill will against those men, but I do need them, and since they are inside me, I will do with them as I please.

You're insane.

No Mathias...I'm alive. More alive than I ever felt living in squalor, pleasuring men to afford a scrap of food to eat at night. Living that way cost me my first life, but I have a new one now, and I'm going to live it to the fullest.

These men are innocent.

I WAS INNOCENT!

I'm terribly sorry for what happened to you but... more throbbing pulsed through Mathias' brain, swimming around it like sharks in water circling their prey.

I know you are. That's why I'm asking you to step down. Let me do what's necessary for me to be happy. I don't want to hurt you. You were my savior, but I will not hesitate if you force my hand.

Somehow Mathias knew she was lying. She wouldn't be ablet to hurt him even if she wanted to. He had no idea why he felt that way, but he thought it might have something to do with the connection she spoke about. If she could read his thoughts and feelings, then there should be no reason why he couldn't do the same to her. Before he could ponder it further, she spoke again. He was certain it was to cause him pain and make him lose focus more than anything else. If that were true, then it also meant his hunch was likely correct.

Anyone who tries to leave I will deal with before their time.

But their time will come regardless, right? So, it should be up to them if they want to take their chances.

Do as you wish, but I've warned you.

Someone outside started banging on the cabin door. Mathias expected each strike to resound within his head, but there was no pain. The throbbing disappeared and the voice along with it. He tried calling out to it with his thoughts, but his efforts were fruitless. She wouldn't respond, or more likely, could no longer respond.

Vincent burst into the room. He looked around the cabin furiously but at first glance he was unable to find the captain. His first thought was that the ship had taken him, since the factor linking men to disappearing was isolation. His heart skipped a beat until he looked behind the door to find Mathias sitting in a fetal position in the corner.

"Oh, for heaven's sake." Vincent closed the door and knelt down next to Mathias. "What was that about? You just shambled off without saying a word. It's a riot out there so I hope you have a plan."

"We sit tight. The ship's not going to move. We have to hope that another ship comes by so we can try to swim or paddle over to it." Mathis spoke, no emotion in his voice.

"I hope you have something better than that up your sleeve. These men are not going to sit around and wait for nothing to happen. If you thought they were restless on an eventless voyage, you know what they will do if we don't make any progress for weeks, sitting in one spot eating all of our rations. They will have cabin fever and be killing each other within a week."

"They'll die regardless." Mathias refused to look at him, keeping his forehead pressed against his knees.

"What has gotten into you? You've never given up before. What's changed?" Vincent asked.

"Nothing's changed. The ship is going to kill everyone on board and anyone that tries to leave and we're powerless to stop her."

"How could you possibly know that?" Mathias was hesitant to answer, but he'd already said more than he wanted to but there was no reason to hold anything back.

"It told me...well, *she* told me."

"The ship?"

"Aye, the ship."

"You can talk to it now?"

"Have been able to for a while apparently. I didn't fully comprehend it, and I still don't fully grasp every concept, but it seems we can communicate with each other. Not out loud, but through our minds, or my mind in particular, I'm not really sure. She speaks to me directly though. I didn't understand how strong of a connection we had until now."

"You were holding more back, even though you'd said you'd told us everything." Vincent let himself fall back to sit on the floor. "It's the migraines, isn't it? You've been acting weird every time they've started up."

"That's how it starts, yes. The pounding begins and she speaks soon after. That's how I know what she's planning. The ship won't move, and anyone that tries to leave will be killed. I don't know how; I only know they will."

"Maybe she's bluffing? How do we know she even has the power to do what she claims she can?

"Seeing as how she controls the rudder and has somehow rotted our food supply; I don't see how we have much reason to question her. If she's able to keep us in this spot or drag us farther out to sea, does it matter what else she can do? It's enough, isn't it?"

Vincent thought about it. He was still convinced they could beat her somehow. It seemed too early to be giving up hope completely. If they were all going to die anyway like the captain said, they might as well try everything they could to escape, or even fight back if possible. He wanted to say more, but it was clear there was no getting through to the captain, at least not yet. He stood up and opened the door outside to the main deck.

"I know you're terrified like the rest of us. But I've never known you to be a coward. Otherwise, I would have never agreed to be your ship's physician. When you are ready to stop feeling sorry for yourself and lead us again, we will be waiting. Until then, stay out of the way."

Mathias said nothing and listened as Vincent left his quarters, closing the door behind him. He was alone again in the dark. It was better than having to look every man in the eye knowing they would all be dead in a matter of days.

13

Frederick Howser

The main deck was in worse shape than it'd been when the Vincent barged into the captain's quarters. Sailors were yelling at each other and arguing over what, he wasn't even sure anymore. It was apparent that unbridled panic had taken over everyone on board. No one knew what was going on and the search of the ship seemed to only create more questions than it provided answers.

When the men were tired of arguing with their words, they turned to their fists. Multiple brawls were beginning to break out between groups of men all throughout the deck. Vincent had to actively dodge a few blows that were meant for other sailors but were coming in close contact with his own head. He was surprised to see Frederick involved in one of the fights. He'd come down from the helm, most likely to confront an insubordinate sailor, before finding himself in a fist fight against three opponents simultaneously. Vincent was impressed with how well the man was holding them off, but he needed the first mate's help. Otherwise, there was little hope of quelling the violence.

"C'mon ya sacks o' shit. I'll knock the block off this entire crew if I have to." Frederick was ready to swing another punch, but Vincent managed to catch his wrist before he could release it. The first mate wheeled around ready to pummel the man foolish enough to stop him. He lowered his fist when he spotted his friend.

"Oy, I almost clobbered ya one." Frederick warned.

"I'm sure it would've hurt like hell too."

Frederick smirked. He hated to admit it, but he enjoyed a good brawl from time to time. He knew it wasn't civil and it was certainly bad for a ship's morale, but damn if it wasn't a terrific way to let go of pent-up frustration. "So, what's the capn's plan then?" He asked.

Vincent frowned. "I'm afraid we're on our own for now. Mathias is convinced there's nothing we can do and the ship's going to kill us off at its leisure."

"How does he know that? What's gotten into that boy?" Frederick tried to push past Vincent, but the man stood firm.

"He says the ship told him. Apparently, that woman he saved the morning we set sail has somehow taken over the ship. They talk to each other, and she told him we were all going to be killed off, whether we sit here or try to leave. So, I say we make her work for it if we have to."

"To the depths with that! It will be a frigid day in hell before I let a glorified floating piece o' wood decide how I die." Frederick's determination was admirable, if a bit misguided in Vincent's opinion.

"That's what I said too, but there's no convincing him otherwise at the moment. I think we need to try and get everyone off the ship, and we'll grab him last. Even if it means some men have to swim for shore. You know what waters we're in and every day we sit here brings more risk of us getting attacked, starved out, or driven mad from dehydration."

"That's a plan I can get behind. Let's get the hell off this floating coffin." Vincent nodded and they shook hands. "Oy listen up you lot!" Frederick's shouting fell on deaf ears.

While they were having their private conversation amidst a brawling deck, more than a dozen men were knocked unconscious from their fights. Those that decided not to partake in the violence were more than happy to sit on the yardarms or rope ladders, cheering and shouting on their friends and shipmates below.

"Damn it all." Frederick grumbled as he grabbed a ring of keys from his pants. His fingers flipped through each one before landing on the one he was looking for. It was easy to find, since it was a bit smaller than the others. He stepped over to the cabinet sitting beneath the stairs that led up to the helm and put the key in. A half turn of the wrist and the cabinet opened, revealing a small array of weapons. A few pistols hung on hooks, a musket sat propped up in the corner, and a few cutlasses standing blade down were in the other corner. He grabbed one of the pistols, a piece of wad, a small flask of gunpowder, and a single bullet from the small shelf sitting directly underneath where they were hanging. He flipped open the flask, pouring some powder down the barrel, then placed the wad on the opening of the barrel, and finally put the bullet on top of the fabric before pressing it with the pistol's push rod all the way to the back.

The doctor had barely enough time to cover his ears before Frederick cocked the pistol, raising it into the air, and pulling the trigger. The shot sent a shockwave through the ship. The fighting ceased immediately, and Frederick had everyone's attention once again.

"Listen up you lot! I'm getting off this ship and heading for land, any land. Anyone who wants to stay behind is more than welcome to do so, but I'd highly suggest otherwise. I don't fully understand what's happening and frankly at this point I don't give a damn. All I know is I'd rather take my chances out there, than sit around here. If you agree, start rigging some boats and let's get off this floating nightmare."

At least half of the crew must have agreed because they were already rushing to opposite sides of the ship to prepare the small boats for launch. Men threw oars into the dinghies haphazardly and a couple of them ended up with extras. Frederick figured extra was better than not having enough, unless they wanted to spend half their time moving a single oar from one side of the dinghy to the other to prevent paddling in circles.

Not everyone was on board with the plan. A few men disappeared below deck. Some went back to sleep; others were looking for something to eat or drink. With less crew on the ship, it meant there were more rations for them. It was a fine idea, assuming their leadership was wrong and there wasn't anything on the ship killing men off by ones and twos.

For the less superstitious members the answer was easy. A few sat atop the yardarms and watched everyone scurrying down below, like rats clambering over each other to run and hide, as if someone had found their nest and meant to do them harm.

Frederick was working on untying the lines that used to lift the boats over the ship's railing. A dinghy on either side of him was already hoisting into the air. Men were grunting "heave-ho" with each synchronized pull. Their boats lifted above the deck, hovering over the railing. A couple men below each, were pushing them over the side so that they would land in the water when lowered. They shouted out "clear" and each dinghy began descending towards the water. The sailors who hoisted them up were now carefully letting them down, hand over hand to prevent scorching their palms with the rope. Once the line was loose, they knew the water was fully supporting the boat's weight. One man tied it off so that it wouldn't float away before they could climb down to board it. They took turns climbing down a rope ladder, sitting down to balance the dinghy while making room for the others when they reached the bottom of the ladder.

Three other boats had already dropped and loaded before Frederick had his in the air. He guided them, lifting it above their heads, and helped to push it over the side before telling them to lower it down. As it touched the water he looked towards the surf. Two other boats were almost fully loaded on either side of his own. He started having feelings of doubt about the ship's ability to do them harm.

"What if all this was bullshit after all?" Frederick asked aloud, heavily considering the possibility, but knowing it was too late to back out. He'd united the majority of the crew to the common idea that this could save their lives, and it would be much harder to convince them to stay than it would be to continue onward with the current plan. *Point of no return.* He thought.

With his own dinghy now tied off and ready to load, he grabbed the rope ladder sitting next to the railing and chucked it over the side. It unfurled down the side of the Anne-Marie, making a small splash as the end snapped open, slapping against the ocean. He directed sailors to start climbing down. They did by twos and threes, most of them not waiting for the man before them to fully mount the ladder before they were mounting it themselves. Frederick had grabbed one man by the arm, helping him over the railing, when the ship began to groan.

Frederick and the man stepping on the ladder looked at each other. The boards creaked and squealed as the Anne-Marie started rocking back and forth. It was hardly noticeable at first and it felt like normal pitching in less than calm seas. The only issue was that there was no tide or current to move the ship. The surface of the water was smooth as glass.

As the rocking grew more aggressive, men both below in their boats and on the ship began shouting. The ones already in their dinghy were yelling up for someone to cast them off, untie the lines, or at least cut them loose so they could paddle away. The ones on board were trying but the rocking was preventing them from securing a solid footing so they could get to the ropes undone.

Frederick was still holding onto the man mounting the ladder, but he knew he needed to make a split decision. Even if the sailor was able to get onto the rope it would slam him into the side of the ship every time it rocked back the other way. The only other options were to let him fall into the water or pull him back on deck. To the first mate, the former sounded safer.

Despite the man's reluctance, Frederick pushed him away from the railing. The sailor tried to grab a nearby length of rope hanging down from the yard arm. He missed it by a good two meters and frantically tried to grab the railing of the ship as he fell overboard. It seemed lucky for him that the side of the Anne-Marie he fell over on was dipping lower than the other side, so his fall to the water wasn't far. However, since the ship was on its way down, it added extra acceleration to the man's descent, throwing him towards the ocean's surface. Unprepared, he hit the water flat on his back. The impact knocked the wind out of him, and he lost consciousness a few seconds later.

Frederick felt regret, certain that he got the man killed. He'd never seen anyone hit water that hard and he was convinced he even saw the man bounce back up some before falling down again, ultimately sinking below the surface.

14

Henry Smith

Henry sank below the surface quickly; his clothes soaked through and dragged him down below. As water entered his mouth and filled his lungs, he regained consciousness. The shock of waking up underwater made him swallow a mouth full of salt. The taste was overwhelming and unmistakable. He closed his mouth and righted himself, looking around for the sun to indicate where he needed to swim to. He'd only ever heard stories, but supposedly on cloudy days or at night when there was no moon, it was easy to start swimming in the wrong direction and end up drowning for the effort. That wasn't the case as the sun shone proudly in the sky, lighting up the ocean's surface. Streaks of light shown underwater like beacons leading Henry towards salvation.

The water grew choppy from the ship lurching back and forth. It was creating small tidal waves and surf that you'd normally only see in an early storm. Henry wanted to get as close to the ship as he could before heading upwards, to avoid having to combat the artificial waves. The hull of the Anne-Marie was unmistakable against the blue-green backdrop of the open ocean. Her hulking bottom stood out like an upside-down island below the water's surface.

Now holding his breath, Henry started swimming towards the ship's hull, surprised that he'd drifted as far away as he had, in the brief time he'd been unconscious. He watched as the bottom of the ship rotated back and forth. After being thrown off, the Anne-Marie's pitching and yawing had picked up considerable speed. The keel was swinging back and forth like a pendulum, only instead of gradually slowing down, the pace was quickening. When the ship was in full swing, small splashes started appearing on either side of her hull. Henry imagined this was what it must look like when cannonballs hit the water after missing their target. Only these weren't cannonballs, but his fellow shipmates forcibly thrown into the sea by the ship.

Henry swam straight upwards towards the sun. The closer he got to the surface the warmer the water became. When the water felt the warmest his head exploded through the ocean's veil and his lungs instinctively gasped for air. The sea water mixed with the air in his nose and mouth. It was the sweetest and saltiest taste he'd ever experienced. He spat out all the salty water, leaving only the sweetness of fresh air behind as he kicked his arms and feet to begin treading water. He twisted to face the Anne-Marie and quickly understood why men were being plunging into the water around it.

Men hung for their lives on the railings, yard arms, and any length of rope long enough to wrap their hand around. The ones on the main deck were able to hold on fairly well, managing to keep from being thrown off each time their side of the ship slammed down towards the water. The ones higher up, towards the crow's nest and the colors were not so fortunate.

Henry never fully understood the physics, but he'd been in enough storms to know that the higher up you were on the ship while it was rocking, the faster you moved each time the ship changed direction. This was no regular storm either, he could only fathom the amount of force enacted on the two men who found themselves unfortunate enough to be near the crow's nest.

Both were holding onto the main mast in a bear hug, trying to wrap their arms all the way around but only managing to reach about halfway. Every time the ship swayed in their direction their grip on the pole loosened. After roughly three cycles one man lost his hold completely. The Anne-Marie threw him a good hundred meters away from the ship. The other, thinking he was clever, had tied a safety line around his waist. When his grip failed him, the ship cast him off just like the other, but the tied down rope caught hold like it was supposed to, slamming the sailor against the exposed hull. He died instantly from the impact, crushing over 32 bones in his body, including his skull.

Henry was glad to be on the opposite side of the ship when the Anne-Marie threw the sailor into her side. As he looked on, the situation grew more dire.

While the Anne-Marie rocked at full speed, she sucked up water into her hull. The men in the rowboats were the first to notice as they were nearly crushed every time the ship pivoted back towards their side. All of them were still yelling up to the main deck to loosen their line or at the very least cut their ropes. Their cries fell on deaf ears as everyone on the ship was now completely incapable of moving around without either being thrown off or slammed repeatedly into the railings. Everyone except for Frederick.

It was slow progress, but he managed to shimmy across to the first dinghy line. He tried to untie it, but only had one hand to work with, as the other was too occupied holding onto the railing. The sailor who tied the dinghy down had used the wrong knot, so instead of it easily coming undone, it only got tighter every time the ship rocked away from the tiny boat.

Frederick unclipped the small knife from his pants loop and started sawing away at the line. He had to wait for the ship to lower on his side in order to cut. Every time the Anne-Marie rose up to his side, it took all of his strength to keep from falling off.

Cut, hold, cut, hold. The process was maddening. The knife almost refusing to cut at some points and only a strand or two snapped away from the rest with each cycle. As Frederick held on for another session, he noticed there were only a couple braids left of the rope holding the dinghy. He'd be able to finish it off on the next cycle. The ship was lowering his side once again when he heard shouting from below.

"Move! Get off! Go!" There were mixed commands and screaming.

Frederick heard the cracking and splintering of wood during his descent and a sound he wasn't familiar with. A squelching noise, like an overripe fruit squeezed to the point of bursting. The wood splintering was the same sound as a ship crashing into rocks, or the hull being torn open against a coral reef. It was one Frederick had experienced a few times and it never got easier to listen to. The cries ceased as his side of the ship dipped low. He focused on cutting the line again, but realized it was a pointless effort.

The dinghy he'd been trying to cut the whole time was nothing but floating debris. Anne-Marie's hull had crushed it completely. Sailors who were lucky enough to jump off in time were treading water nearby, at least those that could swim. The others flailed desperately towards pieces of the dinghy or anything else to hold onto so they could stay afloat. Even more disheartening than the small, destroyed boat, was the blood staining the clear blue water, turning it a gut-wrenching burgundy. The mystery of the squelching noise solved. Frederick would've preferred to have lived the rest of his life not knowing the answer.

"Damn it!" Frederick cried out, chucking the knife into the ocean out of frustration. It plopped into the water and started sinking. There wasn't anything else he could do as the ship began to rise once again on his side. All of his strength and focus moved towards holding on for his own life. To his dismay he heard shouts from the other side of the Anne-Marie. More sounds of shattering, splintering wood followed. At least he was far enough away to not hear the squelching noise of men crushed between the hull and their dinghy again.

Only one boat managed to cast off before the Anne-Marie decimated it. The men aboard didn't care to wait around for anything else to happen. They were already rowing due east towards the nearest shoreline. Men floating by on wreckage called out to them, begging for rescue. Their pleas fell on deaf ears.

Henry continued to tread water, witnessing the small rowboats being crushed while men jumped off of them. Most were able to quickly find wreckage to latch onto or were able to swim on their own. A few he saw floundering, but they began to slip beneath the water's surface. He swam towards them as fast as his limbs would allow. The surf was getting choppier with every passing second, slowing his progress. The man closest to him had managed to keep his head above water for a minute or two before sinking.

Henry dove down, grabbing the drowning man by the waist and pulling him back up to the surface. There was a large chunk of debris bobbing close by. He dragged him over to it and placed both of the sailor's arms over the wood. He waited a couple seconds to make sure it would hold him before looking for the next sinking man.

Henry worked his way closer to the ship, pulling up anyone who wasn't too deep to reach. Periodically he'd duck his head below the water to see if anyone was struggling just below the surface. A couple times he looked towards the ocean floor and saw silhouettes shrinking smaller and smaller before disappearing completely. He knew there was nothing he could do for them. His focus was on the ones that had a chance to survive.

Henry found another one nearby who was desperately trying to climb atop a barrel. Every time the man attempted to climb on top it rolled out from underneath him, making the sailor slip off. Henry held the barrel still from the side so the other man could get on. Once he managed to clamber to the top he breathed a sigh of relief, thankful to be alive.

Henry held onto the barrel a little longer, trying to regain some strength and catch his breath before moving on.

At first, he thought it might've been his imagination, but after a few minutes the choppiness of the surf began to die down. He looked towards the Anne-Marie and saw that the rocking had slowed, to almost nothing. The last of the tidal waves gently passed by him and the ocean was calm as glass once more, except for the men trying to stay afloat, or reach wreckage.

Henry took this opportunity to get closer to the ship. He let go of the barrel and made his way to a man that was beginning to lose his battle with keeping his head above water. After a final flail of the arms, the sailor slipped from view.

Henry got as close as he could to where he saw the man starting to drown. He took a deep breath and dove straight down. The drowning man was sinking quickly, and Henry kicked like hell to reach him. When he got close enough to put an arm around his waist he was about to head back up.

A shockwave of noise slammed into them. The force was strong enough that Henry could see the ripple from the sound moving away from them. If they were on the surface it would've sounded like a cannon blast, only it one came from the bottom of the ship, not her sides. With the man still wrapped in his arm, he turned towards the Anne-Marie. More shockwaves exploded out from the ship in perfect circles. Henry floated in place, suspended in water and unable to tear himself away from what he was witnessing.

With each *boom* the hull of the Anne-Marie split farther apart along her keel. It started in the bow, a few sections at a time. The wood tore away from where it attached to the hull, splintering as it forced itself apart. This continued down the length of the ship until reaching the stern. A thundering shockwave exploded out from the ship as the gap down the keel became a ravine, the hull opening like a mouth. All the boards still attached to the hull appeared as sharp, jagged teeth.

Henry watched the sinking debris and bodies floating closely around the bottom of the ship start to move towards the opening. Water sucked into the ship, along with everything floating around it. What he couldn't see was what was happening on the surface.

15

Frederick Howser

Frederick was sitting on the main deck, exhausted from holding on to the railing that he was now using as a back rest. His heart was pounding and breathing was difficult. He forgot about all of that when the shockwaves started. They resounded from below, soft at first but growing louder and more frequent. The wood all around him creaked and groaned as it had done before the Anne-Marie started to rock back and forth.

The bloody hell is 'appening now? Frederick asked himself.

It was difficult to move. His sides were aching from holding himself on the railing. The final explosion from below got him moving though. He rolled over, grabbing the railing for balance and looking over the side of the ship. Torrents of water began pouring out of the portholes like waterfalls. He couldn't fathom where it was all coming from and watched with awe. He wouldn't have been so impressed had he known what was happening to the men beneath his feet.

16

Henry Smith

Henry paddled furiously away from the Anne-Marie. The last thing he wanted was to find out what happened when sucked inside the ship's gaping maw. Like the undertows he'd dealt with as a boy, he could feel himself and the man he still had an arm wrapped around, slowly sucked towards the ships keel. At first it seemed he might get away. The man he was dragging along didn't seem to be weighing him down as much as he'd expected. The two of them appeared to be making progress even if it was only a meter or so at a time.

If the ship had maintained its initial level of water consumption, the results would've been different. Like with the rocking though, the intensity only increased over time. Now everything within a hundred-meter radius, whether it was floating on the surface of the water, or a league below the water's surface moved into the Anne-Marie. The jagged, wooden teeth of the hull flexed and folded, pushing debris into her bottom like a shrimp grabbing food particles. Water had filled every level up to the main deck, so it had no option but to spill out of every open port and knot hole possible. Frederick watched seawater bubble up out of the stairs leading down from the main deck like a natural spring, spilling out the top.

Henry kicked and paddled with his one free arm as hard as he could, but at best, he made no progress, and at worst…he didn't want to know. The last thing he wanted to do was to let his fellow sailor go, but there seemed to be little choice in the matter. His lungs were on fire from trying to swim free of the current. No matter how much effort he added, the ship's suction managed to add a little bit more resistance than he could escape. He was now losing this personal battle and after a moment's hesitation, he released the grip on his fellow sailor.

Henry watched as the body drifted towards the Anne-Marie, the only consolation being that the man was unconscious and had no idea the fate that would befall him a minute later. No longer encumbered, he made for the surface. If he was going to have a chance to escape, he'd need air to do it.

The sun was still shining bright overhead, even though it was beginning to turn red as it descended towards the edge of the horizon. The sailor wasn't complaining though, it was a blessing that he used to quickly bust his head out from underneath the water. He once again took massive gulping breaths of air. There was no time to enjoy it though, as he continued to feel the undertow pulling at his legs. He could now see what was happening topside. The Anne-Marie, obscured from the water pouring out its sides and the spray splashing up from the waterfalls coming down hid most of the ship's shape. He swam with all his might in a direction directly away from the Anne-Marie. Only when he no longer felt the tug on his legs did he dare to pause and turn around.

A few minutes later, the water pouring out of the Anne-Marie began to recede. The waterfalls near the top of the ship petered out to nothing more than a dribble. The ones below did the same as the ship groaned. Crackling booms, like wood exploding from cannon fire resonated beneath the water again, sending shockwaves out in all directions.

Henry was fascinated, but decided it wasn't worth the risk to return to the ship. Without waiting for anything else to happen, he started to swim away from it towards dry land, and the hope of rescue. He found a large piece of floating debris that somehow managed to get far enough away to not avoid the ship's sucking hull. He grabbed on and kicked with his legs towards shore.

Frederick Howser

Frederick was sitting down, one arm curled around a beam of the railing and breathing heavily. His disbelief went beyond anything he thought capable. Part of him wondered if he hadn't already died and he was living in the circle of hell ordained to him. The events of the past half hour soaked through his clothes, a fact that seemed trivial as he started to look around the main deck. The Anne-Marie felt as empty as she looked.

A couple of men laid out on the deck, unconscious. Their legs and heads lolled with the gentle rocking of the ship. The ones that managed to stay aboard and conscious, were doing the same thing as Frederick. Sitting still, processing what had happened, thanking their maker for somehow allowing them to survive when so many others didn't.

There was a thumping on the side of the ship as the Anne-Marie rocked every few seconds. Frederick didn't get up, he laid down instead, poking his head out between two rails. The sailor who'd tied himself off in the crow's nest was hanging down the side, the rope still wrapped around his waist. His body was limp, arms and legs were flaccid, hanging down around him like a human anchor.

Frederick threw up over the side. He couldn't remember the last time he'd upchucked from something other than an infection around the age of twelve. When there was nothing left in his stomach, he hacked and spat anything left over in his mouth and pushed himself away from the edge. He slowly got to his feet, using the ship's rails for support. His legs and arms were almost too numb to do any good, but he managed to stand.

Vincent was sitting across the ship from Frederick. Their eyes met and each of them raised a hand halfway up. They were glad the other was alive, but neither was overjoyed at having survived given the cost. Vincent had a slightly easier time standing up, hobbling over to the first man he could find. He checked their pulse and provided any medical attention he could under the circumstances, which wasn't much more than turning their head to the side, so they didn't choke on their own vomit or drown in a puddle's worth of seawater.

Frederick left Vincent to do his work. He had his own job to do. He took a quick mental inventory of the situation. There were approximately a dozen men on the main deck. Any that were below had most likely drowned and any that'd managed to get away from the ship were long gone. He knew there was no chance of those individuals coming back and he'd secretly wished he was among them. There was no telling how many supplies they'd lost either. With the meat and fruit rotting below, it didn't seem to matter much. Clearly, Anne-Marie wanted them dead, and she was surprisingly efficient at accomplishing that goal. Not knowing where else to go, he walked painfully towards the captain's quarters.

You better be alive in there. Frederick though. He pushed on the door, but it remained shut. Frederick dropped his shoulder and pushed with the little feeling he had left in his legs. Progress was slow, but he moved the door enough to squeeze his body through. On the other side he saw the armoire that'd broken loose and slid to block the door. The room was in better shape than he would've expected. All the furniture was still in place, other than the armoire, and the only debris on the floor were a few maps, pens, and bottles that'd most likely been sitting atop the captain's desk before the ship started its rocking. He looked around for the captain.

Mathias was no longer sitting in the corner Vincent left him in. Frederick was worried that he'd come out at some point and the ship had thrown him overboard like the others. That was, until he saw the hammock swinging in its normal spot, pulled tight and dangling with what he could only assume was the captain.

"Sir…? Are you alright?" Frederick asked, genuinely concerned.

A muffled voice replied from within the hammock. "What's the damage?"

Frederick could barely make out the question. His mouth and lips were dry. He flicked his tongue against both, trying to get some moisture back before replying.

"Don' know the full extent yet. It's not good though. Maybe a dozen or so men alive. The rest I assume are dead or lost. There's the damage to the ship and cargo to consider too. Most of it probably ruined now." When there was no reply, he decided to ask about something more personal. "Did ya…did ya know?"

"Know what?"

"Know…" but the words didn't come out. For the first time in his life, Frederick was struggling to find the right thing to say when talking to Mathias. Ever since they'd started sailing together over a decade ago, he'd looked after Mathias, as if the lad were his own son. Somehow this voyage changed all that in the span of a month.

"Know what she was capable of?" Mathias finished the question for him.

Frederick nodded. There was a heavy pause before Mathias answered.

"No. I didn't know the extent. I do now though. The entire time I was here, I could feel what she was doing, and what was happening out there. When I realized what was going on, it was already too late, there was nothing I could do."

"Aye, that I believe." Frederick felt awkward standing in the doorway, so he pushed his way inside. "We have to try though."

"That turned out well for you last time, did it?" Mathias questioned.

That stung Frederick, but he wasn't willing to back down. "Aye it ended up bein' a right mess, but I'll tell you what. I'd do it again without hesitation. I'm not goin' to lay down and let the bitch win. I thought you'd do the same. If she's controllin' the ship, she must be doin' it from somewhere. If we can' stop it, then maybe we only need to stop *her*?"

The question sent a shot of pain through Mathias' head. He rolled over in the hammock, squeezing his skull between his hands. It felt like the normal headaches that came before she'd speak to him, only this time it felt different. The throbs were sharper, and he felt something else. At first, he thought it might've been a vision. Instead, it was more of a sensation. A feeling of something Anne-Marie was worried about and needed to protect. Mathias could feel the location on the ship like he could feel a certain part of his body being in pain, almost as if he could put a hand on it.

"I think I know where she's hiding." Mathias tried to climb out of the hammock. Another shot of pain thumped in his brain making him misstep. He tumbled out of the fabric and fell to the floor.

"Come again?"

"Below deck. Near where the boy mentioned. I could feel it. She's hiding or protecting something down there. She didn't want me to know, but I think she told me by accident when you asked the question." Mathias got to his feet and went to open the armoire. Inside he grabbed his sword still attached to its leather sheath and tied it around his waist.

Frederick remembered Vincent mentioning something about the captain being able to communicate with the ship or rather, the woman controlling the ship. As unbelievable as any of it sounded, there was no point denying it after what he'd witnessed.

"So, you know where she is?" Frederick asked, almost excited.

"Kind of, it's more of a feeling but yes, I think I know where she is."

"Then let's go get the bitch."

"Aye, let's."

Frederick once again saw the fire in Mathias' eyes. The same look that made him believe weeks ago that Mathias was in fact ready to take charge. They clapped each other on the shoulders and exited the cabin.

17

Mathias Crane

Vincent was waiting outside for them, cleaning fresh blood off his hands with a rag already soaked through with crimson.

"I've tended to the wounded, all the ones I could find at least. Not like there are many left. There's only maybe a half dozen still on board and breathing, not including us. I sure hope you have a plan Mathias."

Mathias answered. "We do. Grab a couple barrels and some repair boards from the deck below. Strap them together to get us a makeshift raft together. Something we can at least hold onto while we swim for land. Then grab a couple oars or scrap wood to paddle with. Once that's done, get the wounded on it. I have a feeling we're going to need to leave in a hurry. After that, grab three hatchets and meet me in the storage deck."

"And what will you be doin'?" Frederick asked.

"I've got some preparations of my own to make." That was all Mathias would tell them before leaving the two to complete their tasks.

The men split into two groups. Frederick and Vincent started collecting the required materials to make their modified dinghy, while Mathias disappeared below to find satchels of black powder.

Two decks down, the cannons were all pulled back from their portholes and set into their secured positions. The water had flooded the level completely. Droplets still fell from the ceiling and ran down every available surface, pooling on the floor in large puddles. Bodies of drowned men littered the floor.

Poor bastards. Mathias thought. He checked for a pulse on the first few men he came across. He grabbed their necks and wrists to see if he could feel anything. There was no movement, no steady and rhythmic thumping of blood to indicate they were still alive. All he felt was their cold flesh, sucking the warmth from his fingers. He gave up after the fifth body and returned to his prior task.

Crates of wad, shot, and powder sat next to each cannon inside crates. Sailors had left some of them negligently open from their encounter with the French schooner, their contents soaked through. The powder satchels inside became useless.

Mathias began opening the still sealed crates. The first couple had allowed water to get in and the outer black powder bundles soaked through. There were a few in the center however, that still looked dry. The outer bundles had made a barrier that seemed to absorb the majority of the water, keeping those in the center untouched. He grabbed as many as his arms could carry, ferrying them two decks down and piling them on top of the supply barrels a deck below. He managed to make two more trips before his head started throbbing. This time, he resisted the pain, mentally forcing it away so it wouldn't get in the way. There was still too much that needed doing and the last thing he could afford was Anne-Marie, or whoever she was, slowing him down.

After the sixth trip he had to pause a moment. Running across the deck, up and down the stairs with awkward bundles carried in his arms, was exhausting. He leaned against the main mast, the shirt on his back soaked through instantly from residual water, but he hardly noticed. His chest was heaving up and down, which took the majority of his focus. He looked around wondering if Vincent and Frederick had finished yet. It only now dawned on Mathias that he was inside the ship alone, and it was getting dark.

Another sharp pain shot through Mathias' head. He pushed it away before it could manifest into more. That's when he heard a soft *meow.* Mathias couldn't tell exactly where it was coming from, but it sounded like Lucy. "You bitch. How dare you take her and try to use her against me." Mathias thought Anne-Marie was trying to slow him down. All it managed to do was piss him off and get him moving faster. He completed three more trips before Frederick and Vincent came down to join him.

Both of their arms were full. Frederick had a lantern, and several pistols bundled in his arms. Vincent was carrying down two lanterns and three hatchets. They caught Mathias before he was able to start heading back down to the storage level on another run.

"We're all set topside." Frederick told him.

They all met next to the main mast; Mathias dropped the powder bundle on the floor in the only available dry spot he could find. Vincent handed Mathias one of the extra lanterns, nearly dropping the hatchets in the process. "Figured you'd want one of these, it's getting dark out there."

"Down here too." Mathias added. He grabbed one of the hatchets from Vincent and a pistol from Frederick, tucking them both in the waist of his pants. With both hands free, he grabbed the extra lantern.

Vincent and Frederick exchanged supplies as well until they were all kitted the same. Mathias held his lantern up so they could all see each other's faces clearly. The soft orange glow revealed their features and each man's resolve. "I'm sorry I got you both dragged into this. I never meant for any of this to happen."

Frederick clapped a hand on Mathias' shoulder and squeezed. "We know lad. Neither of us blame you. Not a bit."

Vincent nodded in agreement.

Mathias appreciated everything they'd done for him. There were no two other men he'd rather have at his side than them, which is why he was going to do whatever he needed to get them off the ship safely. He grabbed the still dry powder off the floor and headed for the stairs. The other two men were right behind him. They descended in a single file line; Mathias was in the front with Frederick behind him and Vincent trailing.

"The smell's worse than before." Vincent commented.

Mathias had gone up and down the steps a dozen times in the past hour and hadn't even noticed. He did now though, only after Vincent had mentioned it. The rotting fruit had spread from a single barrel to the rest of the supplies. The scent of spoiling food mixed with seawater that flooded the deck, made for a pungent and distinct odor none of them had the displeasure of experiencing before.

Their lanterns weren't effective enough to light up the entire room of the hold. They only managed to breach a small circle around their group, reaching the first set of supply crates and barrels, while only making the ones behind them appear like distant shadows. Mathias' pile of black powder bundles sat on top of the barrel closest to the stairs. He was able to get roughly a dozen piled onto it before the others had joined him. Mathias hoped it would be enough.

Mathias set his lantern down next to the pile. He grabbed the hatchet from his pants waist and cut a small slit in the side of the satchel he was holding. Small black particles, like sand, began pouring out of the cut and onto the floor.

"Is this your plan?" Frederick asked.

"Only if we don't have any other choice. I'd rather not have to light it, but she may give us no other option."

"We better be well on our way before that goes off then. Goin' to need a long trail leading up to that. If it goes off at all given how wet the area is down here."

"It should suffice." Mathias assured him.

Frederick gave Mathias a disbelieving glance but didn't push the matter any further. "Alrigh' so where is she?" Frederick asked.

Mathias pointed to the wooden wall standing directly behind the staircase. "Remember what the sailor said about the ballast area, sealed off from the rest of the ship? A large empty space where you could hide and not found by anyone, no matter how long you searched for them? It's because she's behind that wall."

Vincent raised his lantern, illuminating the surface of the wall. He carefully examined the wood for any indication of a door, latch, hinge, or anything that could provide them with easy access into the hidden area but found nothing. He pressed his ear against the wood. The texture was wet, and the cold started numbing his lobe. There were no sounds, so he closed his eyes to concentrate on listening. A few seconds of silence passed. Then there was a thump. It felt distant and shallow, but another thump followed shortly after the first, and then two more in quick succession. He pushed away from the wall.

"There's definitely something in there. Can't say what exactly, but it sounds like you were right captain." Frederick grabbed Vincent by the arm and pulled him aside.

"Let's get this over with, shall we?" Frederick set his lantern down in front of the wall. He pulled the hatchet from his pants by the blade. He gripped the handle in a fist and started swinging. Small bits of splintered wood fell with each swing. The wood was sturdy, and the first mate only accomplished cutting small slits in it with the first few attempts. Once he got a solid chunk out, the rest started coming apart easily.

Mathias and Vincent joined in on either side of him, hacking away, yanking up and down on their hatchets when they got stuck. They worked in silence, their attention completely focused on the task at hand. All they heard was the *thunk* of the hatchets on the wall and the occasional creaking of boards as splinters of wood were torn away from it.

Frederick was the first to break through. The head of his hatchet lodged all the way to the back of its head. Now that he had a hole to work with, he started hacking down the newly formed gap, trying to free up as much of the wood as he could on either side.

A few more minutes of exhausting swinging and the gaps were big enough to almost squeeze their bodies through. They dropped the hatchets and started pulling the boards on either side of the slit. At first, the boards didn't pull free. The wood bent but refused to break. The three of them grabbed onto the same board and pulled. It began to wobble before breaking off from the rest of the wall. They threw it behind them and worked on the other side. This board came away without much effort, and they tossed it next to its kin on the floor.

They stared at the hole they'd created. It was wide and tall enough for them to slip through one at a time. Mathias offered to do the honors. He traded the hatchet for his lantern and started squeezing himself through the gap. His pants caught on a sliver of wood, as if it were trying to prevent him from going in. He wiggled a bit, and it released him disappointedly.

Mathias investigated the area in front of him but was afraid to go deeper until the others had joined him. They forced their way into the hole, their pants snagging in much the same way Mathias' had. Mathias held up his lantern, but the soft glow wasn't powerful enough to reach the stern of the ship. The other two added their lights to his and it added another meter or so of light in front of them.

Their eyes all locked on the floor simultaneously. To Mathias, it looked like the root of a plant, a thick, tubular shape that tapered off to a point going into the floor. It reminded Vincent of a vein running along the contour of the ship, only they were on the underside of the skin instead of seeing it from the outside. The three of them stood clustered together, not moving, only staring at the root, waiting for it to move.

It thumped. They all watched it bulge, starting from the tip that dove into the wood of the floor, up the root, vein, whatever it was, and towards the back of the Anne-Marie. The hairs on the backs of their necks all stood up on end.

"Whatever's back there...the ship's feeding it." Vincent explained. He was surprised at the steadiness of his voice. Somehow analyzing it from a medical perspective kept him grounded enough to not run away immediately. He'd always had a morbid fascination with the unknown and this was no exception. He knelt down to get a better look, running a finger over the surface like someone checking for dust on a table. "It's wet, and slimy. Not sure whether it's from the ship flooding or not. It definitely feels alive though." The root thumped again, making the doctor jump away to rejoin the others.

"We might as well see where it goes." Mathias suggested. "Won't do us any good standing here talking about it." Frederick nodded in agreement, pushing past them to lead the way farther into the dark room.

As they approached the rear of the ship, the root continued to grow larger. It was almost as thick as a man by the time they ran into more of them sticking up out of the floor. Their tendrils were weaving back and forth like snakes desperately trying to slither away from the intruders. A few more paces and the few tendrils turned into a dozen and that dozen turned to hundreds. All of the smaller root offshoots began converging into one main mass. This major root was beating almost once a second, pulling in nutrients from all of the smaller offshoots.

The three men were having trouble walking farther towards the back as the roots became too large for them to walk over. They were almost having to climb by the time they made it to the stern. There was no need for them to make it all the way back though.

Their combined lights shined on the wall opposite the hole they entered from. The masses of roots covered the entirety of the wall. There wasn't a scrap of wood showing through, whatever the roots were feeding on, had allowed them to grow enough to encompass the entire area. All the offshoots led towards the roof, which is where they now directed their lanterns. The light reflected off of a massive dome hanging down from the ceiling. The dome was clear, filled with a yellow liquid like a freshly cracked egg that'd been open and poured out above them.

"Vincent, you have any opinion on this?" Mathias asked.

The organism was a mystery to the physician. There wasn't anything close in any of his years of study and personal experience that remotely compared to what he was witnessing. The roots were one thing, understandably natural, like a plant, mold, or fungus, growing throughout the ship. The thing that these roots led to though, was unrecognizable.

"Uh, no. Can't say I've seen anything like it/in all my years. There's certainly nothing about this in my academic records either. I'd want nothing more than to study it given any other circumstance. Right now, though...every fiber of my body is urging me to destroy it." Vincent's spoke quietly, afraid to disturb the organism.

"Aye, so let's do that." Frederick still had his hatchet held firmly in his hand. He'd been ready to use it the second they squeezed through the small slit in the wall. Now his arm cocked back and prepared to throw it at the dome. Vicnent caught his arm before Frederick was able to release it.

"Hold on. That might not be the smartest move here. Whatever is in there could come pouring out if you were to puncture it. God knows we probably don't want to find out firsthand what's inside as it splashes down on top of all of us."

Frederick lowered the hatchet. "Yer right 'bout that. Sorry, got carried away."

While Vincent and Frederick discussed it further, Mathias' eyes never left the dome. He watched it with increased fervor every time the roots surrounding the base of it pulsed. He watched the tendrils expand and contract, pumping unknown nutrients into the egg like dome. The dome itself was clear, but inside was a cloudy liquid, with three dark and distinct objects floating around. One of the patches started to grow larger the longer he stood there watching. The three of them shifted around inside the cloudy, yellow dome. When it moved into position towards what Mathias considered the top of the dome (at least from their perspective underneath it), he interrupted his companions' conversation.

"Look!" Mathias demanded.

With all three of their lanterns held above them, there was enough light to clearly see the top of the dome. They watched as the largest of the three shadowy objects inside descended towards them. It reached the edge of the half circle, thumping against the gelatinous wall making the entire container wriggle in place.

"My god is that...?" Vincent was afraid to complete the sentence.

"A ship." Mathias finished for him.

The hull of a ship sat on the bottom of the dome, like a sunk vessel sitting on the sea floor. It rocked back and forth for a moment, before the top part, with a complete set of sails and rigging, fell over and rested on the wall of its sac.

"It looks identical to the Anne-Marie." Mathias commented.

"Not identical." Corrected Frederick. "The body and hull look the same as the Anne-Marie, but the rigging...is different. That yard arm and dual mast configuration is like that French schooner we encountered." That's when it clicked for all three of them.

They stood there for a minute, staring slack jawed up at the floating hull. The mini ship bobbed a couple more times before the bow turned upwards and floated once again out of sight.

Mathias' head began to throb. The sharp intensity forecasting the approach of Anne-Marie's phantom manifestation. He tried to fight it, falling to his knees, and gripping the sides of his head to force the pain away. Frederick and Vincent both bent down to put a hand on him, but Mathias raised one of his own to stop them. She was trying to force her way in. Mathias knew if she was able to break through that he'd be powerless to stop her.

Before he managed to fully suppress her influence, he saw flashes of the Anne-Marie sailing on the open sea, with three smaller, full-size renditions of the ships floating above them, at her side. Anne-Marie spotted a fishing vessel along the coast. She sailed towards it, raising her bow into the air as she approached, and crushing the defenseless fisherman beneath her hull. The three smaller ships moved over the wreckage, cracking open their hulls and consuming the remains. He saw himself standing at the helm, watching the scene unfold around him.

With a final effort Mathias threw his head back and screamed into the dark. He thought he'd failed to hold her at bay, but a few seconds later the pain began to subside. The hammering pressure faded, and he collapsed on the floor.

"Cap'n, oy are you alrigh' lad?" Frederick lifted Mathias off the floor, placing the captain's back on his own knee to keep him supported.

Vincent was checking Mathias' vitals, looking for anything out of the ordinary. Other than the bout of fresh sweat beginning to bead on his forehead, he otherwise looked fine. The physician wiped the sweat away with the sleeve of his shirt.

Mathias swatted at Vincent's hand. "I'm alright." Vincent wasn't convinced, his brow furrowed in concern. Mathias saw the expression and it irritated him. "Seriously I'm alright."

"What happened?" Frederick asked.

Mathias lifted himself off of the first mate's leg and sat upright on his own. "I saw everything this time. I know her end goal and it's horrid if we don't end this here and now."

"Say no more." Frederick pulled the pistol from his pants, cocked the hammer back and pointed it at the peak of the dome. His movement was quick and precise. Mathias barely had enough time to react.

"No!" Mathias yelled, jumping up and grabbing the first mate's arm as his finger squeezed hard enough on the trigger to fire a shot. The small room exploded with sound and the lead ball flew wide of its target, hitting a thick piece of root. Their ears were all ringing, but they could discern the sound of wood creaking in protest as the dome and all of its tendrils convulsed in protest at being struck. Mathias continued to hold Frederick's arm until the room settled back down to the constant rhythmic thumping.

"The hell was tha' for?" Frederick asked.

"It's not enough to stop those, we need to stop the ship as a whole."

"How are we supposed to accomplish that?"

"I have an idea, but I need you two to trust me."

Vincent and Frederick gave each other curious glances. The physician shrugged and the first mate reluctantly put the pistol back in his pants.

"Alrigh' fine. Let's 'ave it then."

When Mathias was convinced that Frederick wasn't going to try attacking the dome again, he loosened the grip on his arm.

"The only way we can be certain that the Anne-Marie won't be able to continue wreaking havoc is to destroy her completely. That leaves few options other than burning her down to nothing but rubble, along with *whatever* those are." He motioned in the general direction of the dome. "I need you two to get on the raft and paddle as far away from the ship as you can. I'll get a good fire going and abandon it as soon as I'm sure she'll catch fully. I shouldn't have any trouble finding you if you hang a couple lanterns up. I'll swim like the devil, and we'll all get our asses to shore."

"And why you? Can't we help you get it started then hop on the raft and paddle like mad?" Vincent suggested.

"No. You need to be long gone before I set the fire. She's going to be terribly angry, and I have no idea what she may do, especially now, knowing what she's guarding. I know she won't hurt me. I can't say the same about you two. So, it has to be me."

"I still don' like it." Frederick protested.

"Damn it Frederick, listen to me!" Frederick recoiled. "Get the hell off the ship. That's an order!"

Frederick looked in Mathias' eyes. He *really* looked at them for the first time in a while. Raw determination reflected back at him. With a heavy sigh, he resigned.

"Alrigh'. Fine. 'ave it your way. Give us five minutes to cast off and you do wha' you have to. Once we see her go up in flames, we'll be waitin' for ya."

"And I'll be on my way." Mathias added, flashing him a convincing smile.

Frederick doubted Mathias meant what he said. He felt that this was probably the last time he'd get to see his friend.

"Aye, you better." Frederick clapped a hand on Mathias' shoulder and squeezed the way he always did.

Vincent offered Mathias a hand. The captain took it, and they shook. The physician gave him an affirming nod, not knowing what to say before joining Frederick.

18

Frederick Howser

The two of them left Mathias alone, squeezing back through the small gap in the wall they'd entered through. It'd felt like hours since they entered the small room, but it'd been merely a few minutes.

They reached the main deck and headed to the port side railing. The sun had fully set, and the raft was hardly discernable from the water surrounding it. The only real indicator that it was still down there came from the small bumping noises each time it drifted into the side of the ship.

Vincent was the first to descend. He climbed down the rope ladder and hopped onto the makeshift raft upon reaching the bottom.

Frederick tied a couple of lanterns to one end of a length of rope, slowly lowering it down towards Vincent, who untied them as soon as they were within reach. He then climbed over the railing, grabbing onto the rope, and working his way down the side of the ship. By the time he'd reached the raft Vincent finished attaching the lanterns to a couple of posts sticking up in each corner.

Frederick untied the line holding the raft to the ship but couldn't bring himself to let go. "Are we really goin' to leave him in there alone?" Frederick asked without looking at Vincent. His eyes fixed to the side of the Anne-Marie.

"Yes, it's his decision." Vincent assured him.

Frederick reluctantly dropped the rope. It fell into the water and made a small splash. With both hands he pushed off the hull of the ship. The two of them, along with the other survivors, floated away. They each grabbed a wooden board and started paddling east, using the stars as a guide. When they were far enough away that they could no longer distinguish the silhouette of the Anne-Marie from the backdrop of the night sky, they stopped.

They sat quietly, each of them counting seconds in their head. Waiting for the five-minute mark to come. They each expected to slowly see orange light break through the darkness as the ship caught fire.

Frederick counted aloud in a whisper. "32…33…34…35…"

White light filled the horizon as the belly of the Anne-Marie exploded outward, sending hundreds of wooden shards and scraps careening out towards the water around it. The boom was followed by the worst, blood curdling scream they'd ever heard. It sounded like a woman, but also a beast in its final throes of life, mixed with agony. It made their skin crawl. Deep down though, there was a sense of relief and satisfaction.

Wooden fragments continued to rain down as the fire started to catch on the rigging. Frederick and Vincent watched as the Anne-Marie went up in flames. Frederick had been worried that it wouldn't fully catch, given how wet it'd been a few hours before. His concerns proved unwarranted as the fire raced towards the crow's nest of the main mast. The Anne-Marie fully engulfed in flames, burning like a torch on the surface of the water. There was another explosion near the bow of the ship as the fire reached the black powder stores. The screaming stopped soon after.

The ship broke in half, the front piece bobbing above the surface for a while, but the back filled with water and sank into the darkness within minutes of the initial explosion.

The two of them watched the last embers burn on the crux of the figurehead, before it too disappeared into the depths. They sat motionless, only the glow of the lantern light and the stars to keep them company. They waited, neither fully knowing how long, hoping for their captain to come swimming into view, but they knew better.

Without a word they each grabbed the boards they'd been using to paddle and dipped them into the water. They each pushed, forcing the water behind them, and propelling the raft towards land and hopefully within a few days, rescue.

Printed in the USA
CPSIA information can be obtained
at www.ICGtesting.com
CBHW011537111224
18826CB00056B/933

9 798991 988728